LUCKY
STUFF

SHARON FIFFER

LUCKY
STUFF

minotaur books ❧ new york

LUCKY STUFF. Copyright © 2012 by Sharon Fiffer. All rights reserved. Printed in the United States of America. For information, address St. Martin's Press, 175 Fifth Avenue, New York, N.Y. 10010.

www.minotaurbooks.com

Library of Congress Cataloging-in-Publication Data

Fiffer, Sharon Sloan, 1951-
   Lucky stuff / Sharon Fiffer. — 1st ed.
       p. cm.
   ISBN 978-0-312-64303-4 (hardcover)
   ISBN 978-1-250-01489-4 (e-book)
   1. Wheel, Jane (Fictitious character)—Fiction.   2. Women private
investigators—Fiction.   3.   Antique dealers—Fiction.   4.   Illinois—
Fiction.   I.   Title.
   PS3606.I37L83 2012
   813'.6—dc23

                                                          2012014698

First Edition: September 2012

10 9 8 7 6 5 4 3 2 1

In what three ways do I count myself lucky?
Kate, Nora, and Rob.
And this book is for them.

ACKNOWLEDGMENTS

When it comes to actually producing a novel, a writer probably should thank everyone she has ever encountered—from those who have passed by her office window, wearing a too-big yellow coat, to those couples upon whom she has eavesdropped in coffee shops. In my case, I thank Don and Nellie, proprietors of the EZ Way Inn in Kankakee, and all of those regulars who peopled my life and upon whom I eavesdropped for most of my childhood. Additionally and specifically, in random order, thanks to those who have aided me with answers to my research questions, created a beautiful Web site, read early sections of *Lucky Stuff* and all those who support my storytelling and Jane Wheel's collecting habits. I present a virtual four-leaf clover to: Dr. Dennis Groothuis, Judy Groothuis, Susan Phillips, Walter Chruscinski and the crew at New Trier Sales, Cas Rooney, Muggs Rooney, Emory Schmidt, Kris Schmidt, Steve Bertrand, Allison Beasely, Betty Schatz, Bill Yonkha. I thank my husband, Steve, for his unconditional support and superlative editing advice; my children Kate, Nora, and Rob and their significant others, Chris, Adar, and Kim, for patiently listening to ideas, paragraphs, pages, and chapters. I thank all of the other

Fiffers young and old, for always being supportive and cheering me on. Thanks to my wonderful agent, Gail Hochman, and also Bill Contardi, Lina Granada, Marianne Merola, and Jody Klein at Brandt and Hochman who have helped Jane Wheel find an even larger audience. A four-leaf clover and a lucky horseshoe to my editor Kelley Ragland, who makes the hard work of writing a book the pleasure I always hoped it would be.

LUCKY STUFF

1

"I'm sorry," she whispered, as she struggled to close the lid of the wooden trunk. A middle-aged woman's face stared up at her. "It won't be forever . . . I'll let you out again," she promised.

While fighting against the old hinges, Jane Wheel had stopped to admire the milk paint that softened the look of the wood, made the trunk look like whatever it held would be old and precious. As she paused, the relatives being packed away shifted their weight and resisted the lockdown of the heavy wooden lid.

"Aunt Bessie, I am so sorry," Jane repeated as she smothered Bessie with a small autograph quilt made from men's suiting fabrics. The houndstooths and tweeds and scratchy woolens might not feel soft to the touch, but they would protect the family members jammed into the wooden box from scratches and breakage. At least Jane hoped the framed photos would be well protected. Aunt Bessie, Uncle Titus, the cousins who worked at the Iowa State Hospital, the 1912 firefighters from Des Moines, the twelve grown men riding on a child-sized train ride somewhere in a leafy park. None of these photos were of people blood-related to Jane Wheel. Aunt Bessie and Uncle Titus were christened on the days Jane gathered them from far-flung rummage sales and flea markets, rescued them from the oblivion of thrift stores and estate sales. *Aren't we enough for you?* Jane's ex-husband Charley, would ask. *Of course,* she would answer, beaming at her husband and son, Nick, as she unpacked photo albums and yearbooks and unknown ancestor after unknown ancestor when she returned from Saturday sales. These people needed rescuing, she explained to Charley.

"If I don't save them, who will?" Jane asked.

And now, as she packed away the faux family, she could point out to Charley, who wouldn't hear her since he now lived most of the year far from Evanston, Illinois, in Honduras, that the adopted relatives would come in handy to keep her company these days. Nick had been a wonderful companion and it was with great mixed feelings that she celebrated his acceptance at a math and science academy for high school. It was Nick's dream school—one that would actually sanction time with his father at the dig site if something exciting turned up during the school year. Nick would board at a school with other students like him, brainy and funny and motivated, all on a full scholarship. He had left two weeks ago and Jane still teared up when she thought about his whispered good-bye.

"A text every night, Mom, if there isn't time for an e-mail, okay? And don't worry about the house or packing up. I'll help you do it all at Thanksgiving—Will's mom said nothing happens in real estate this time of year."

Nick had hugged her ferociously and for just a second, Jane thought about asking him to give up Lakewood Academy and stick to boring old high school at boring old home with boring old her. But as ferocious as his hug had been, she could see the absolute joy and excitement in his eyes. He was headed to the place he was meant to be.

And Jane? Where was she headed?

"Trouble. You are headed straight for trouble," said Nellie, talking out of the side of her mouth as she always did when she thought Don might hear and contradict her. Not that Nellie ever cared who contradicted her.

"I'm headed toward fiscal responsibility," said Jane. She had caller ID; she had seen that it was Nellie calling. Jane had chosen to answer the phone and had no one but herself to blame.

"You're a single woman now and your son is off to boarding school. If you sell your house, you'll be homeless. Hell's bell's, Jane, isn't your life pathetic enough?"

"Thanks, Mom, got to go. Another call—probably someone from the soup kitchen wanting to know if they can deliver my meals or if I'll be shuffling down to the church basement on my own."

Jane pushed END and her mother's voice was gone. How she longed for a sturdy Bakelite telephone receiver that she could slam down into an even heavier Bakelite base. Hanging up on someone used to mean something, used to have a kind of sound and fury to it. Ending a conversation with a silent click had no panache and gave Jane little satisfaction. In fact, it was such a quiet ending to the phone call that Jane had no doubt her mother was still talking on the other end, railing about Jane's decision to sell the house and find a smaller place to live. She would be enumerating all the reasons it was too soon to make a change—the reverse of all the reasons she had enumerated twenty years before when she told Jane and Charley they should not commit to buying the house in the first place.

Buy it they did—for a good price that felt impossible to manage at the time. But the house, the beloved old four-bedroom with charming stone fireplace and ancient hot-water heater and rattling furnace had appreciated—the property's value had risen up and up to a figure too good to be true. That peak was eight years ago and the figure was indeed too good to be true—in fact, it wasn't true at all. *Poof*—like a puff of smoke from the working-but-always-problematic stone fireplace, the imaginary profit had vanished and their beloved albeit drafty old house had become one more sad listing on the overcrowded housing market.

"Pack this junk up. Every bit of it," said Melinda, Nick's friend's mom, the realtor who had come over to list the house. "I got phone numbers of people you can hire to come in and have a sale."

Jane stared at her. Melinda was a sturdy attractive woman whose blazer pulled a little tight in the shoulders, but whose pricey blond highlights and good gold jewelry supported her claim to being a top producer at her realty firm, even in this depressed market.

She was probably a swimmer, thought Jane, unaware that she was staring at Melinda's shoulders.

"What? What's back there?" asked Melinda, turning to look behind her shoulder where she thought Jane was staring. "Oh yeah, you're going to have to clean up all that luggage. What's the deal? Packing for a vacation?"

Jane looked at the vintage suitcases stacked behind Melinda's back. Two drunken pillars on either side of the fireplace, the cases were turned this way and that, brown and red, a few that were striped or plaid and displaying the scars of travel and the tattoos of stickered destinations. They made for interesting storage of old tax information, auction catalogs that Jane used both for reference and her own continuing education as a picker. A brown leather bag with a Bakelite handle contained twenty-five high school yearbooks from the thirties. Jane figured someone who loved cool graphics and vintage photos would buy them in a heartbeat—but that would involve taking them out of the case and actually pricing them for sale.

Melinda had given her a week to clear out the main rooms, offering over and over to help her find a service to do a clean-out.

Last night she phoned Jane to tell her she wanted to bring by a potential buyer in two days.

"I've worked with hoarders before," said Melinda. "I can find you someone to help. Someone who runs estate sales. They know how to get rid of the crap."

No they don't. They just bring it all to their homes, thought Jane.

"What do you say?" said Melinda.

"The house will be ready for showing on Wednesday," said Jane.

"If you promise . . ."

"Afternoon. Wednesday afternoon, okay?" Jane could hear Melinda chewing something. She was eating while on the phone. Okay, so maybe Jane looked like a hoarder, but she wasn't a phone-eater.

"I'll call you with the time. Get it cleaned out, Jane. If you want to sell this place, clear the decks!"

So, in her best *aye, aye captain* mode, Jane Wheel, Picker and Private Investigator, was spending this warm September evening clearing the decks. She was packing the smalls: the vintage glass and pottery flower frogs that dotted shelves and served as punctuation marks between rows of books in the cases; the McCoy flowerpots that held fistfuls of number-two pencils as well as old plastic advertising pens and mechanical pencils; the small copper vessels in which she had planted bouquets of old pairs of scissors; the Depression glass and mason jars, which bloomed with bunches of wooden and Bakelite knitting needles; the glass apothecary jars that held swizzle sticks and wooden spools of thread and several pounds of old silver and iron and brass keys. A basket of doorknobs stood in the corner and an antique fishbowl sat on the trunk used as a coffee table filled not with koi and guppies, but rather board-game tokens, dice, and orphaned Scrabble letters.

"Am I a hoarder?" Jane asked herself out loud.

Jane sat down on the trunk that now held all those made-up old relatives and gave her living room a long hard look. Stacked cardboard boxes, taped and labeled with a black Sharpie, replaced the vintage luggage stacks. Now packing cases held old flowered tablecloths, napkins adorned with initials not even close to Jane Wheel's, and tatted doilies, antimacassars and crocheted tea cozies.

One lone black garbage bag sat in the middle of the room. Jane had put it there for any items she came across that she no longer wanted. Movers were coming in the morning to pack up all the boxes and nonessential furniture and driving it to a storage locker in Kankakee—in a facility that Jane's friend, Tim, used.

"It's dry and clean and I got you space on the first floor next to two of mine," said Tim. "You can drive right up to it, open the garage door, and visit your stuff anytime you want. From seven AM to ten PM. Except on Sundays when it closes at six," he added.

Jane peered into the garbage bag. One lone flour sack pot holder lay at the bottom of the bag. Shaped like a pear and embroidered with a cheerful smile and long curly eyelashes that gave this 1940s handmade kitchen collectible a feminine, flirty air, it was lightly padded, Jane guessed, with a piece of old recycled wool sandwiched between the soft cotton fabric.

"How did you fall into that throwaway bag?" Jane asked the pot holder.

It was the second question she had asked herself—or an inanimate object—out loud.

Quickly she stuffed the cloth pear into a box where the tape was not totally sealed and snatched up the garbage bag. There were some old shirts and pants, Charley's clothes he had left behind that he asked her to donate and get rid of. Okay, she could do that. After all, answering her first question, it wasn't like she was a hoarder.

By the time the Wednesday showing of her Evanston home arrived, Jane had watched movers fill a large truck with trunks, luggage, and box after box of stuff that they drove off to Kankakee. Jane had already decided to let Tim receive the stuff on the other end while she stayed behind to wrap up some business at the bank and have lunch with her partner in the PI part of her PPI professional life, Detective Oh. Jane's plan, after lunch, was to head home and pick up her dog, Rita, and head down to

Kankakee. There she would be reunited with her boxes and cartons and bags and suitcases. And, of course, her parents, Don and Nellie. Jane would remain there through the weekend since the open house was scheduled for all day Sunday.

Melinda would shepherd the lookers, the gawkers, the curious neighbors, and one or two potential buyers who would descend upon her now sparsely furnished space. Jane could hardly believe anyone would find the house appealing without its character-building clutter, its rich textural personality, but according to Melinda, Jane had done a spectacular job of de-cluttering.

"A for effort," she had announced when she made a quick inspection early on Wednesday morning. "Don't forget to take all the family photos out of the den."

Jane had showered and changed into a clean pair of jeans and a soft navy V-neck sweater. She grabbed her giant leather tote bag—what she referred to as her "just-in-case," which held everything she might need . . . *just in case*—and prepared to leave to meet Oh, when she remembered that she hadn't removed the family photos. Not wanting her grade to drop down to a B, she dashed into the now almost empty room.

When Charley left, his den became a resting place for old library items—book carts and card files—all of which Jane snapped up when a suburban branch moved its location. Jane thought she might find a good use for the comfortable trappings of a library, all worn and wooden, and they had given the room a cozy, if cluttered ambiance. Now that the den was emptied of all but a leather chair, ottoman, and lamp, strategically placed on a lovely old semiworn Persian carpet, Jane found herself a little breathless at how peaceful it looked. What did it remind her of? Oh, yes. A den.

She took all the photos off the built-in bookcases that flanked the fireplace. With only a few books remaining on the shelves, old leather-bound sets of Dickens and Alcott, books that felt as warm and soft to the touch as a pair of ladies' kid-skin gloves, and the brass lamp next to the chair turned down low, the room gave off such an appealing glow that it was all Jane could do to resist curling up in the old leather chair with one of the books. She steeled herself against the house love rising up in her and grabbed the photos, stuffing them into her "just-in-case."

Whistling for Rita and giving her big dog a decent head rub before sentencing her to a few hours alone in the backyard, Jane threw herself into her car and pulled it around to the front. She sat parked in front of the house for a long look. Each red brick stair that led up to the oak front door held a terra-cotta pot filled with rust-colored mums. The window boxes were still filled, but the greenery was dying, spent from a summer of blooming. The stucco was in good shape and the stained timbers that framed the house, giving the illusion that the all-American four-square had English Tudor roots, were solid. It had been a good house and although waves of sentiment, feeling vaguely like the flu, washed over Jane as the years of Nick growing up, learning to ride a bike on the front side-walk, kicking a soccer ball into a net Charley had set up alongside the house, dashing out the front door to trick-or-treat dressed as a dinosaur or a gila monster flashed by in a slide show, making it hard to swallow for a moment, Jane wasn't really sorry about selling the house. It was the right thing to do. It was time for a new family to plant flowers and to play catch in the yard. Charley had moved on and Nick was firmly launched.

Time for Jane to move on, too.

Jane walked into the Deadline Café at three minutes past noon, almost exactly on time, but, of course, Detective Bruce Oh was already sitting at a table by the window, He rose slightly as Jane approached and she smiled at him, wondering if younger men were learning to do that, to stand when a woman came in the room or, as in this case, approached the table. Why would they? Who would teach them? She felt a little panicky that she had never mentioned it to Nick, that maybe he should stand when a woman enters the room, then wondered if women today wanted men to stand. Would everyone have been better off if no one stood for everyone or everyone stood for everyone?

". . . and so I ordered the tea. I hope you don't mind," said Oh.

Oh looked at Jane, and realized that she had been carrying on one of her conversations with herself when she arrived at the table.

"I ordered a pot of Earl Grey, Mrs. Wheel," said Oh. "Would you prefer coffee?"

"Tea's fine," said Jane, glancing at a menu, but fully aware that she would have a veggie club sandwich, which is what she always ordered at the café.

Tossing the menu aside, Jane looked her partner in the eye.

"We've known each other for a few years now," she said, stirring a packet of sugar into her tea. She always drank her coffee black, but loved to load up her tea with sugar or honey and as much lemon as a waitress offered. "And I think we . . ." Jane hesitated, hoping Oh would read her mind as he frequently did and bail her out by finishing her sentence.

Oh, however, never finished her sentences or anyone's, even if he could read minds. "Listening, Mrs. Wheel, is a lost art. People will always tell you more and tell you precisely, if they are allowed to tell you themselves."

Jane took another sip of her tea, admiring the mismatched vintage cup and saucer that the café used.

"We've been through a lot together, and I think you and I, we should . . ."

"Hey, Jane, want the club?" asked Lissa from behind the counter.

Jane looked at Detective Oh, who nodded.

"Two," said Jane, holding up two fingers.

She had thought about this conversation for several days. Since she would be going to Kankakee and staying over the weekend she knew she wanted to say it now, before she left town, and get the hard words behind her.

"We both know we have a special rapport and I . . ." said Jane.

"Extra pickles?" yelled Lissa.

Jane nodded, but then saw that Lissa was, as usual, doing four things at once and not looking in Jane's direction. "Yes, pickles," said Jane.

"Perhaps," said Oh.

"Yes?" said Jane. He was going to bail her out after all.

"You should just say it, Mrs. Wheel. Perhaps we are of one mind."

"We usually are, don't you think? And that's why I think, we should begin . . ."

Lissa set the plates down in front of them. Their sandwiches were perfect, giant slabs of whole wheat bread, with avocado, cheese, tomatoes, sprouts and cucumbers, and smoked tempeh. *Fakin Bacon*, one of Jane's favorite food groups. Once she took a bite, the moment would be lost forever, since beginning a sandwich like this was a commitment. One bite and all serious conversation would be lost to shredding and swallowing. That was true for Jane, anyway. Oh was deconstructing his sandwich and, using a knife and fork, managing to consume the components with his usual grace.

"It's nothing," said Jane. She shook her head. There would be other opportunities to have this discussion. In fact, what she had been about to say wasn't even important. Jane was going to simply suggest that they call each other by their first names. A simple request, perfectly appropriate for their friendship, their business partnership. Why did she find it so difficult to simply say, *Please call me Jane?* As she looked at Detective Oh, his knife and fork held aloft over his plate, his dark eyes staring frankly into her own, she smiled. Maybe she couldn't bring herself to say it because she liked the way he called her *Mrs. Wheel.*

Looking down at her plate piled high with her most favorite lunch in the world, she realized she had completely forgotten to eat breakfast. She picked up her sandwich and took an enormous bite.

Jane was on her way to Kankakee one half hour before the showing of her house was to begin. Driving through Chicago in the early afternoon was painless. Light traffic, a clear day, and although Jane couldn't quite see forever, she could see the Chicago skyline as perfectly carved into the blue sky as one could hope. Curving and swerving into, and then around the city, taking an almost straight line south to Kankakee, Jane felt that she had driven the I94 to I57 route so often, her car could autopilot her to Kankakee.

This was an oddly carefree trip. Jane wasn't rushing to put out any fire set by Nellie, she wasn't flying down to fix any of Tim's problems, she wasn't being lured into a fake murder mystery that all too often turned real when she hit Kankakee County. Nope. This was just a girl and her dog heading down to visit her hometown on a clear September day. This would be the perfect visit. She had left her house in order, the realtor would host the open houses, and Jane wouldn't be there to mess up anything between today's showing and the weekend open house. Her packed treasures had already arrived in Kankakee, several hours ahead of her. Tim would supervise the unloading into the storage locker. Her son Nick had her on speed dial—*an archaic expression if ever there was one*, thought Jane. What was today's smart phone equivalent? Detective Oh could take care of any little thing that came up at their office. Over the summer, the initial gloom and doom of Charley's departure had lifted, Jane's adjustment to this new chapter in her life was complete, and by golly, life was, or at least could be—no, *would be*—good. Jane turned on the radio, hoping some oldie would come on so she could sing along and make this little moment complete.

"Uh-oh," said Jane out loud when "Love the One You're With" came on.

Singing along, Jane started planning. There was an auction scheduled for the weekend. It was taking place at a farm just west of Kankakee and it was a complete household. The farm equipment would be sold out in the barns and the house would be turned inside out, its contents displayed under tents out in the yard. Tim had been invited in early to look at a few of the antiques and he had advised sending two of the pieces out to special sales for the best prices.

"But there's plenty for us, Janie. How long since you've been at a country auction?"

Too long, thought Jane.

Even Nellie had seemed welcoming when Jane told her she was coming for a long weekend.

"Yeah, I guess it's okay if you come. Bringing the dog?"

That was practically a welcome-home banner strung across the lawn in Nellie language!

Speaking of banners, or thinking of them, as Jane was, she saw something flapping in the breeze on Court Street as she made her way through downtown Kankakee. Held taut by wires across the street from the courthouse, there was a bright yellow banner.

"Maybe there's a big church rummage sale this weekend, Rita," said Jane, feeling like everything was going her way. Maybe this would be her first visit to Kankakee where nothing terrible happened. Her parents would stay well, she wouldn't discover any new relatives, no skeletons would be unearthed, no beams would fall on anyone, no one would discover an old body, an old theft, an old forgery, no poisonings would occur, no nail guns would be fired, and no schemes to liven up Kankakee would be hatched by Tim. Maybe she would go to an auction and find a box of vintage pottery, a bag of Bakelite bangles, and, for good measure, an old sewing box with a sterling silver thimble case. Maybe this would be her lucky weekend.

Jane stopped at the red light and looked over at the banner.

LUCKY KILLED THEM IN LAS VEGAS!

Jane could see from where she sat at the light, there was another banner planted on the parkway a few buildings down.

LUCKY KILLED THEM IN BRANSON!

"What the hell does that mean?" Jane asked. Rita pulled her nose in from her window and turned her head to Jane. She looked as puzzled as her mistress. On the next block was another banner.

NOW LUCKY'S GONNA GET KILLED IN KANKAKEE!

Maybe some football player from a rival team? Was there some big game? Would they actually allow the kids to put up signs about being killed?

KANKAKEE'S FAVORITE SON'S COMEDY ROAST

TAPED LIVE—IN KANKAKEE, ILLINOIS!

Under the words of this next banner was a caricature of a man with a cigar in his mouth, a pouf of black hair and a toothy grin.

"Well, Rita, that must be Lucky," said Jane, and added, "whoever the hell he is."

Jane was at another stoplight, staring at this last banner when her phone rang.

Jane clicked it on speaker to answer.

"Are you driving, Jane? Pull over," said Melinda. Jane could hear her chewing something crunchy.

Jane did as she was told. What could have happened? Did a water pipe burst? A fire? Gas explosion?

Jane parked in front of a lawn sign that had been stuck into a large concrete planter in front of what used to be Kresge's Dime Store.

TODAY'S YOUR LUCKY DAY read the sign with that same grinning, cigar-smoking face outlined underneath the lettering.

"Today's your lucky day," said Melinda.

"How did you know?" asked Jane, thinking somehow she must be sending a picture of what she was looking at. Just how smart was this smart phone?

"How did I know?" asked Melinda, chomping away at what sounded like two stalks of celery. "Find a new place to live, Jane Wheel, because you just sold your house!"

2

"I knew something like this was going to happen," said Nellie.

Nellie always knew what was going to happen. She'd see someone trip on the sidewalk, two cars crash at an intersection, lightning hit a rooftop, and shake her head.

"I knew that was going to happen."

During what experts call the "magic years" of childhood, when children believe in impossible behaviors and events, Jane truly thought her mother had special powers. As Jane grew into the less magical years, she grew slightly more judgmental.

"If you knew it was going to happen, Mom, why didn't you stop it?"

Nellie shrugged. Her powers could not be explained.

When Jane spilled a cup of coffee, ripped the hem of her skirt, or lost her job, Nellie, in the same monotone, would chant, "I knew that was going to happen."

When Charley left? "I knew that was going to happen."

And if there was an earthquake on the other side of the world? Nellie knew that was going to happen, too.

From the smallest accidents to the largest acts of nature, Nellie knew.

Five minutes before Nellie made her most recent assertion of prescience, Jane had let herself in to what she thought was her parents' empty house. Don and Nellie would be at the EZ Way Inn and although the tavern was generally Jane's first stop, she had no desire to walk into the barroom, make small talk with Francis the bread man or Boxcar or anyone else sitting at the bar, halfheartedly watching the Cubs lose.

Instead, Jane and Rita had walked into the house through the back door, directly into the kitchen, where Jane was examining the contents of Nellie's refrigerator and Rita was sniffing around for nonexistent crumbs on Nellie's antiseptic floor. The shelves in the refrigerator, often still referred to as the icebox by both Don and Nellie, were spotless and the condiments were lined up in an orderly fashion, not a drip of catsup, not a dried spot of mustard to be seen. Orange juice and milk standing sentry on the top shelf, butter and eggs in their assigned niches. Dill pickles, olives, and jam in the side pocket. One meticulously rewrapped package of turkey, one package of muenster cheese in the cold drawer, and a loaf of bread tucked into the middle shelf. Jane had the feeling she was looking at a museum display—so clean, so predictable—as if it should be titled "Contemporary Refrigerator" and protected behind two stanchions and a velvet rope.

Yup . . . all the normal stuff of Don and Nellie's daily lives . . . except for the magnum of Veuve Clicquot.

Veuve Clicquot? Jane took out the bottle and studied the label. What were Don and Nellie doing with a bottle of French champagne?

"What the hell you looking for?" said Nellie, in a kind of low growl.

Jane nearly dropped the bottle.

"When will you stop scaring the hell out of me?" said Jane.

"You're the one snooping. Put down my wine, it's too early to drink."

Jane forced her mother into a kind of hug, although Nellie dodged and ducked out of it as quickly as possible. It was highly unusual for Nellie to be home in the middle of the day. Although Jane had never known a germ to dare settle on Nellie— she had never sniffled, sneezed, or missed a day of work that Jane knew of—she did have to acknowledge that her mother was getting older. Maybe she had started coming home for midday naps?

"I came home to mow the lawn," said Nellie. "Want to do the edging?"

"Thanks for asking, but I have to run over to Tim's and print out something and then I guess I have to sign it and . . ." Jane stopped, finally letting it all sink in. She looked at her mother. "I think I just sold my house."

"I knew something like this was going to happen," said Nellie. "You're homeless."

And with Nellie's pronouncement, which Jane knew was going to happen, Jane felt herself go a little weak in the knees.

"Do you know how freaking lucky you are?" asked Tim. Although he was phasing out of the florist business, he still operated his estate sale business out of the flower shop, partially furnished with antiques and special treasures from the estates he had helped liquidate for clients. Today, behind the long iron and butcher-block worktable he had scavenged from an old garment factory, Tim looked every inch the florist he was when he had first opened the shop. Wearing a white apron with bits of fern and foliage stuck to it, his workspace was covered with raffia and stems, and his giant coolers were filled with mixed bouquets.

"Last minute favor for a friend," Tim said, waving his hand in the general direction of the coolers. "Bit of a splashy party and I agreed to do flowers."

Jane pulled out one of the bouquets for a closer look. It was tied with a green ribbon; a few charms hung from the bow. A four-leaf clover and a fake rabbit's foot.

"What?" asked Jane, pointing to the bow.

"Lucky charms," said Tim with a shrug. "Theme party. Here's your offer. I'll print it out for you, then you can sign and fax it."

Jane was silent as she replaced the flowers.

"You *are* going to sign it," said Tim. "Aren't you?"

"What's with all of this Lucky stuff all over town. I saw a bunch of banners across from the courthouse."

"You *are* going to sign it, right, Janie?"

Jane paced around the office of the shop and looked over Tim's shoulder.

"How did you get into my e-mail? I didn't log in yet."

"Honey, I set up your e-mail in-box, remember? It's not like you ever changed your password or anything," said Tim, as the printer started spewing pages. "Stop avoiding my question. You got a cash offer in a rock-hard, rock-bottom market. You'll be more financially solvent than you've been in years." Tim started picking up the pages and arranging them in a neat stack. "Charlie has a new home in Peru or wherever . . ."

"Honduras," said Jane.

"Wherever. And I got an e-mail yesterday from Nick. He's happy as a clam at school. Loves his classes, likes the kids. He sounds perfectly at home. He'll be relieved when he doesn't have to worry about you all alone in that house," said Tim.

Jane nodded.

"So let's read this baby over and then sign it. I'm a notary, you know," said Tim, hunting for something in his desk drawer.

"Why?" asked Jane.

"Because even if it's the best deal in the world, you still have to read the contract, honey."

"No. Why are you a notary?" asked Jane

"Why are you avoiding the subject at hand?" said Tim, standing and walking over to Jane. He put his hands on her shoulders and looked her in the eye.

"I'll be homeless," said Jane.

"Nellie," said Tim.

"What?"

"You're talking like Nellie. Here's what's going to happen. You're going to sign this deal before the buyer wises up and actually looks at the real antiques in your house—the hot-water heater, the furnace. According to the date on this offer, they want to close in a week if they can. The company's buying the house for the family and the wife wants their kids in school asap. They've been in a hotel in downtown Chicago and . . ." said Tim, looking for the exact wording from Melinda's cover letter he'd printed out with the offer, ". . . the wife wants Evanston, wants your house because it's a giant corner lot, and she wants the location, both the elementary and middle school districts and plans on redecorating, but slowly, and wants your furniture, all your stuff, beds, bureaus, dining room furniture, all of the big stuff, to use as her temporary furnishings until her decorator takes over and gets in the real pieces she wants." He scanned down the page. "Listen to this. She told Melinda she thinks your eclecticism is charming, but feels that bringing the house back to a true Arts and Crafts consistency will make it a more peaceful space in which to raise her children."

"Where should I live?" asked Jane, slowly warming to the idea that she was going to have some interesting choices.

"How about a condo in the city. Make Millennium Park your front yard?"

"Maybe I could find a sweet little place in Lakeview. When Nick's home, he could walk to Wrigley Field?"

"You could go way suburban, babe. Find a cool little ranch house on a big lot west of the city and fill it up with mid-century modern."

"Or I could find one of those places off the Red Arrow Highway in Michigan on the lake, a kind of winterized summer cabin," said Jane. "All knotty pine and Pendleton blankets in the winter . . . all votive candles anchored in tin sand pails in the summer. Or a little farmhouse with a barn and outbuildings . . ."

Jane picked up a stack of Bakelite ashtrays from Tim's desk and separated them, laying them out in a line. Red, yellow, green, black. She restacked them slowly, each one making a kind of sucking sound as they came together.

"I could leave altogether," said Jane. "I don't have to stay in the Midwest. I mean, Nick's going to spend more than half of his vacations with Charley and he'll be happy to come to me wherever I am, he loves change, and I could pick him up at school and we could go somewhere together and . . ."

Jane stopped talking and looked at Tim, who had grown completely still. Until Jane started daydreaming, neither of them had ever thought that Jane would leave the Midwest, leave Evanston or Chicago, or be more than an hour or two's drive from Kankakee. Or the EZ Way Inn. Or Don and Nellie.

"It's not like you have to decide where you're going to live right this very minute," said Tim.

"Of course not," said Jane.

According to Melinda, although the buyers legally had five days to have their lawyer review the contract and arrange for an inspection of the property after Jane accepted their offer, they had assured her that they had an inspector ready to go, and that the contract review could be done in half a day. The family had moved from a company rental in Dubai and had not owned one stick of furniture in their cavernous house. Now, back in the States, they wanted cozy, they wanted livable, they wanted homey and although they planned to redecorate, some quality they saw in Jane's house made them want the place. Right now.

Melinda had written that the wife had opened the linen closet, seen the towels and sheets folded and stacked, and told her to write everything into the contract. It wouldn't be a deal breaker if Jane wanted to take her own linens and pots and pans, but they would pay top dollar to have everything in place when they moved in. Melinda's words practically vibrated on the page. *You could walk away—just walk away with a giant check in your pocket!* Where Melinda had left a space to *except* anything, Jane printed that she would be taking all of the books in the library and her desk and leather chair and the rug on the floor. Those were the only items she could think of that were special, that she hadn't already packed up and sent ahead.

Jane signed on the line, as the buyer, accepting the offer and Tim signed as a notary. He scanned the document into the computer and with a few clicks, and a SEND, Jane's house was under contract.

"Tim, with this offer, I could buy all new stuff if I wanted. I mean, I could get stuff that matched and . . ."

"Way ahead of you," said Tim, who had already read everything onscreen as it printed out and he handed the pages to Jane. "Look, I know you don't buy retail, but sheets and towels? We could go to Crate and Barrel and pretend we're getting married, you know, . . . go to one of the bridal registry parties they have on Sunday mornings and pick out all the stuff you'll need."

Tim was glowing as he described the joy of traipsing through the store before it opened to the public. "And there's a brunch, too," said Tim. "We get to walk through the entire store with our coffee and use our own handheld scanner! For what we want our friends to buy us!" Jane allowed herself to bask in the glow for a moment before she reminded Tim that she couldn't very well pick out furnishings for a new home, if she didn't have the home first.

"Okay, no rush, though. You can live with me or your folks while you decide."

Jane took a deep breath. She wasn't sure she could last more than a day or two in her old room at Don and Nellie's. And the back room of the tavern would be a dimly lit, grim alternative. Tim had a big four-bedroom on the river. She could camp out there for a few weeks, that was true. It might be fun actually. And there was no better partner for dreaming up one's home-selecting and decorating future than Tim Lowry.

"Well, our stuff is living side by side in the storage lockers, so I guess there's no reason we couldn't give actual living together a try. Besides, as much as I've loved all my stuff around me, the idea of starting with nothing and building . . . rebuilding . . . has always been appealing. And you know, the whole metaphor of this—Charlie gone from my life, Nick otherwise occupied, just me and now . . ." Jane stopped when she saw the horrified look on Tim's face.

What had he just seen on the computer screen? Had he lost an eBay bid on the Art Deco daybed he had his eye on? Did the Kalo bowl he had been visiting online for weeks get sold? Did his favorite *Project Runway* finalist have to clear off his workspace and go home?

"Oh, Jane, I am so sorry. I am so, so, so sorry."

"What?" asked Jane. What could be so terrible? "Oh Tim, if you can't put me up for a while, it's okay. Did you forget about other company, did you . . . ?"

Jane looked at her friend's handsome face. His wide-eyed terror had given way to a kind of frantic eye-darting pinball panic. He had turned to the computer screen and was furiously typing. As the soft *tap-tap-tap* of the computer keyboard grew more and more staccato, Jane looked around the shop. All those flowers in the cooler! She knew what had happened. The meticulous bouquets, neatly trimmed and decorated, meant that he had gotten this order, this favor for a friend had been called in. Tim said he had been finishing up everything that morning, tying up bouquets and attaching tiny little lucky charms. In the flurry of activity in the shop, Tim had forgotten his promise to Jane.

Instead of meeting the moving truck at the storage locker, directing the two burly workers to gently stack her boxes, her treasure chests filled with vintage photographs, crates filled with tin lithoed recipe boxes, her old suitcases packed with vintage tablecloths and kitchenalia, her red Formica-topped kitchen table, Arts and Crafts tiles, art pottery vases and flowerpots, file boxes filled with vintage maps, postcards, paper calendars from the twenties and thirties, metal boxes filled with hundred of keys, baskets filled with vintage padlocks, a collection of over one hundred advertising yardsticks, and carton after carton of vintage, collectible books, Tim had been here, making floral arrangements.

Jane had taped bubble wrap around knitting needles and sewing gadgets, advertising tape measures and paper-wrapped sewing needles from England. She had boxed boxes—carved wooden jewelry caskets and tea caddies, tramp art frames and whimsies, cast-iron banks, and a wooden chest filled with her vintage office supplies—tiny cardboard boxes shaped like miniature books that held paper fasteners and gummed reinforcements and labels and pencil leads. Leather bookmarks, coins, silver charm bracelets, and container after container of Bakelite buttons had been loaded into that moving truck. Jane had waved good-bye to decades of treasures she had hunted and gathered, knowing they would find a safe home at the other end, in a dry and well-lit storage locker in Kankakee, right next to the one where her friend Tim kept his own treasures.

In addition to all of those priceless treasures? Jane had packed up most of the clothes in her closet, since Melinda had advised clearing out half the stuff in every storage space. Nick's closet was already empty, since he had taken everything that mattered with him to school. But Jane's closet? It had been jammed with vintage beaded sweaters, swingy wool coats from the thirties and forties, plus her favorite professional clothes that she couldn't part with even after she stopped going into an office on a daily basis. Shoes, scarves, expensive bags, everyday jewelry. It was true that for picking, for weekend rummage and Dumpster diving, she only wore jeans and sweaters and boots and running shoes with the occasional pair of Birkenstocks thrown in for good measure, but in her past life? She had never gotten rid of the clothes she loved because, after all, who knew? Maybe she would wear them again?

Melinda had suggested packing everything away in large cardboard storage closets that could be taken to the locker she was renting and Jane had filled two of them with all of her clothes, leaving just a coat and jacket or two, a few shirts and dresses hanging, waving in the breeze of her now spacious closet. Besides those few personal pieces, the contents of her bureau drawers and bathroom cabinet exempted in the contract, all Jane now owned for sure was in a small duffel bag in the trunk of her car.

"I've used these movers before. I mean they're offbeat and alternative, but they're good, they're reliable. I will track down your stuff. They probably just went to get lunch and then . . ."

"They had your cell phone number, Tim. They would have called you, right? Maybe they were delayed since they didn't call?" said Jane, with a question mark built tentatively into her phrasing.

Tim's face lit up for two seconds, then his features flickered and went dark as he slapped his pocket, then realized he wasn't wearing his sport coat. He still had on his white apron.

"I left my jacket in the . . ." Tim dashed out the door, and through the wide picture window that fronted the store, Jane could see him throw open the door to his T & T Sales van and grab his jacket, feel in his pocket for his phone. He stayed outside while he listened to his voice mail and Jane read his shoulders. Hunched up around his ears as he listened, then with a slight dip as they relaxed just a bit, then they slumped—low and discouraged. Jane watched Tim gather himself and turn and walk back into the shop.

"They gave me thirty minutes to contact them and meet them at the locker. When they couldn't reach me, they had to proceed to their next location. Your stuff was a half load and they had another half load to deliver so they went on to do that, then I have to reschedule with them, since they'll be picking up more stuff at the drop off and . . ." Tim sat back down at the computer. "I just have to call them and work out a new schedule, that's all."

"Where?"

"At the home office," said Tim, almost in a whisper as he picked up the landline at his desk to call the company. "It's not exactly an office, it's . . ."

"No. Where? Did they mention *where* the other half load was going?" asked Jane.

Tim nodded, but didn't speak.

The door to the shop opened, startling both Jane and Tim, who were so wrapped up in the drama of the missed delivery they had not noticed a rented white catering truck pull up outside.

"That you, Jane? How are you? Just saw your mom and dad over at the tavern, I was dropping off some cocktail napkins with Lucky's logo on them and they were talking about your good news."

Jane looked at Baby B. Berteau, whom she and Tim had known in high school. He did deliveries for Tim and house clean-outs after sales. Apparently he did other freelance deliveries, too, since he had just said something about dropping something off at the EZ Way Inn.

"Yup, nobody sells a house in just one day, except somebody very L-U-C-K-Y," he spelled out, turning his back so they could read the word LUCKY on his jacket. "Seems like all the luck around here is rubbing off."

Tim gestured to the cooler and Baby B. started loading the boxes of floral arrangements into the truck.

"I'll make this up to you, Jane," said Tim.

"Where's that other delivery?" asked Jane.

"Omaha," said Tim.

"Omaha," repeated Jane.

"Yeah, then they pick up a quarter load in Lincoln, and probably another quarter somewhere else on the way back this way. They cover about five or six states," said Tim.

Baby B—what was his real name? Jane could hardly call a grown man with two-day stubble on his chin Babyface—picked up the last box of flowers and turned to Jane before heading out the door. "You sticking around for Lucky Days? Might as well, huh? I mean if you don't have a house to go home to, like Nellie was saying."

Jane Wheel, homeless and unencumbered, with only the clothes on her back (and in her duffel), unburdened with the materialistic woes of the world . . . stuffless . . . sat down at Tim's desk and began to rapidly click an old ballpoint pen

before taking a breath and replacing the pen in a vintage Mc-
Coy nursery planter shaped like a lamb.

"I knew something like this was going to happen," said
Jane.

3

Jane Wheel did not like being told to *take a deep breath, count to ten, step back,* or *relax.* To her, those admonitions sounded condescending, judgmental, patronizing. Jane was perfectly capable of breathing and not letting the top of her head fly off like some cartoon of a pressure-cooker head wearing a hat and glasses. She knew that in tough situations, the tough got going.

That is why, after absorbing the news that she had sold her house and everything in it except for what might be left in her underwear drawer, and then discovering that the truck with all of the prized possessions she had quickly but carefully culled from her house was more than one state west of where she currently stood, Jane Wheel got into her car, locked the doors, checked to make sure all the windows were tightly shut, and opened her mouth to scream. She planned to belt out every vile, despicable word she had ever heard. She would invent new words—graphic portmanteau words combining anger and venom and despair. She would wail and moan and rend her garments.

But the scream would not come. In fact, Jane felt eerily calm.

"Isn't 'calm' just 'numb' with a positive spin?" she asked. *Whatever,* she thought. *For now, I'll go with calm.*

"I can't rend my garments anyway," said Jane, again out loud, "since I don't have any garments to spare."

Jane chose to ignore the fact that calm people didn't talk to themselves out loud and turned right on Station Street, heading toward the EZ Way Inn. According to Baby B, Don and Nellie were both there. Nellie must have abandoned the lawn mowing in order to rush to the tavern and tell Don about the miracle of Jane's house being sold. Jane pictured her nondriving mother hustling the eight or so blocks to the tavern, pedaling Jane's old bicycle. If Rita were a little shaggier and a lot smaller, Jane could imagine her head poking out of the handlebar basket and Nellie would be the spitting image of the determined, upright Miss Gulch taking off with Toto in the *Wizard of Oz.*

Driving west on Station Street, an illuminated sign caught her eye.

MACK'S CAFÉ OPEN 24 HOURS!

Mack's Café hadn't been open for years. Thinking about Nellie on a bike reminded Jane that Mack's was one of those childhood bicycling destination spots, offering milk shakes, Cokes in glass bottles, and a candy counter. The diner had closed its doors before Jane finished high school. The storefront had remained vacant as far as Jane knew. Why would Mack's reopen now, since all of the businesses that provided the lunchtime customers, the stove factory and appliance store down the road, had closed their doors?

Jane was in no rush to arrive at the EZ Way Inn, and answer questions about her house or lack thereof. She would have to tell her parents and anyone else who lounged at the bar about her wayward possessions. Knowing how Nellie felt about her stuff, her collections, her treasures, her rescued objets d'art, Jane was in no hurry to hear her mother say "good riddance" when Jane told the story of the runaway truck.

So why not stop at Mack's and see if someone still knew how to make a milk shake?

Several booths were filled, which surprised Jane for two reasons. It was late afternoon, almost dinnertime in Kankakee. Jane knew her parents—if not working at the tavern or waiting for Carl, their longtime evening bartender, to arrive—like their fellow Kankakeans, preferred to have dinner between five and six. Once, when Jane attempted to cook her parents a special dinner and told them it would be ready at seven, Nellie had snorted. "What do you think we are, French?" "Or Italian?" Don had added. The customers who filled the booths at Mack's were drinking coffee or sipping milk shakes. It was too late for lunch, too early—even in Kankakee—for dinner, but as far as she knew, this area of West Kankakee, mostly residential except for the businesses located few and far between on Station Street, didn't support a big "coffee-break" or "afternoon-teatime" crowd. This all felt suspiciously European.

Who were these people, wearing baseball caps or sunglasses on top of their heads? Jane saw that most of the tables had one person who was writing in a notebook, taking down what others said. Although laughter occasionally erupted, the faces of these people looked dead serious. At the counter, a waitress had been bending down, picking up her order pad from the floor. When she straightened and looked at Jane, both of them gasped—one with recognition, the other with simple surprise.

"Ruthie?" asked Jane. Ruthie had been a waitress at Mack's thirty years ago. Same white uniform, same striped apron, same pin with red rhinestones that spelled out RUTHIE. Jane did some quick calculations. Could Ruthie be the same Ruthie? Of course not. Wasn't Ruthie Mack's wife or sister, and wouldn't that make her at least sixty now? Maybe seventy, eighty? This Ruthie, couldn't be more than twenty-five.

"You startled me, didn't hear you come in, honey," said time-warp Ruthie. "Want a table? Or are you joining some-body?" The waitress waved her hands around the room.

"Chocolate shake to go, heavy on the chocolate, light on the whipped cream, please," said Jane, automatically ordering just what she ordered when she was ten years old. Something threw Jane off—maybe it was being called "honey" by some-one considerably younger and infinitely perkier than herself.

"Sure thing," said Ruthie, repeating the order to a young man farther down the counter whom Jane hadn't even seen before. She was relieved it wasn't a thin prematurely white-haired man with the name MACK stitched across his pocket. "Sam makes a great milk shake. Just be a minute."

"I used to come here when I was a kid," said Jane. "There was a waitress named Ruthie," Jane pointed to the pin. "Was it your grandmother or . . . ?"

"No, but you're close. I was hired because I looked like Ruthie. At least that's what Bill said when I got the gig." She pointed to an old photograph hung behind the counter. Ruthie, and Mack, and three others were all leaning in close to a covered cake stand with what appeared to be a four-layer coconut cake protected inside the dome.

The girl picked up a full coffeepot and ran over to a booth whose occupants had been waving at her.

"Top you off, sugar?" she asked, with no trace of irony that Jane could detect.

Two guys sitting at the counter smirked. "Overkill, yes?" said one, peering over his glasses, watching her make the rounds with the coffeepot.

"Method," said his companion. "I heard her say her 'dogs were barking' a few minutes ago.

Sam came over and delivered her milk shake. Jane glanced up at the menu board to see the price. Some things—prices, for example—had to have changed, even if the new owners of Mack's, if they were in fact new owners, were trying to keep the waitress looking the same as she did twenty years ago.

"Lucky Burger?" asked Jane, reading it off the menu.

"Sorry, grill's off right now. We had a little problem back in the kitchen. Up and running by breakfast tomorrow morning. You signing for this?"

Sam had shoved a clipboard in front of her. The top sheet was divided into a kind of grid where one could sign his/her name, then there was a space for crew name, then date and time.

"I was going to pay cash," whispered Jane. She leaned in, knowing that she was in some *Groundhog Day* scenario and wasn't sure she wanted all the baseball caps and sunglasses to notice her confusion.

"You're not with the show, are you?" asked Sam, also leaning in.

Jane shook her head, trying to formulate the first of approximately a hundred questions lining up in her head.

"You knew my great-aunt Ruthie, didn't you?" asked Sam, still speaking low.

Jane nodded.

"So the milk shake's on the house," said Sam. When he said that, the young man smiled and Jane could see the familiar grin of old Mack, handing her extra pennies for the gumball machine.

"What the hell is going on here?" said Jane, then realized she sounded exactly like Nellie and corrected herself. "I just got into town to visit my parents and I'm a little confused."

"Who are your parents?"

"Don and Nellie. They run the EZ Way Inn about six blocks west of here."

"Sure, I know it. Home of the Lucky Duck."

"Home of the frosted mug," corrected Jane.

"Not anymore," said Sam. "Look, they'll explain it to you. I got to clean up in back from the grease fire. Actors don't know squat about being grill cooks."

A few years ago, a couple of con men came to Kankakee and offered to turn the town into some kind of theme park. Jane thought it unlikely that they would come back and try the same con. Then again, things were looking suspiciously bright and cheery and wholesome around town. Passing the gas station just before she turned into the EZ Way Inn, Jane almost drove on to the sidewalk when she saw a gas station employee actually pumping gas.

What the hell was going on? Jane knew what it was to be haunted. When she shopped an estate sale, she was overcome with a feeling that the former owners of the stuff she was handling were smiling at her, explaining what drink they had poured into that highball glass, what flowers they had placed in the cream-colored, two-handled McCoy vase. But this haunting was different—much more like a Hollywood feature film possession. Shortly after hitting town, Jane was overcome with the feeling that she was being held hostage inside of a movie. At Tim's shop, it was that movie about identity theft with Sandra Bullock—or maybe that one where somebody wakes up from a coma and his life has been erased. That's what losing track of all her possessions felt like. At Mack's she had walked into a scene from *Groundhog Day*, where her life would be played out over and over until she got it right. And now, watching that gas station guy with a big grin on his face wash the car windshield? Jane was smack dab in the middle of *Back to the Future*.

The EZ Way Inn looked unusually crowded. The parking lot was almost full. Jane checked her oversized man's watch. Even though Nick told her that no one wore a watch anymore since every man, woman, and child was always checking his or her phone, Jane preferred a glance at her wrist to a dig into her tote bag or even a dip into her pocket. And the giant numbers on this watch didn't lie. It read 5:15 P.M. Shouldn't everyone be home eating dinner?

"Janie!" said her dad, coming out from behind the bar to give her a giant hug. "Your mother told me the good news. Congratulations, honey."

Don's words were kind and celebratory, but he looked his daughter over carefully and said in a softer voice, just for her, "Are you okay with selling the house? That's a big change for you and Nick."

When Nellie hit certain trigger points in conversation with her daughter, Jane could feel her hair stand on end. When Don, a kind old bear on the outside, an equally kind and somewhat shrewder bear on the inside, hit those same trigger points—filled with concern about Jane's welfare—Jane could feel herself go all soft inside. Tears came quickly and right now, in front of a full barroom where Nellie was having a tug-of-war with Vince over a beer bottle that she claimed was empty and he said had a little left in it, Jane did not want to cry on her father's shoulder.

Jane tried to focus on something, anything other than Don's face with those eyes that looked right into her heart and demanded nothing but the truth. Just over her dad's right shoulder, she spotted a banner. HOME OF THE LUCKY DUCK!

"What the hell is a Lucky Duck?" asked Jane, curiosity canceling out tears.

"It's a drink I invented for Lucky Days," said Don.

"Okay, maybe we have to go a little further back on this one," said Jane. "I need a little fill-in on Lucky Days, too."

"Who invented the Lucky Duck?" asked Nellie. Despite the beer bottle throwdown with Vince halfway across the bar, Nellie's batlike radar picked up on Don's remark.

"Well, Nellie, you helped with the recipe," said Don, "but I—"

"Helped with the recipe? You wanted to use vodka in it, for God's sake," said Nellie, grabbing the beer bottle from Vince once and for all when he got distracted, anticipating the storm that was about to rain down on all patrons of the EZ Way Inn. "He said vodka was what the young people drank and we had to have a vodka drink."

"Jane drinks vodka, Nellie," said Don.

"So?" said Nellie. "Look at her shoes. She's a smart girl, but she's no trendsetter."

Jane felt a little giddy as she looked down at her Birkenstocks. Okay, clunky shoes, but Nellie thought she was smart and Jane needed a little boost after her day. And, let's face it, when a girl is hovering around forty—either side of it—a girl likes to be called a girl.

"I wanted it spicy," said Don. "Worcestershire sauce and—"

"He made a Bloody Mary, that's all," said Nellie.

"No, I had a secret ingredient," said Don.

"It was tasty," said Francis the bread man. "I tried out the recipes."

"I bet you did," said Vince.

Nellie poured a brown opaque liquid into a glass, picked up a cocktail shaker, and gave it two no-nonsense shakes, and added a small amount of red liquid to the brown. She placed a wooden stick that had what looked like it might have been a baby carrot stuck to one end in the glass, tossed a few ice cubes in, and handed it to Jane.

"Try it," said Nellie. "This is my recipe."

"What's this?" asked Jane taking the carrot-on-a-stick out of the drink.

"When I got time, I carve those things to a point so they look like a duck's beak," said Nellie, with what Jane could only assume was pride. "Your dad's drink didn't even have a garnish."

Don poured Jane what looked like a glass of orange juice, perhaps a little paler, and threw in a shake or two of grapefruit bitters.

Jane sat down at the bar next to Francis and stared at the two glasses. Nellie came over and placed a napkin next to her concoction. It was white with black block printing: TRY NELLIE'S LUCKY DUCK. Don came over and slipped a paper coaster under the diluted orange juice. Printed around the edge of the circle was: TRY DON'S LUCKY DUCK.

"They're both real good," said Francis.

"You haven't ordered either one since we stopped giving free samples," said Nellie, picking up his beer bottle and pouring out the last few drops into his glass, before whisking it away.

"You let him finish his beer," whined Vince.

Jane had had the kind of day that called for a drink at the end of it. She wouldn't have chosen either her father's screwdriver—even though Nellie kept insisting it was a Bloody Mary—or her mother's swamp water, but what the hell? How often do you sell your house and divest yourself of almost all worldly goods?

Jane sipped Don's Lucky Duck.

"See, Nellie, I don't need a garnish because mine's the color of a duck," said Don.

"Where the hell you ever seen an orange duck?"

"Not bad," said Jane. It was actually refreshing. The mixer with the vodka was orange juice and grapefruit juice with some fresh lemon. Something was a little sparkly in there, too. Club soda? And Jane noticed only when she sipped, that Don had rimmed the glass with Margarita salt so it had a tart and savory taste with just the slightest sweetness from the orange juice.

"It's kind of like a mimosa, Dad," said Jane.

Don shook his head. "Nope, no champagne."

Jane raised an eyebrow. Don had been reading his bartender's guide.

Nellie handed her a glass of water.

"That's enough of that breakfast drink. Mine's the real Lucky Duck," said Nellie.

The song on the jukebox ended and the sound was muted on the television. The barroom had grown so quiet, Jane expected to hear the scraping of a chair on the floor as one of the cowpokes fled the scene before the shootout.

Jane sipped Nellie's thick brown goop. Salty, savory, and hearty with a kick. Jane took a small bite of carrot and another sip.

"Delicious," said Jane, completely surprised. "It looks vile, but it's delicious. Like spiked vegetable soup or something."

"So whose drink is better?" asked Vince.

Jane scanned the room. All of the regulars and many of the strangers—more baseball caps and sunglasses, Jane noted—waited for her to make the pronouncement. Nellie, all steely springs and coils, and Don, all smiles and hope, watched their daughter's face.

Jane pointed at Don's drink. "Daytime Lucky Duck . . . serve before five P.M. and"—she added, pointing to Nellie's recipe—"Lucky Duck After Dark . . . serve at dinnertime and beyond."

Jane felt like Solomon the Wise, but Nellie wasn't having it.

"You got to pick one or—"

The front door to the EZ Way Inn opened and a tall man in jeans, boots, and a linen shirt walked in. He gave a one-fingered salute to Don, who nodded, and two more strangers came in behind him, one with a camera and one holding lights and portable stands for setting them up.

"I give up," said Jane. "What is going on in this town? What's with all the Lucky stuff?"

"Lucky Miller, hon," said Don, as if he were explaining two plus two equaling four.

"He's shooting a television special here in Kankakee, a comedy special on HBO, and he decided to do it from his hometown," said Barney, another EZ way regular, over his shoulder as he began feeding coins into the jukebox.

"They're shooting little bits for the opening all over town and tonight, Lucky's coming in for a Lucky Duck," said Don.

"My Lucky Duck," said Nellie.

The men who had come in to set up the cameras started laughing and one or two of the folks at the bar, whom Jane now realized were part of Lucky's crew and staff, laughed with them.

"Not HBO," said the cameraman.

"Yeah, it's Comedy Central that does them roasts," said Vince.

"Not Comedy Central, either," said a thirty-something-year-old with thick glasses, wearing the ubiquitous baseball cap, which Jane now saw had a four-leaf clover logo on the front. "In fact, you see that bin you got with all those aluminum beer cans in it for recycling?" Some of the regulars at the bar—the ones who could understand the man's thick British accent—nodded, thinking they were getting some new information about the exciting event taking place in their very own town.

"You put those cans out with some pieces of string and

you see if you can pick up any stations, because that's the only place that's going to air this special."

A few people facing the front of the bar snickered, but all of those sitting on the other side, facing the back door kept their faces completely neutral.

Jane supposed their completely humorless faces had something to do with the fact that a man in a bright red shirt and a leather blazer was standing in the kitchen doorway facing into the barroom. Although he didn't look exactly like the caricatures on the banners, Lucky Miller was recognizable. He did have a mop of black hair—although it didn't actually appear to be his hair—and he also had a cigar, unlit, sticking out of the side of his mouth. It must have been a permanent fixture because Lucky could talk perfectly well with the cigar glued into place.

"Malcolm, that you made that wise-ass remark?"

"Shit," muttered Malcolm. "Yes, sir, testing it out for the show, Lucky, just like you told us to do with the new material."

"Good boy," said Lucky, "good boy."

The jukebox roared back on with some country song that Jane was surprised Don allowed on the machine. He was a music lover, but couldn't stand country. *Love songs to trucks*, he always said, although he admitted to a soft spot for Willie Nelson's voice.

Lucky pointed to the jukebox and the cameraman pulled the plug, shrugging his shoulders at Barney, who protested that he had just played that song.

"Got to do a sound check. Drinks are on us while we're here, though," he said, patting Barney on the shoulder.

Everybody relaxed when they heard that. Jane realized

that's why everyone was here. Lucky came in to shoot a little B roll for the special and when he stopped into a place, everything was on the house. Free drinks would keep a lot of Don and Nellie's customers in the bar past their dinnertime.

"Free drinks, huh?" said Nellie. She had been staring at Lucky Miller since he walked in. "You going to pay that bill tonight or run up a tab?"

A pretty blonde in a short denim skirt and a red T-shirt came over to Nellie with a clipboard and began to explain the system they were using around town.

"We ask that you invoice us at the end of the evening for everything used or consumed during the filming; we'll sign a copy, and your reimbursement check will arrive before the end of the month. My name is Brenda and I will be personally responsible for—"

"I'd like Lucky to pay us tonight," said Nellie, her arms folded.

Lucky had been consulting with another baseball cap, who seemed to be feeding him lines and suggesting the best place for him to sit, but when Nellie made her pronouncement, he looked at her.

"You've got to be the famous Nellie," said Lucky. "I've heard about you."

"Yeah? You've heard of me but you don't remember me, huh?"

"Nellie, let it go," said Don.

Lucky shook Don's hand, but never took his eyes off of Nellie.

"We know each other?"

"You lived just off of Fifth Avenue when you were a kid, right?"

"For a couple of years, but then the family moved to—"

"Remember a little guy who lisped? Everybody called him Boing Boing?"

"Sure," said Lucky, "I mean, who could forget a kid named Boing Boing, right?"

"You stole his lunch money and I kicked your ass and got the money back," said Nellie.

"Nellie," said Lucky, "Nellie!" He tried to give her a hug, but she ducked out and grabbed a glass with her Lucky Duck concoction doing its best to imitate pond water.

"So, you know what I do when somebody tries to cheat somebody, right?" said Nellie, handing him the drink.

Jane was surprised that Don was letting Nellie get away with so much trash talk to a celebrity who was bringing so much business to the EZ Way Inn at dinnertime on a Wednesday night. Don, however, didn't look disapproving at all. Instead, he was doing all he could to stop himself from laughing.

"Got it all," said the cameraman.

"Jeez, Nellie, you're great! You're a natural," said Lucky. "I was pretty scared."

"See, your mother was supposed to go on the attack when he came in the door. Like she didn't know who he was or she didn't like him as a kid or something. She made that all up herself," said Don.

"That was an improv?" asked Jane.

Don nodded, although he didn't look completely comfortable with the term. "It was a bit," he said. "They call it a bit."

Jane looked at her mother, who was now pouring pond water for the camera crew. Lucky had moved over to a table where they were going to film him tasting each of the Lucky Ducks.

Jane walked over to her mother and patted her shoulder.

"That was great, Mom. You got me," said Jane.

"Yeah."

"I mean, Boing Boing? How did you make that up?"

"I didn't make it up," said Nellie.

"What's in your Lucky Duck?" asked Brenda. "Lucky has some allergies."

"Secret recipe," said Nellie.

Brenda whispered something in Lucky's ear.

"Any peanuts in this drink?" asked Lucky.

"Nope," said Nellie.

"Who the hell would put peanuts in a drink?" said Nellie to Jane. "These people are idiots."

"So Lucky really did steal Boing Boing's lunch money?"

Nellie looked at her daughter as if she had never seen her before.

"What are you talking about, Jane?"

"The story, the improv you just did. You said it was true."

"Lucky Miller only lived in Kankakee for a few years. He didn't know his ass from a hole in the ground then, and he doesn't now.

"What about Boing Boing?"

Jane would have to find out later. Two chairs toppled over as Brenda jumped up and ran for her purse. "Call 911, Lucky's having a reaction. Where's the goddamn EpiPen?" Brenda found what she was looking for ran back and jabbed Lucky. He began breathing regularly and his red face calmed slightly.

"Damn it," said Nellie. "Now your dad's going to say his Lucky Duck won."

4

Lucky refused to go to the hospital.

"Let's not overreact, everybody," he said, replacing the cigar in his mouth.

Don brought water to the table and scanned the adjoining tables for any open bags of cashews or beer nuts. He apologized and pointed out that he had removed the snack rack entirely after receiving the advance memo that Lucky's production team had sent out.

"Cashews are no problem, buddy, don't be so spooked about this," said Lucky. "Everything's good. We got me sipping the drink, right? Now I'll just sip the orange crap. No need to change the bit," said Lucky to the production assistant, who was leaning over him, whispering.

"What the hell?" asked Don.

Jane thought her father might be reacting to his concoction being referred to less than respectfully, but Don hadn't heard the remark.

"Why can he eat cashews?" asked Don.

"Tree nuts," said Nellie.

Jane and Don both looked at Nellie, who had watched

the scene unfold from a few feet away, her arms folded and her eyes still trained on Lucky Miller.

"What?" asked Don.

"Cashews are tree nuts and peanuts aren't nuts at all," said Jane.

Don shook his head in admiration for his wife. Jane, too, was admiring and, she had to admit to herself, shocked. How did Nellie know half the stuff she did? She hadn't graduated from high school, she had gone out to work as soon as she was able, and Jane had never seen her mother read a book. What was her secret?

The camera rolled as Lucky, patted down and powdered, raised Don's Lucky Duck to his lips. Jane winced as the comedian licked the salt off the rim with a wink and a kind of leer at one of the lighting techs. Was there anything more disgusting than an overage lech?

Nellie remained where she was, staring at Lucky, as the crew packed up their gear to move on to the next bar where Lucky would taste a drink invented in his honor. Lucky finally looked up from the notes thrust under his nose by an eager writer—not Malcolm, Jane noted—and saw Nellie staring at him.

"Still thinking about Boing Boing, Nellie?" asked Lucky. "Convince yourself I really did bully some guy you knew?"

"Nope," said Nellie. "I know for a fact you didn't."

Lucky took a few steps closer to Nellie, slipping one arm back into his leather jacket. "So why you giving me the fisheye? Something's on your mind."

People were ordering drinks fast and furious since the Lucky crew was getting ready to leave and one more free drink would have to be poured and served pretty quick to make it onto the TV show tab. Don was bouncing back and forth behind the bar, but Nellie stayed where she was, eyeball to eyeball with Lucky. Only Jane paid attention to their conversation.

"We didn't even start calling him Boing Boing until he . . . until after seventh grade," said Nellie. "And we were doing it behind his back." Nellie waited to add that piece of information until Lucky was almost finished putting on his jacket.

"What'd you call him before that?" said Lucky. He was no longer paying close attention to Nellie, just continuing the conversation halfheartedly, as his assistants gathered up bags and briefcases and props for their next stop. Although just two steps away from her, Lucky turned his back to Nellie, not expecting her to answer and began waving toward the customers at the bar who were raising their glasses. Jane noted that Lucky looked hale and hearty for a man who had recently been struggling for breath on the floor of the EZ Way Inn.

"We just called him his name. Dickie," said Nellie. "Dickie Boynton."

Lucky was a pro and he didn't stop waving or smiling while the camera was running, but Jane saw his shoulders go back and his head move slightly to one side when he heard Nellie say the name. No peanuts in sight but at the mention of Dickie Boynton, Lucky Miller appeared to be a man who had trouble trying to catch his breath,

"I'm sure I'll see you all again," said Lucky. "Won't be able to resist stopping back at the EZ Way Inn for a nightcap. Thanks for the Lucky Duck, Don." Lucky turned and faced Nellie. "Sure there weren't any peanuts in that drink, Nellie?"

"Not this time," said Nellie.

And just like that, with the slam of the screen door in the kitchen leading out to the parking lot, all the glitz and glamour of baseball caps and sunglasses and free drinks for all were out the door and on their way to the next saloon where the owners and bartenders were vying to become the inventor of the Lucky Miller–sanctioned Lucky Duck cocktail.

And now, Jane thought, *time to get to the bottom of all of this Lucky Miller stuff.*

Nellie placed her jars and bottles of secret ingredients along with a fifth of Jack Daniel's on a vintage high-rimmed metal beer tray that Jane recognized as a bar collectible she had given to Don last Father's Day. She threw a clean dish towel over what she called the "fixings" and placed it on a low shelf in the back room off the kitchen.

"I told you, Janie, it was a bit. I was making up a fight with Lucky, just like that skinny producer told me to do."

"Yeah, but that Boing Boing stuff? Seemed real to me," said Jane.

"I'm a hell of an actress," said Nellie.

Jane decided to work this story from another angle. Nellie wasn't going to spill the beans until she was good and ready, so Jane would have to play a "just the facts, Ma'am" game as well as her mother did. And was that possible? Not in a million years. No one defined "need to know basis" as well as Nellie. Even when Jane used to ask her what the family was having for dinner, Nellie would give her a look.

"Who wants to know?"

So Jane decided to take her questions into the barroom while her mother cleaned up in the kitchen.

"Dad, what exactly is going on with all the banners downtown and what just happened here?" Jane made herself comfortable on one of the padded bar stools and out of habit Don placed a cardboard coaster down in front of her. Jane knew her dad didn't carry Grey Goose vodka, so she nodded toward the tap and Don drew a textbook glass of beer—frosted mug, perfect amount of foam and icy cold. The snack rack was back, so Jane grabbed a pack of beer nuts and tore it open, offering the bag first to her dad, then to Francis on her right. Both shook their heads.

"I thought your mom told you all about this. Pretty exciting for everyone. Lucky Miller grew up here . . . at least until sixth or seventh grade. His family lived over near Saint Stan's. He hit it big as a comedian and now they're doing a comedy special, like one of those dinners where everybody insults the guy who's being honored, and he's filming it here in Kankakee."

Don crossed to the other side of the bar to draw a beer for Bobby, one of the lingering few who didn't disappear for dinner when the free drinks ended. Francis nudged Jane and nodded.

"Pretty exciting, Janie."

"How can they be shooting everything here?" asked Jane. "Where is there a studio or a soundstage or a—"

"They're fixing up the old stone factory over there on Water Street. Making it just like a New York loft," said Francis.

"Francis," yelled Nellie from the kitchen, "what's a loft?"

"Mmmm-mm-mm," (Kankakeean for I don't know) muttered Francis, reverting to his native tongue.

"What I thought," said Nellie, still working in the kitchen.

"Yup," added Don. "That factory's been empty for thirty

years and now it's getting some life again. I heard they got the rental for nothing, just a promise of cleanup and bring the electrical up to code."

Jane sipped her beer. Now that beer had become the new wine, everybody rattled off special brands and brews and labels and batches, and discussed hops and barley and malt the way they used to talk about nose and fruitiness and cru and clarity. Last time Jane had met some of her old advertising colleagues in Chicago, they had pressed upon her red ales and Michigan breweries and seemed to really know the difference between lagers and IPAs. Everyone now seemed to know the difference between hoppy and *very* hoppy. Jane wished she could just treat all the new beer afficionados to a perfectly drawn ice cold American lager from Don's immaculately clean tap system.

"Perfect, Dad," Jane said, holding up her glass and toasting her father. "I'm still not sure I get all the fuss about Lucky Miller, though. I've never heard of him."

"Aha! Finally! An honest citizen of Kankakee!" The writer who Lucky had called Malcolm slid over from the dark corner near the cigarette machine. Jane figured all of the out-of-towners left when Lucky and his followers sashayed out the back door, but apparently, Malcolm had chosen to remain behind and, hidden behind the bulk of Bobby on the bar stool to his right, he had been drinking and listening. Now, it seemed, he was ready to talk.

"I bat cleanup for Lucky and the crew," said Malcolm, dipping his head in an introductory bow. "Correct American baseball reference, right? I make sure that the bills get signed, or in this case, paid, and the talk stays positive after he's come in to mark his territory, so to speak."

Malcolm held up his glass and waggled it for a refill. Don reached under the bar for the whiskey and poured another shot while Malcolm took a quick peek at his phone, which was vibrating steadily. He shrugged off whatever message was buzzing in and turned his full attention on Jane.

"Tell me everything you don't know about Lucky Miller, you gorgeous woman."

Jane smiled, not at the gorgeous line, although those lines are almost always nice to hear, but rather at Malcolm's obvious delight that someone in Kankakee wasn't fawning over Lucky.

"I'm not a big television watcher," said Jane, "but I keep my hand in. I used to work in advertising; I supervised the production of several commercial campaigns for a big agency and we looked at talent all the time. I knew TV lineups and names from casts, even if I didn't exactly follow sit-com plot lines. And before my professional life, there was college life and I was a theater major. Even if we didn't watch television, everyone knew someone who knew someone in the business and was hoping to get a leg up in New York or L.A. I know a ton of names of B- and C-list actors and comedians, even if I might not know everything about their work. I have a great memory for names. And, finally, I grew up in Kankakee where we try as hard as the next guy to claim celebrity connections . . . ."

"Fred MacMurray was born here," said Francis.

"Do you kids know who Fred MacMurray is?" asked Don.

Jane smiled at her dad, thinking that Malcolm might not realize that anyone near his daughter's age was a kid to Don.

She and Malcolm answered at the same time, respectively.

"Double Indemnity!"

"*The Shaggy Dog!*"

"*Son of Flubber,*" they then shouted together.

"Yeah, Fred MacMurray was born in Kankakee, but his folks were just passing through," yelled Nellie from the kitchen.

Jane turned back to Malcolm. "So you can see, I know my celebrity trivia, past and present, but I have never heard of Lucky Miller."

"He's a Las Vegas act," said Bobby from across the bar.

"You've never been west of the VA hospital in Quincy," shouted Nellie. "What do you know about Las Vegas?"

"I saw him on the *Love Boat* once," said Don.

"Bingo!" said Malcolm. "A true Lucky fun fact!"

"I remember because there was an article in the paper about him being from Kankakee and having a guest-star part on the show."

"I shall educate you," said Malcolm. "I will tell you the Lucky Miller story in a nutshell. Lucky, born Herman Mullet, in Lima, Ohio , was the son of a salesman who moved around a great deal. The family never remained in any town more than two years and Herman, also known as Hermie, spent his sixth and seventh grade years in Kankakee, where he made few friends and, as far as I've been able to determine, left absolutely no lasting impression on anyone."

"I could have sworn he lived here for—" began Don.

"Aha! Of course you could have!" said Malcolm. "That's the whole idea."

Malcolm stopped for air and when he had taken a breath, threw back another shot, replaced his glass on the bar, and signaled for another pour.

"Herman ended up in Los Angeles and went from bit part

to bit part, occasionally doing stand-up in strip joints or opening for singers. The singers who went on to bigger and better things immediately got better opening acts. Then Lucky's big break came along. He got cast as a has-been comic on the *Love Boat*. Lucky fed the publicist on the show a lot of guff about his once-promising career, the guy wrote it up, and Lucky started believing he really had been somebody and decided to stage a comeback."

"From where?" asked Francis.

"Exactly," said Malcolm. "He needed a biography that was just truthful enough to pass while he rebuilt his image as a small-town boy with big dreams who could have had it all, but for a few wrong turns and bad breaks. His bio mentioned lots of big names in lists with his, but never actually said he'd worked with them. It stopped just short of saying he wrote for Milton Berle and Red Skelton when he was barely out of his nappies. It implied, though, that he had studied at the feet of the masters and could have been a contender."

"How do you know all this?" asked Jane. "Makes more sense that Lucky would surround himself with young writers who believed the bio and wrote for the character he created."

"True," said Malcolm, nodding.

Jane felt the lightbulb switch on over her head "You wrote it. You created the bio. You're—"

"Dr. Frankenstein, at your service."

"I am so lost," said Francis. "Lucky did horror movies, too?"

"May I buy you a drink, sir?" Malcolm asked, patting Francis on the shoulder. "It is Lucky Miller fans such as yourself that make my job so rewarding."

5

Nellie emerged from the kitchen immediately after Malcolm's cab arrived to take him back to the Lucky Miller Motel—actually the B-Back-Inn south of town, renamed in honor of Lucky Miller week.

"You believe that guy?" asked Nellie.

Jane shrugged. What was not to believe? She had watched him drink four shots of whiskey and who knows how many he had downed before that? Why would he claim to write the official fake bio of Lucky Miller? Not exactly like claiming screenwriting credit for *Chinatown*.

"Don't you?" Jane countered.

"Few holes in the story, that's all," said Nellie with a shrug. "Besides, the guy's a lush. And—" Nellie dragged out the syllable for effect—"he had an English accent."

"Yeah, Nellie's right. He did talk a little funny," said Francis.

Nellie nodded and looked Jane in the eye.

"There's something else that doesn't add up," said Nellie.

Don had finished giving Carl the instructions for the night, taken most of the cash out of the register, and told the bartender he could lock up early if there were no customers at eleven. Carl nodded, not a word waster, and dragged a bar stool behind the bar so he could perch comfortably and face the television between drawing beers and pouring shots.

Jane had offered to treat her parents to dinner out to celebrate the selling of her house, even though she wasn't sure how much she felt like celebrating.

"Okay, Mom, I'll bite. What doesn't add up?" said Jane, grabbing her purse and keys. "Wait, I know. . . . Where's the money coming from? If he wasn't ever a success, how can he finance a comeback . . . or who's interested in financing a comeback for a has-been who's really a never-was?"

"Now you're talking like a detective," said Nellie, flicking off the light in the kitchen. "No sandwiches, Carl. Don't make any food for anybody. I don't want to have to clean up the kitchen in the morning,"

Carl nodded without taking his eyes off the television set. He had worked for Don and Nellie as their night bartender for over thirty years. He had heard the same instructions thousands of times. He had quit at least fifty times. Don had fired him at least twenty times. Nellie had fired him over one hundred times. No matter who fired who or who quit, Carl always showed up shuffling through the back door around six every evening.

Jane pulled up in front of Mack's Café and suggested they get a hamburger and a milk shake. She had wanted another milk shake from Mack's as soon as she finished the first one.

"What the hell, Janie? Mack hasn't been open in twenty years," said Don, pointing to the darkened interior of the storefront.

"It was open this afternoon . . . something for the Lucky

Miller show. The sign said OPEN TWENTY-FOUR HOURS. It was filled with writers working and they had a waitress in there doing a fifties shtick. The milk shake was great. And it was Mack's grandson running the place."

"Got to cost a lot of cash to reopen a place like that and get it all back up to pretty and polished," said Nellie. "Follow the money, Janie."

Nellie had her face pressed against the car window, staring into Mack's Café window. Without turning to look at either Don or Jane, Nellie added, her breath fogging up the window glass, "Besides, you see how Hermie caved in on himself when I said Dickie Boynton's name? Something fishy going on with that guy and all the money he's tossing around town. Or," she added, "pretending to toss around."

Jane nodded, then realized she was agreeing with some kind of conspiracy theory of Nellie's that she didn't even get. What was wrong with turning Kankakee into a soundstage for a week or so? Even if Lucky was overspending his producer's money, it was still going into pockets in Kankakee, and a lot of those pockets could use filling. Jane also suspected that L.A. or Vegas money, even the amount earned by a B-list comedian like Lucky Miller, went a long way in Kankakee, Illinois, in terms of rent and housing and production costs.

Jane and her dad got her mother to agree to dinner at the Steak and Brew. Nellie thought it was too nice a place for a Wednesday. Besides, when they ate at a tablecloth restaurant, Don always ordered a martini and Nellie didn't approve. But Jane decided that selling one's house in this economy for asking price plus was worth the judgmental stares of Nellie. Jane ordered a martini, too.

"What's he got? A radar chip in you?" said Nellie, counting the pieces of celery in the relish tray and comparing it to the one on the next table over.

Jane raised her hands in surrender.

Gesturing with a nod of her head, Nellie muttered, "Lowry."

Tim walked directly over to their table and pulled up a chair without being asked.

"Steak and Brew on a Wednesday, eh? Pretty fancy."

"I told you we shouldn't come here," said Nellie, putting the menu in front of her face.

"Carl told me he overheard Janie saying she wanted to eat at S and B," said Tim. He called over the waitress, ordered a gin and tonic and asked for a menu.

"Why don't you just make yourself at home and join us, Lowry?" said Nellie.

"Thanks for asking. How about if I order some appetizers for the table?"

Jane wished she knew if Tim chose to ignore Nellie's sarcasm or if it truly went over his head.

"Oh, for God's sake," said Nellie, trying to slink under the table. "Who do you think we are? The king and queen or something?"

"Hot artichoke dip does not a princess make, Nellie," said Tim. "Besides, the dinners take a while and I am starving. And"—he added putting down the menu—"I've got some good news to share with you, my lovely adopted family."

"What's up, Timmy?" asked Don, savoring his second olive.

"Don't *we* have to *agree* to adopt *you*?" asked Nellie.

Tim spread out four bright yellow rectangles on the table. Then, with a flourish, he laid down four more, almost identical, although these were a bright green.

"Who else would I share these with, if not my adoptive family?" asked Tim, his smile at about seventy-five watts and growing.

Don picked up the yellow rectangle, which Jane realized was a ticket, and read aloud, "VIP seating for the preview show/dress rehearsal." He then picked up a green ticket and in a slightly louder voice read, "VIP seating for *LUCKY GETS ROASTED.*"

Don clapped Tim on the shoulder. "How did you manage this? I didn't think even you would be able to get VIP seating for either one of these, but to get both?"

While Nellie asked the waitress just how well done she could assure her that her steak could be cooked, Tim explained to Jane that the seating in the converted factory was going to be limited and the audience would be made up of Kankakee movers and shakers like the mayor and editor of the newspaper and the Kankakee merchants who had won Lucky Miller competitions. In other words, if Don or Nellie won the Lucky Duck drink contest, one of them would get two tickets to the event—either the dress rehearsal or the actual taping.

Tim's floral arrangements had been much appreciated by the hotel that was hosting a dinner tonight in Lucky's honor. Because the flowers had been a last-minute order and Lucky's staff had absolutely loved them, preview tickets were bestowed upon Tim and four tickets to the actual roast were given to the party planner who had an out-of-town wedding next week and couldn't make the show.

"Did you notice the little lucky charms I put on the bouquets?" asked Tim. Not waiting for Jane's nod, Tim turned to Don and Nellie.

"Seems like Lucky is really superstitious and for some reason, all of those little tokens like rabbits' feet and lucky pennies and four-leaf clovers, horseshoes, all that crap really rang the bell for him. He made a big deal, said whoever thought of that was going to get a big raise and the party planner pointed to Lucky's assistant, Brenda, who had hired him and said it had all been her idea, thinking Brenda would be able to get him more work, would make a good contact if he ever made it out to California and so she comes out smelling like a rose and lays these tickets on us." Tim finally stopped for a breath and took a big sip of his drink.

"I'm good at four-leaf clovers," said Nellie.

"She is," said Don. He pointed at his empty martini glass and the waitress nodded. Nellie snorted and shook her head. "Oh come on, Nellie, we're celebrating."

Nellie bent over, digging for something in her purse. Don's second martini arrived along with appetizers and for a moment all was quiet, except for the gentle sighing that went along with people being served just the right thing at just the right time.

After trying one cracker thickly smeared with the warm dip Nellie declared too salty, she slapped down one small piece of waxed paper in front of Jane on her right and one small square in front of Tim on her left.

"Don't say I never gave you anything," said Nellie.

Jane picked up the square and held it close. Pressed between the two pieces was a real four-leaf clover. Tim had one, too, although his was slightly smaller.

"I find them all the time."

"It's true," said Don. "We go out to work in the yard and before I mow, your mother goes through the grass on her hands and knees and finds three or four of these every time."

Jane was used to odd statements and off-the-wall predictions and declarations from her mother. Nellie had always had her peculiar catchphrases—her "I knew that was going to happens"—but this was the first she had heard of her mother's ability to find four-leaf clovers.

"It's like having a truffle pig or something," said Jane, finishing up her drink.

"A what?" said Nellie.

"A highly trained specialist who can find rare things," said Jane.

Nellie stared her down. "Better be respectful, Jane, because if I can give you good luck, I can take it back, too."

"I'm sorry, Mom, I didn't mean that as an insult. Truffles are special and—"

"Forget it, I don't really give a damn. Eat your dinner and let's get the hell out of here because I've got more to say about this good luck and bad luck business."

Jane looked over at Tim, who was cutting into a steak and chatting with Don about gin martinis versus vodka martinis. She wanted to ask him about the errant moving truck, what he had heard, *if* he had heard. She thought about her stuff, boxes and boxes of random finds, taking a road trip through the Midwest. What were the odds that these boxes, the old wooden trunks, the cardboard wardrobes, the vintage suitcases would make it back to her? Dropoffs, pickups, changes of drivers would all contribute to chaos. And she hadn't even labeled all of the boxes that well. Why did she have to? It was going to be one load, traveling one and a half hours south and being met by its godfather, Tim Lowry. These were the objects Jane had collected and curated for years, ever since she began picking up the oddball find in college. Now her treasure trove was circling around a five-state area, alone and unprotected. Jane felt oddly light and slightly dizzy. She was positive the second martini she ordered had nothing to do with it.

Tim ordered an after-dinner drink, which set Nellie off on a lecture that had something to do with overdrinking, overspending, showing off, and taking a table in a busy restaurant for too much time.

"People waiting in the bar want to sit down, too, Lowry. We had our turn."

"Our waitress is delighted that we're here and continuing to spend money, Nellie. This will be her biggest tab all night. Plus," he added, "I'm a big tipper."

"I'm treating tonight," said Jane. "Celebrating the house sale."

"Yeah, but I owe you after my screwup and I'm buying tonight," said Tim, as the waitress set down his brandy.

"Let me see that dessert menu again," said Nellie.

Don asked for more coffee as did Jane, and they settled in to wait for Nellie's hot fudge sundae to arrive.

"Why are there so many people here so late on a Wednesday?" asked Don.

"This is what time people eat," said Tim.

"Not in Kankakee," said Don and Jane at the same time.

"But it is in L.A. or Las Vegas or wherever all these writers and production people are from," said Tim.

Jane looked around. Tim's observations were correct. These were non-Kankakeeans ordering multiple drinks, specifying brands of vodka and gin, people who requested wine lists and ordered two shrimp cocktails instead of an entrée. Waitresses were confused, but delighted. The bartender looked like he needed to call for backup. Jane was about to tell Tim that he was right about the clientele but wrong about their own tab being the priciest. Records might be set at the Steak and Brew tonight.

"So what's your screwup this time, Lowry?"

Jane began to shake her head, but she had spooned up a giant bite of coffee ice cream and hot fudge from her mother's dessert and couldn't protest out loud quickly enough to stop Tim.

"Didn't Jane tell you most of the stuff from her house, the stuff she packed up for the showing, is lost somewhere between here and Colorado?"

"You said Nebraska before! Colorado?" Jane exclaimed. *And you never said lost before either,* she added silently.

Tim knocked back the rest of his brandy and leaned forward. He explained that the truckers were independent fellows who made short hauls from place to place, referred by bigger outfits who didn't want to take on half and quarter loads and short hops. So, sometimes, if they had room in the truck and they could find new contract drivers when they needed them, they took on jobs as they came along and didn't drive in necessarily straight lines.

"He screwed up, but you're the one who's screwed," said Nellie, taking another bite of whipped cream.

"These guys looked like real movers," said Jane. "How can they be so . . . random?"

"Actually, they're used to moving band equipment. See, they're part of a band that was on hiatus, but then they ended up getting some gigs through this small college booking . . ."

Jane stopped listening. As Tim laid out the details of these full-time roadies, part-time movers who gave him incredible rates, explained what a great and talented band they were a part of, and how the group was finally getting some breaks and taking on moving jobs was how they paid for their truck and expenses and how they had promised to store Jane's stuff at a storage space in Nebraska—Tim had already called to put the monthly rental on his credit card—while they loaded up the band stuff and played a few gigs, then they would pick up Jane's boxes and come back to Illinois, just about the time she had decided where she was going to settle . . . While Tim explained all of that and more, Jane stopped listening and accepted the rest of her mother's sundae, which Nellie pushed in front of her.

"Eat the rest of that fudge. You're going to need it."

Don said that he was happy they would have Jane with them for a while and Tim interrupted that Jane would stay with him since he had so much more room.

Nellie watched Jane eat the last bite of ice cream and said nothing.

Jane finally looked up. Before she could begin telling them she'd prefer to sleep in her car, shouts from the bar interrupted.

"Call 911. He's choking, call 911."

A busboy ran over, prepared to give the Heimlich maneuver, but was stopped by a burly teamster who told him it was an allergic reaction, not a lodged food particle.

"He's got a peanut allergy, he shouldn't even be in here,"

he yelled, pointing to a small dish of nuts at the other end of the bar.

Jane almost turned over her chair rising and running into the bar. She would be too embarrassed to admit that someone else's emergency had saved her from thinking about her homeless, stuffless self, but she was weirdly grateful that someone urgently needed something.

The bartender shouted that the paramedics were on their way.

"I don't think he's breathing," said the woman on the floor next to the unconscious young man.

"If he's not breathing, we have to start CPR," said Jane, trying to move some of the people in the crowd who had turned to stone. "Let me through."

"Oh God, thank you," said the same woman who had shouted out that he wasn't breathing.

Jane looked away from the statues she was trying to budge out of her way and saw Nellie, who had threaded her way through the eight or nine men and women standing slack-jawed and frightened on the other side, drop to her knees, support the man's head, and bend her head down to breathe life into this stranger.

The paramedics burst into the barroom and were at the man's side immediately and Nellie popped up without having to begin the treatment. They backed people away, trying to give themselves room to work and the man air to breathe.

"I told you we shouldn't come here," said Nellie. "Your dad looks like he's going to faint."

Two peanut allergies in one night? thought Jane. *Did Lucky have some fetish about hiring people who have the same health problems?*

Jane saw that Tim had left a wad of cash on the table and she followed her parents out to the parking lot.

Don leaned against Tim's car, parked closest to the door.

"Nellie, what were you thinking?" said Don, taking a few deep breaths.

"Mom was doing the right thing, Dad," said Jane. The only thing stranger to her than witnessing two reactions to peanut allergies in one evening was the fact that her mother knew CPR and was willing to perform it on a stranger. "That was gutsy."

"You never fail to surprise me, Nellie," said Tim. "I've got to admit, I was impressed with your quick thinking and—"

"Jeez, Nellie, what *were* you thinking?" said Don.

Jane was relieved to see color returning to her dad's face, but surprised at how harshly he was speaking to her mother. He usually championed Nellie no matter what sort of nonsense she spouted and now when she was about to be a real hero, he looked like he wanted to ground her for life.

"Oh c'mon, Don, I seen it on TV a million times," Nellie said with a shrug. "How hard can PCR be?"

6

Jane had looked back and forth between Tim and Nellie, deciding where to spend the night. Tim was perky and bubbly, describing the bedroom he had readied and her own private bathroom he had supplied with her favorite shampoo.

"Your old room and you share the bathroom with me," said Nellie. "And I use the store-brand shampoo," she added, glaring at Lowry.

Don had hugged Jane and said she was welcome as long as she wanted, though he admitted he had no real estate to share since he had long been relegated to the bathroom in the basement. He had tiled it and built a shower in the small bathroom next to the area where he kept his beloved, if not often-used, exercise bike. No one would mistake his small corner of the basement for a man cave, but it served as a fairly sound-proof hideaway for Don.

"And," Nellie added, "no matter where you stay, Rita stays here. I know how to take care of her."

Jane kissed Tim on the cheek.

"I'll move into that lovely suite later," said Jane. "But tonight I want to catch up on some stuff with Don and Nellie."

Tim was still shaking his head as he jumped into his car and roared off. Jane didn't blame him. It was crazy. But she didn't want to chat all night about where she was going to live and what she was going to do next. She had enough of it for now.

Jane wanted to hide out in her old bedroom, read a good-night text from Nick, and answer him with a long e-mail about how lucky they were that they sold the house, She needed to ask him what he wanted her to save from his closet. She needed to know if there were any old soccer balls or baseball cards, anything that she needed to rescue for him. Although she knew she could do that at Tim's house, she also knew that if she decided to cry, just a little, before falling asleep, Tim would be listening at the door and fall all over himself fussing and trying to make her feel better.

Nellie, on the other hand, would leave her completely alone.

Jane closed her bedroom door and opened the large bag she always carried—her just-in-case—and inventoried her possessions: one toothbrush; one half tube of toothpaste; Kiehl's lip balm and moisturizer; hairbrush; large silver hoop earrings, pajamas, silky kimono; two changes of underclothes; spare blue jeans; navy turtleneck; black turtleneck; good black pants; blue oxford cloth tunic; gray cardigan; brown lace-up hiking shoes; plaid wool Pendleton shirt; two pairs smart wool socks; gold and black patterned pashmina; one black jersey dress with a V-neck, three-quarter sleeves, and a wrap style that incorporated baggy pockets; black strappy flats that could pass for dress shoes. Jane laid all of these things out carefully on the extra twin bed. From the outside zippered compartment she removed a pair of leather driving gloves, an extra lipstick, and a carved red Bakelite bangle. She sniffed the bracelet, hoping for a whiff of formaldehyde, the comforting eau-de Bakelite that she loved so much, but smelled nothing.

"You might be the only one I have," she whispered.

Patting her not-too-worn Coach briefcase, which she had picked up at a house sale for three dollars—*three dollars*—she felt for her laptop and notebook and pens. She felt for the cords she used to her charge her computer and phone, then slapped her pocket to make sure she did, indeed, have her phone.

Jane looked in the mirror. She was wearing dark jeans, short Frye boots, a navy V-neck sweater, a chain around her neck with a few silver medals and a baby ring—all rummage treasures—and an old buttery leather jacket that she had bought when she and Charley were in New York, for their fifth anniversary. It had been way too expensive but Charley had insisted she buy it.

"It will never go out of style," he had said.

Jane knew that wasn't exactly true. The jacket had gone in and out of style, several times actually, but she wore it through its ins and its outs. Every September, she took it out of her closet and put it in her car, or folded it into her just-in-case, so she would have it with her when the sun went down.

"Thanks, Charley," Jane said. "I'm glad I bought it."

"Did you say something?" asked Nellie, walking in without knocking. Jane wondered how long her mother had stood outside the door, waiting for Jane to sigh or groan so she'd have an excuse to come in.

"Just taking stock of my worldly possessions," said Jane. She waved her arms over the bed. "Except for my books at home and very few clothes in my closet and drawers and maybe a few other odds and ends, this is it."

Nellie looked over everything on the bed.

"What do you need two turtlenecks for?" she asked.

Jane opened her mouth but couldn't think of anything to say. Instead she started laughing. At first, it was that sad laughter, the prelude to hysteria that Jane had heard in so many others when she and Oh were working on a case. Then, as Jane looked at her things arrayed before her, the laughter became real, genuine, joyful laughter. She picked up the navy turtleneck and handed it to Nellie.

"Can you use an extra?"

"Sure," said Nellie, snatching it up. And then a small miracle occurred on the south side of Kankakee. Nellie smiled. Jane saw it. She wanted to grab her phone and snap a picture of it, but it was gone too quickly. No matter. Jane saw it and she wouldn't forget it.

"You working on a detective case right now?" Nellie asked.

Jane shook her head.

"Good. I got a job for you," said Nellie. "And you only got a few days to get it done because I'm not paying out-of-town expenses."

Jane sat on her bed and patted the spot next to her.

Nellie ignored the invitation. A smile was one thing, but cozying up for a conversation was another.

"I want to know what Lucky Miller's up to," said Nellie.

"Other than staging a comedy roast in a charming little town that gave him pleasure as a child?"

"Bull," said Nellie. "Hermie Mullet wasn't charmed by Kankakee. And Kankakee isn't charmed by Hermie Mullet.

There's something fishy going on here. Lucky Miller's a crook of some kind and I want to know what he's up to."

"Mom, I can ask around, but—"

"Use that computer of yours and find out stuff about Hermie Mullet. Maybe Bruce can help you on this."

" I can call him and ask him to check on the family. You'll have to give me the year they left. He was in your class?"

Nellie nodded.

"Just one year, then the nuns and priests split up the boys and the girls in different rooms."

"Yeah, but you were in the same grade, that's all . . . wait a minute. You call Detective Oh . . . Bruce?"

"That's his name, ain't it? Just find out what Lucky Miller's up to," said Nellie.

Jane finished hanging up her clothes and stowing away her bags, and climbed into bed. She expected it to feel too small and hard, but it was cozy. She had e-mailed Nick about what happened, even about the moving truck and found herself smiling through the story. She didn't have the slightest urge to cry herself to sleep. Instead, she closed her eyes thinking about Nellie wanting to know about what Lucky Miller was up to. Questions swam below the surface of her thoughts: Of all the towns Hermie Mullet had lived in, why Kankakee? Why all the re-created stuff of his childhood? Then the current brought her right back to Nellie and her obsession with Lucky Miller. The last question that finally floated to the surface just before sleep?

"What was Nellie up to?"

7

On Thursday morning, when Jane woke up in her old bedroom, she lay perfectly still, making a list in her head. It was a habit that served her well as far as giving her a few extra minutes under the covers. It didn't help her organizational skills all that much, since she found that a day usually unfolded demanding that its own list be obeyed.

She got as far as Mr. Toad—or was it Frog who wrote "1. *Get up*"—before she heard Nellie yelling at someone or something. She pulled on yesterday's clothes as quickly as she could and ran out to the living room, where her mother was hanging out the front door, yelling at children on their way to school.

"I don't like it when they cut through the yard. There's a sidewalk there and they ought to be using it," said Nellie, offering the explanation without turning to look at Jane standing behind her.

"How do you get all the eggs off your house on Halloween?" asked Jane.

When the phone rang and Nellie, still busy giving the evil eye to fourth graders, made no move to answer, Jane ran to the kitchen to grab it.

"Put your mother on, honey," said Don.

"You kids use the sidewalk. That's what it's there for."

"She's yelling at the neighborhood, Dad, what's up?"

"It's Carl."

Jane heard the break in her father's voice before he cleared his throat.

"I found him when I got here. He had closed and locked up the front, but the back door was still unlocked. He was on his way out. He had his jacket on and that little cap of his. He was sort of awake, but . . ." Don broke up midsentence and cleared his throat. "Doc says stroke."

"He's dead?"

"He's in intensive care, but they don't seem very hopeful he'll come out of this one."

Jane pulled her mother in from the doorway and closed it behind her. She told her as gently as she could that Carl was at the hospital and it was serious.

Nellie continued to stare out the front door.

"So Carl's dying?"

"Maybe," said Jane. "I'll get dressed and drive you to the hospital."

"Nope. You finish getting dressed, make yourself look presentable, and go tend bar while Dad and I go to the hospital. Carl hasn't got any family but your dad and me so we should be there together, not one at a time. Hurry up."

Jane ran into her bedroom to put on her boots. She ran a comb though her hair and put in her hoop earrings. While she helped herself to a quick swipe of Nellie's lipstick in the bathroom, she heard her mother's voice coming from the front porch.

"That's right, go around and use the sidewalk. Grass won't grow there if you wear out a path."

Jane drove to the tavern, and got a quick lesson in drawing a beer. Jane thought she had enough practice, but her dad gently shook his head.

"You're tilting the glass too much. Just like this," he said, helping her hold the glass correctly in her left hand under the tap while drawing the beer with her right. Don picked up a coaster and smoothly slid it under the glass.

"You won't have too many people, Janie," said Don. "And if you have any questions, call this number."

Don withdrew a cell phone from his pocket, looked at a piece of masking tape on it, and copied down the number, then placed it by the landline phone behind the bar.

"When did you get a cell phone?" said Jane, letting beer run all over her hand as she backed away from the tap to face her dad. "And why don't I already have the number?"

"I got it last week," said Don. He looked a little flushed and Jane wondered if the pressure of finding Carl had been too much for him. Then she realized her dad was blushing.

"I haven't told your mother yet. I just thought we ought to have them. I got her one, too, but I wanted to get used to it . . . you know, figure out how to use it myself so I could teach her when I gave it to her," said Don. "I want you and your brother, Michael, to be able to reach us. With you all alone up there in the city, I thought it would be good for us all to be able to get in touch easier."

"It's a wonderful idea, Dad. But if I call you on it this morning, won't Mom catch on pretty quick?"

"Got it on vibrate and I can just excuse myself and call you back. Doesn't really matter, I'm ready to start the battle with her to use one. I'm getting pretty good. See? I got your number, and Nick's, and Michael's, and the EZ Way Inn on my favorites. And Carl's," he added.

Don's voice got husky and he went around to his desk to pick up his keys and hat. He was swinging by the house to pick up Nellie and together they would go spend a couple of hours at Carl's bedside. To anyone watching, they would make an odd triangle of a family.

Jane watched her father put on his hat, tilt it back at an angle, and felt tears coming. She had known Carl forever. He was cranky and usually silent behind the bar, and a terrible hypochondriac. He called in sick a few times a month, always with a specific array of symptoms.

"I have a rash on my left arm, an earache in my right ear, and both of my eyelids are twitching," Carl would report.

"For God's sake, Carl, put on a long-sleeved shirt, take an aspirin, and get your ass in here," Nellie would tell him.

"I quit," he'd answer.

"You're fired," Nellie would answer back.

Around six o'clock, Carl would come in through the back door, wearing a long-sleeved shirt and sunglasses. He and Nellie would shrug at each other and Don would repeat the closing instructions he had give him every night for thirty-odd years.

Jane could see that her father was tired. He was tan and healthy-looking from a summer of golfing and lawn mowing, but the lines around his eyes and mouth were cut more deeply than Jane remembered. She hugged him as he passed by and promised she would hold down the fort.

The bar was completely empty. After all, it was nine

A.M.—how busy should a neighborhood tavern be on a sunny September morning? Jane took out her own cell phone and programmed in her father's number. *Good for him,* Jane was thinking. He might be embracing technology a little late, but then again, Jane was only a few years ahead of him. She was racing forward, though, what with her smart phone and all. As she admired it in her hand, it vibrated and she saw on the screen that Melinda, her realtor, was calling. Jane steeled herself to hear that the deal had fallen through.

"Everything's a go," said Melinda, all energy with a mouthful of toast.

Jane surprised herself by feeling disappointed and elated at the same time. She couldn't honestly tell which came first or which carried more weight. She opened her mouth, ready to be surprised by whatever words escaped.

"Yay," she said. It came out in a cracked whisper.

She knew her response was anemic, but Jane hadn't received good news in a while. She was out of practice.

"Okay, Janie, you better plan on getting back here to clear out what you want and we'll get all the rest of the papers in front of you to sign. You don't have to come to the closing if you don't want. She's nice, though, this woman who appreciates your stuff. Since this is such a wild offer, I warned her that we hadn't listed any furniture as exceptions since they're never usually included and you might have to do some picking and choosing when you got here. She's cool with it."

"Well, my desk and chair and books," said Jane, "but I honestly can't picture anything else right now. A lamp or two . . . oh there's a hook on the wall in Nick's bedroom, a brass horse's head . . ."

"Don't even think about doing this from memory. You'll forget something. There's going to be some kitchen things, you know, favorite pans and stuff. I don't know, maybe you already gathered up all your faves. Aren't you so glad I made you pack up all that junk you collected? So now you've got all your personal stuff with you and this walk-through and pack-up will be a piece of cake."

Jane agreed, without filling her in on the fact that her personal stuff was on a three to five state tour. She had to hang up. Francis had walked in midway through the conversation and he was tapping all of his fingers, using both hands. Jane could tell he was uncomfortable without Don and Nellie in sight and the fact that Jane was behind the bar talking into a cell phone added to his discomfort. "I'll be there this weekend. Maybe tomorrow. And have I thanked you? I'm so sorry if I haven't, Melinda. Thank you so much."

Jane hung up, slipped the phone back in her pocket, and walked over to Francis. She had tended bar for her parents only a few times and when she had, either Don or Nellie had been working with her. Alone behind the bar, she had to admit she was nervous. And excited. She had been an adult for a good many years, but being on her own behind the bar at the EZ Way Inn gave her such a different grown-up feeling.

"What it'll be, Francis?" she asked, her voice squeaking like a ten-year-old.

"Got any coffee?"

Jane panicked. She had no idea how to make coffee with her mother's contraption.

Looking over at the big metal pot warmer that sat on the

counter next to the kitchen door, she saw that Don had made a pot of coffee before he left. A carafe sat there, full, hot, and ready to strip away any protective lining that might still exist within the interiors of the regular customers.

"Coming up," said Jane. She poured coffee into the thick green jadeite cups that Nellie had used since the seventies.

"Why do I need to get new ones? If it ain't broken, don't fix it," said Nellie every time Jane mentioned that the cups were now collectible and Nellie might want to sell them since she really only needed about six cups and saucers at any one time.

In the case of the Fire-King jadeite, it wasn't likely to ever get "broke." The thick china could be dropped over and over without chipping. *This was a coffee cup that could take a punch,* Jane thought, as she added a few packs of sugar to the saucer and a spoon from the top drawer of the cabinet.

Jane's phone vibrated and she reached for it after giving Francis his cup. She had no idea what Nellie charged for coffee. A tall coffee at her local Starbucks was around two dollars, wasn't it? Doing a kind of Chicago-to-Kankakee math, a designer signature roast ratio to the no-name sludge she just poured, she guessed at a price.

"Fifty cents? A dollar?" Jane asked. "Sorry, Francis, I don't know what to charge."

Jane sent Tim's call to voice mail, then looked up at Francis, who looked wounded.

"I don't get charged a thing, Janie. Your dad never charges any of his delivery men for coffee," said Francis.

Jane did a quick calculation. Francis hadn't delivered anything to the EZ Way Inn in well over ten years. Quite the lifetime perk. Jane smiled to herself thinking about free coffee as a *perk*, even though no one really knew what a percolator was anymore, and her smile was immediately misinterpreted.

"You can ask your mom and dad. I never get charged for coffee," said Francis.

"I believe you, Francis, I was just thinking about coffee . . . never mind. Of course it's on the house. I'm new at this, you know," said Jane.

"You come by it naturally, you'll catch on," said Francis. Then he remembered that this was totally out of the ordinary. "Where are Mom and Dad?"

Jane might be able to sub behind the bar. She could pour a coffee or draw a halfway decent mug of beer. She might even be able to pour a shot of whiskey without spilling too much, but she knew her limits. Breaking the news to the regulars about Carl was not her job. Don and Nellie had been the oddball parents, Carl the weird uncle, to this dysfunctional family for too many years and Jane was not about to be the dreary messenger.

"They had to take care of something important this morning, so I told them I'd fill in," said Jane. Francis accepted the nonanswer and Jane could tell by his scrunched-up eyebrows he was trying to think of anything that he and Jane might be able to talk about.

"How's your son?" asked Francis.

Bless his heart, thought Jane. She filled Francis in on Nick's school and how happy he seemed to be. Just last night Nick had texted about new friends, referring to Alex and Trevor and Ian as if he had known them for years. He would have done fine at Evanston High School, but Jane knew that he was thriving in a whole new way at the academy. Of all the second-guessing she practiced as if it were her own special brand of meditation or yoga, she could let her thoughts about this decision rest. Sending Nick off to this gifted program had been the right thing to do.

Jane went over and wrung out one of the clean white terry-cloth bar rags and started wiping around Francis's cup without realizing what she was doing. It was her mother's "precleaning" routine. Nellie always had a rag in one hand cleaning under and around people's drinks even as they continued to sit and order another round. Nellie liked to stay one swipe ahead of any drips that might be thinking of dropping. Maybe just being behind the bar at the EZ Way Inn conferred a kind of *Nellieness*, a constant motion—even when there was only one customer who, as of yet, hadn't even taken a sip.

Jane's phone vibrated again and she checked to see if it was coming from St. Mary's hospital or her dad's secret number. Tim again. This time, a text.

Wher r u? Pic up phon!!!!

Jane slipped the phone back in her pocket. Yesterday, when Tim's rock and roll movers had been trying to reach him, his phone was sitting in a pocket draped over the front seat of his truck. Let him stew for a while about where she and her phone might be.

The front door swung open and Jane's heart raced. Francis was an easy customer. What if someone came in and asked for something she couldn't make? She knew it wasn't likely, since the EZ Way customers didn't really ask for mixed drinks—they had been effectively trained by Nellie for years. "No blender drinks," she'd growl at the mention of any drink that had a name. *Rusty Nail? Sex on the Beach? Harvey Wallbanger? Rob Roy? A simple Manhattan, for God's sake?* All requests got the same answer from Nellie, wiping her hands on her apron like she had just finished the daily butchering, "No. Blender. Drinks."

Right, so whoever walked through the door at the EZ Way Inn wasn't likely to order something fancy. Especially not this early in the day. Jane was more nervous about not finding something ordinary or, as she realized when she served Francis coffee, collecting for the order. She didn't know the prices of anything. *Old theater improv skills, don't fail me now,* thought Jane, straightening up and smoothing down her plain white apron tied jauntily at the side.

"Got any Bushmills? Shot and a cup of strong coffee, honey, fast. And a word in private, too," said Lucky Miller, as he walked through the door. Before he even took a seat at the bar, he had ordered and looked over his shoulder enough times to make anyone believe he was, indeed, being followed.

"Damn producer has these teenage goons tagging after me every second. I think I escaped for a few minutes. We're shooting some breakfast competition down the street. I told 'em I needed to light this cigar for a few puffs and slipped out the back. Haven't lit this thing in twenty years," said Lucky. He looked over at Francis. "That's why they last so long with me. I've had the same Cuban in my mouth since Desi told Lucy . . ." Lucky stopped talking, looked at Jane, who looked disapproving, and Francis, who looked uncomprehending. He shrugged. "Why waste A material? Just set me up here, honey."

"My name is Jane. I'm not even 'honey' to my friends, Mr.

Miller," said Jane, pouring a cup of coffee. "And, I don't think anyone would mistake that for A material."

"Got some of that Nellie sass in you, don't you?" said Lucky, chomping on his cigar. He knocked back his shot and nodded at the cup of coffee. Grimacing, he took a sip, then slugged back the hot coffee just as he had the whiskey.

"Look, I've got to get back there before they send out the lush police, but I heard you were a private detective or something. That right?"

"Yeah, she's solved lots of murders," said Francis.

"Private conversation, buddy, know what that means?" said Lucky, looking back at the door and then out the window.

Francis stood up, hurt, and prepared to leave by the back door.

"Don't go, Francis." Jane realized she wanted to hear what Lucky was about to say, but in equal measure, she didn't want to be alone in the room with him. "Why don't you see what kind of cream pie is in the fridge? Have a piece with your coffee. It's on me," Jane said, then corrected herself. "I mean it's on Mr. Miller, right?"

"Sure, of course. Sorry," he said, tossing his apology in the direction of Francis, who had already left for the kitchen.

"Look, you're a detective and I need one. Somebody's either trying to mess with my head or . . . look, it's pretty melodramatic to say somebody's trying to kill me, so I'm sticking with mess with my head.

"I got a trunk full of stuff I carry around with me and somebody's been fooling around with it. It's just some memorabilia and, you know, lucky stuff, I like to have with me. I got some superstitions when I perform. Everybody who travels with me knows I carry this trunk . . . and anyway, somebody is taking stuff and switching it out on me. Sometimes I find little notes."

Jane knew he had her at "trunk full of stuff," but she wanted to know a little more before she agreed to help.

"What kind of stuff is missing and who has access?" said Jane, still busy wiping the bar.

"How about you come and work for me, be my new assistant, for a while and I'll fill you in. Brenda has to fly to Las Vegas for the weekend and no one will think anything of it if I hire somebody local to fill in for a few days. That way you can get to know people and see how the operation works. Brenda keeps one of the keys to the trunk, and I have the other one. I'll get you a copy and—"

"Have you considered Brenda?" asked Jane. "Why is she leaving for the weekend."

"No, it's not Brenda. I know it's not Brenda," said Lucky Miller, pointing to his shot glass for another Bushmills.

Jane turned to get the whiskey and allowed herself to smile. If Lucky Miller was so sure it wasn't Brenda, then it probably was Brenda. This might be an easy case.

"I have to drive up to Evanston one day this weekend, probably tomorrow. I'll be gone for six hours or so. I also might have to help out here at the bar. I mean you can introduce me as your assistant, but I might not be able to be around 24/7, so if that's okay, I might be able to help," said Jane.

"Yeah, that's okay," said Lucky. "I mean the stuff's not valuable or anything, but I mean it's pretty weird when someone takes a four-leaf clover and replaces it with a regular three-leaf clover, right? I mean, that's just a head game, isn't it?"

Jane felt in her pocket for the four-leaf clover Nellie gave her. It was still there.

Lucky stood up, then ducked down to look out the front window. Jane could see a production truck parked at the corner restaurant.

"I got to get back," said Lucky, "before somebody tries to claim I broke my contract. Come over to the factory around lunchtime and I'll introduce you as my assistant."

He pulled out two sticks of peppermint gum and stuffed them in his mouth. "Not supposed to drink before five P.M.," he said, shrugging. "I used to have kind of a problem.

"One more thing, huh, Jane Wheel? Your mom, Nellie? She was riding me pretty hard the other night. How about when you're working for me, you find out what's up with her, too? Can you do that?" asked Lucky, as he was walking out the front door. Just before the door slammed shut, Jane heard him repeat the question.

"Can you find out what's up with Nellie?"

Jane stared at empty shot glass and the empty cup of coffee. She knew that checking out Lucky for her mother and checking out her mother for Lucky was definitely not the right thing to do. Conflict of interest, for sure.

But Jane was far too interested in the potential conflict to not take on the challenge. She would find out what was up with both of them.

"Stiffed you?"

Jane jumped. She had forgotten that Francis was in the kitchen eating whatever pie he could find in the refrigerator.

"What?"

"You forget to charge or he forget to pay?" asked Francis.

"Damn it," said Jane, clearing the bar and washing it down.

"If you're starting a tab for him, put two pieces of banana cream pie on it, too," said Francis, picking up his cap. "See you tomorrow, Janie."

"Yeah," said Jane. "See you."

Wiping off the bar and rinsing out the shot glass and dishes, Jane thought about Lucky Miller's offer of a job. Still lost, she answered her phone when it vibrated, without looking at the screen. *Why did Lucky even mention somebody might be trying to kill him? Because somebody stole his lucky clovers? Why hadn't she asked that follow-up question?*

Before Jane could even finish her hello, Tim Lowry was yelling into the phone.

"Why haven't you been picking up? I got us a great job! Meet me at the old stone factory on Water Street where they're shooting the Lucky Miller special around noon, okay?"

"I've already got a job," said Jane. "Two or three as a matter of fact," she said.

"Not like this one, baby!" said Tim, clicking off.

The good news was that Jane had some work to do and work was the consummate distracter. Her collectibles on the lam? Her imminent house closing? No matter if she could keep her head in the game here. Her mother asking for some help? Intriguing. Lucky asking for help with her mother? Irresistible. Tim enthusiastic over a new job? Priceless. All good news

The bad news? That was what was written all over the faces of her mother and father as they walked in the back door. Their shoulders were slumped and they walked more slowly than Jane ever remembered seeing. Don and Nellie were always purposeful, both busy and businesslike. They were always in the middle of doing something. Now they both looked a little lost. Don and Nellie, the longest running show on Station Street in Kankakee looked like they were ready to bring down the curtain.

Don poured coffee for the two of them and held the pot aloft, looking at Jane. "Want a cup, honey?"

Jane shook her head and smiled slightly at the "honey." Yes, there was one person allowed to call her that.

"Tell me what's going on with Carl," said Jane.

Nellie had disappeared into the back room and now Jane could hear her banging around in the kitchen.

"Not going to make it," said Don. "He had a sister somewhere in Indiana and we need to find out if she had any kids. Any nieces or nephews would be his heirs. And since he's connected to, you know, machines and stuff right now . . ."

"His sister died," said Nellie, shouting from the kitchen. "I remember he told me. And she never was married. Carl doesn't have any."

"Heirs?" asked Jane. "Seems odd. All these years I've known Carl and never thought of him with a family or . . . anything to leave to a family. I can't imagine him anywhere but behind the bar."

Jane remembered a big stuffed dog Carl had given her when Nick was born. "For the baby," Carl had said, barking it out sideways. Jane had been so touched she cried. Of course, for a few months after Nick was born, tears were her answer to everything. She cried equally hard when someone beat her out for a parking space and when someone held the door open for her in a department store. Nellie had stared hard at the stuffed dog and then at Carl.

"Wasn't this the prize on the punchboard down at Wally's Pub?" asked Nellie. Carl lived alone in a one-bedroom apartment over Wally's, another tavern three blocks east of the EZ Way Inn on the street Don had named Saloonkeepers Row.

"So what?" said Carl. "I had to spend over thirty dollars in punches to win it for the baby."

"You know, Carl, there are stores that sell things," said Nellie.

Carl shrugged. His tan cotton jacket had come from the EZ Way Inn coatrack, left and lost by a nonregular who had come in before last spring's golf league kick-off party. His cap had come from a baseball giveaway promotion at Wally's earlier in the summer. At the holidays, Carl gave out cartons of cigarettes, boxes of cigars, and bottles of whiskey in festive wrappings, purchased wholesale from one or more of the delivery men he encountered while behind the bar or sitting in front of it. He gave both Nellie and Jane boxes of chocolates won from punchboards at any number of saloons along the row. Of course, Carl had managed to find a baby gift in a bar.

Jane came back to the present when she heard her dad sigh. Don shook his head. Jane knew that for her parents' sake it would be best to find the relatives if there were any life and death decisions to be made. Jane figured Carl must be in his seventies or maybe he was even older. He had always looked exactly the same to Jane, even when she was a little girl. He had always been bald and too thin and near-sighted, with thick dark horn-rimmed glasses that looked too big for his pinched face. When it came down to it, if Carl wasn't going to wake up, would Medicare make the decision to pull the plug or would the doctors ask Don and Nellie? Or would whatever doctor on duty when the insurance ran out be the one given the power?

"Maybe I can help find any relatives?" said Jane. "Or I can call Detective Oh. He can find anyone."

"Who ate all of my banana cream pie?" asked Nellie from the kitchen.

"Lucky Miller stopped in for a couple of shots and he offered to buy Francis some pie," said Jane.

"Lucky Miller was in here?" asked Don.

Jane explained that he was taping down the street. She also mentioned that he asked her to fill in for his assistant for a few days, to help him find a few of his missing possessions. She left out his reference to someone trying to kill him and his request that Jane find out what was up with Nellie.

"They serve liquor at the café. Why didn't he get his whiskey there?" asked Nellie, standing in the kitchen doorway.

"He's got something in his contract about daylight drinking," said Jane. "Says he used to have a problem."

"Used to, huh?" said Don, with his first smile of the day.

Nellie took a metal coffee can out from behind her back and shook it in front of Jane. "So where's the pie money?"

"Your mother keeps her food money separate. So when she orders from the bakery, she can pay it from the kitchen account," explained Don, "and the kitchen account is whatever ends up in that can."

Jane opened her mouth to answer, but was interrupted by Don who had gone over to visit his pride and joy, his ornate polished brass cash register, a part of the EZ Way Inn as long as Don and Nellie had owned it. He looked at the paper tape he still used to keep track of the day's receipts.

"What'd you charge him for the Bushmills? I haven't sold a shot out of that bottle in years. Don't even remember what it cost. I'll have to look it up."

"She didn't charge anybody anything for anything," said Nellie, crossing her arms in front of her. "Did you?"

Jane shook her head. She explained that Francis had informed her of his coffee deal, then Lucky ran out the door so fast, she hadn't even remembered to collect.

"I don't think he's used to paying. Probably his assistant . . ."

"Better fill your purse with money from his petty-cash box," said Nellie. "Sounds like you just took a babysitting job that might cost you money."

Nellie was right. Jane began to apologize, but her mother cut her off.

"No need. Wasn't your fault. I told your dad he should have a price list. Half the time Carl gave away the store. He never knew . . ." Nellie stopped and retreated back into the kitchen.

"I'll make a price list," said Don. "For you, if you help us out. And I'll have to hire somebody for nights, I guess."

Jane realized what an enormous weight had descended on her parents and the EZ Way Inn. Carl might have been a grouch and, on occasion, a grinch, but he was reliable and honest and loyal to Don and Nellie.

"How about Bill what's-his-name, who worked for Wally for a while? Maybe he could fill in a couple nights," said Don.

"Nope. He'll drink too much," said Nellie. "Why do you think Wally got rid of him?"

"There's so many people out of work, Dad, there must be someone," said Jane.

"Hard to find a bartender, Janie. If they're honest, they probably drink. And if they drink, well, they drink," said Don. "It's not exactly an important career, bartending."

"Yeah, but enough people need jobs right now, so there are—"

"Here's what we're going to do," said Nellie, wiping her hands on her apron and grabbing the scratch pad of paper always next to the cash register. "We still open early like the factory's still going, like I have to start my soup and you know goddamn well, there's no need to be here at seven. We'll open at ten and we'll close at ten. That'll keep Francis happy in the morning, he can still get his coffee, just a little later and it'll still give the boys a place to watch the game in the afternoon and—"

"You can't work twelve hours a day! That's ridiculous," said Jane.

Don and Nellie both stared at her.

"We've always worked ten or twelve hours, haven't we?" said Don, looking at Nellie. "And once or twice a week, I come back here and close up when Carl's not feeling so well so I . . ."

Don stopped and Jane knew he was thinking about what might have been prevented if he had returned last night to close up. She was trying to think of something to say that would reassure her dad, when two men walked in through the back door.

Jane didn't recognize them, but Don and Nellie both stood, nodding like they had been expecting them. Don shook hands with both of the men, and although the gray-haired one tried to give Nellie a hug, she ducked out of the way and asked if they wanted a cup of coffee.

"This is our daughter, Jane, Wally. Jane, this is Wally and his brother, Mel. They own Wally's Pub down the way."

Jane put out her hand but both men looked confused. *Really?* thought Jane. *There are still men who are thrown by a woman who offers to shake hands?*

"We know Jane!" said the gray-haired one, laughing at the outstretched hand and grabbing her in a bear hug.

"Yeah, Carl talked about you and your brother, Michael, all the time. He spent a hundred bucks on that stuffed dog when you had your baby boy. Oh yeah, you're part of the family, Jane," said Mel, who, Jane saw, looked just like his brother except for the shoe polish black hair. Their voices were identical, too, and Jane realized, looking back and forth at their faces, they were twins. Mel, apparently, was the vain one, refusing to accept the gray hair his brother wore proudly. Or maybe they just wanted people to be able to tell them apart.

"We just missed you at the hospital," said Wally. "We were bringing you this," he said, holding up a fat manila envelope. Jane could read upside down, all those years of sitting in meetings with the account executives, trying to read their notes and agendas, telling time upside down by the Rolexes flashed across the table, had made her *ambi-optical*, as she called it. The return address on the envelope was that of a law firm, Beasley and Beasley in downtown Kankakee.

"It's Carl's will," said Mel.

Silence. Jane could hear the whoosh of the fan in the big cooler starting up and then a few fat drips of water splash into the rinse tanks.

"What the hell are we supposed to do with it?" said Nellie, but her bark definitely had no bite.

Wally and Mel sat down at the bar and accepted cups of coffee from Nellie, although Mel looked into the cup like he would prefer to refresh his hair color with it rather than consume the stuff. Wally then proceeded to do most of the talking, explaining that Carl hadn't been well for some time. He knew his blood pressure was too high and his heart was weak, but he had told the brothers that he wanted to keep working and die behind the bar.

"He was a professional," said Mel. "They don't make them like Carl anymore."

"They sure as hell don't," said Nellie.

Jane was prepared to give her mother a withering look, but she saw that her mother was dead serious—as respectful as she had ever seen her.

"He was a good saloon man, that's for sure," said Don.

Nods all around.

"Want to know what's in his will?" asked Mel.

Silence. The whoosh stopped, followed by a clunk as the fan in the big cooler turned off. Two more drops splashed into the rinse tank.

"Hell no," said Don. "First of all, Carl's not dead. Second of all, you got no business going through Carl's things or taking that envelope out of his apartment. Being his landlord doesn't give you the right to—"

"Hold on, Don," said Wally. "We didn't snoop. Carl gave

us this and said if anything happened, we were supposed to bring it to you right away. We figured we'd get to give it to you at the hospital, but the doc said you were gone and if it had anything about last wishes, we should find you right away so you could open it. It's addressed to you and Nellie."

Nellie had gone into the kitchen and brought out a fresh cherry pie. Jane was amazed. *Where did she keep them? Was there a magic pie closet back there?* Nellie slid plates in front of Wally and Mel, gave them forks and napkins, and lifted out enormous slices of pie. "Makes the coffee taste better," she said. Then she almost smiled, gave Mel a pat on the shoulder. "You did the right thing bringing that here if that's what Carl wanted. Don and I are just all done in, that's all."

"I'm sorry, Pepper," said Don, looking at Mel, who nodded.

Jane watched her dad take the envelope and open it carefully, affording it the respect of an official document of some kind. There was, indeed, a copy of a will in the sheaf of papers, but there were other signed papers as well.

Don motioned for Jane to look at the pages with him and she stepped to his right so she could see the contents of the envelope. The first paper was a living will, specifying that no heroic measures be taken. After the living will, the pages were all stamped COPY and there was a note saying the originals were all on file in the lawyer's office. The second page was a letter that must have been dictated by Carl to the lawyer since it was signed and witnessed at Beasley's office. In short, Carl named Don the executor of his estate. He specified that everything was to be left to Don and Nellie. He left bank account numbers and specific information and included a safety deposit box key. And in an explanatory postscriptlike note, in Carl's boxy printlike handwriting, he mentioned Jane and Michael. Don pointed it out and Jane read aloud:

> Although I am leaving everything to Don and Nellie, the two people in the world most like family to me, who have always treated me honestly and fairly and who have always helped me when I was down, I would also like their children, Jane and Michael, to share in my worldly goods. Therefore, I authorize Jane Wheel to inventory all of my property and after she and Don and Nellie and Michael take anything they want, they can sell the rest or give it away, whatever they think is best. If any money is raised from the sale, it should go to Jane's son and Michael's boy and girl. I like to think they are like my own children and grandchildren and I would like them to have something from me. If Jane thinks it's okay, her son Nick can have my car if he's now old enough to drive. And now that I must be dead, I'd just like to say, Nellie, you were the only sensible woman I ever knew and Don, you were the most honest man I ever knew, so you deserved to have Nellie. I was proud you were my boss and my friends.

"I'll be goddamned," said Don softly. "This was dated two months ago. Carl knew he was dying."

Nellie had been standing, listening with her arms folded. She scratched her cheek, snaking her finger up to wipe her eye, then cleared her throat.

"Damn fool could have told us. He didn't have to come in every night."

Mel, or *Pepper*, as Don had called him, patted Nellie on the shoulder. She winced but didn't move away. Wally took a bite of cherry pie, then wiped his mouth with a napkin.

"Carl was afraid he'd get the saloon keeper's disease. All the smoke and drinking . . . you know . . . he was afraid of lung cancer. He told me when he gave me all these papers that he was glad that when he went it was going to be quick and a surprise, That's what he said. He had a lot of ailments, Carl did, and he said he was surprised that something he didn't know anything about would probably kill him," said Wally, stopping for another bite of pie.

"Why wasn't he taking blood pressure medication or . . . ?" asked Jane.

Wally and Mel both shook their heads. Jane was struck by how their movements were as much in synch as their appearances. If only Mel didn't have that black hair and Wally that salt-and-pepper gray . . . Then Jane got it. Salt and Pepper. Nicknames. Her dad's mnemonic of choice. Mel dyed his hair, Wally didn't. Salt and Pepper. That's how people kept them straight.

Mel explained that Carl had said he had heart problems and nobody could regulate his blood pressure. He had tried some medication, but nothing was working. The twins finished their pie, shook hands with Don, and dropped the keys to Carl's apartment in Nellie's hand.

"We haven't been up there in years, but Carl was neat as a pin. Probably isn't much stuff up there. Whatever it was, he was anxious for you all to have it. You'll have to talk to the lawyer about the bank accounts and such, but no reason you can't come by the apartment whenever you want," said Wally.

The twins left by the back door and Jane watched them walk in tandem to their car. Don sighed heavily and picked up the living will.

"I've got to get this over to the hospital."

"I'll drive it over," offered Jane. "It's on my way to the factory where I'm meeting Lucky. And Tim. He has a job for me, too," said Jane.

"We do, too, honey," said Don. "If you're going to be around a while, maybe you could help us out a couple of hours a day? I know I always said I didn't want you in the tavern business. It's no place for a woman—I always said that and I still believe it."

Nellie cleared her throat behind him. "What the hell do I look like?" said Nellie, hands on hips.

"Come on, Nellie, you know that's different," said Don. "You're an exception to the rule," he added softly, taking her hand. She let him hold it for a count of three seconds, then said, "Damn right I'm an exception." Nellie than reclaimed her hand and touched it to the top of Don's head. "You need a haircut." Jane turned away, knowing that she was witnessing a moment of Don-and-Nellie-style intimacy.

"I don't want the tavern business for you, Janie. But if you could just help us until we figure this out, I'd appreciate it. Never want you in here at night, no closing up, but maybe a few hours during the day so your mother could go home for a while or I could catch a nap in the back room. That's all. A few weeks."

"Whatever you need," said Jane. "You seem to have caught me at a good time."

9

Jane delivered the copy of Carl's living will to the nursing station at the ICU. A young nurse assured Jane that she would put it into the right hands. Jane, as instructed several times by both her parents, reminded the floor secretary that Don and Nellie wanted to be called when there was any change in Carl's condition, then she peeked in the door to his room. Always thin, Carl now looked skeletal, like he barely took up half of the narrow bed.

"Nicky loved the dog, Carl. It was worth every penny," Jane whispered.

Pushing through the double doors that isolated the ICU, on her way to the elevator, Jane walked down a corridor with patient rooms on either side. She could hear the hospital version of Muzak playing in stereo. The droning television programs, creaking of wheeled carts, whispered conversations, soft weeping, snoring ... then an unexpected new note in the soundtrack.

"Doesn't anybody care that somebody tried to kill me?"

Jane stopped short, just before the doorway to the room. Who wouldn't want to hear the answer to that question? Or at least get a glimpse of the questioner? Jane could see into the half of the room where a lightweight navy windbreaker was thrown onto the visitor's chair. On top of the jacket was a baseball cap. Jane recognized the four-leaf clover logo of Lucky's production company.

"Yeah, well, I didn't sign on for this. No one told me that crazy bastard would get me killed!"

Jane heard the phone slam onto its cradle. Ah, the sweet satisfaction of a landline! She poked her head into the door and saw the man from the Steak and Brew who had suffered the allergy attack.

"Hi," said Jane.

"Who the hell are you?"

Jane introduced herself. She fully intended to tell him that she had been at the Steak and Brew and just wanted to tell him she was pleased to see that he had recovered without the intervention of the television-trained Nellie, but best intentions veered off course as soon as Jane had a chance to digest the fact that Lucky's crew member was claiming someone had tried to kill him.

"I've just agreed to fill in as a temporary assistant for Lucky, so I thought I might just pop my head in and make sure you were being well taken care of," said Jane, with her best executive assistant smile.

"Lucky sent you? I'd say it's the least that bastard could do. I took this driving job in this God-forsaken location because I was promised a little something extra from Lucky. I didn't realize I'd have to die to collect it."

A quick look at the name card to the left of the door should have helped Jane slide smoothly into the conversation, without confirming or denying that she had been sent by anyone, but she couldn't say the name without a follow up.

"Slug? I mean, Slug. They agreed to put your nickname on the door? Slug Mettleman?"

"Not exactly a nickname. Full name is Sluggo," said the patient, who Jane could now see was fully dressed and lying on top of the tangled sheets and blankets. She noted the discharge papers on the bedside table. Someone would be coming to pick him up, so Jane had to work fast in case Lucky really did send someone to the hospital and Jane would be revealed as little more than a curious bystander.

"Yeah, my mom was a fan of the 'Nancy' comic strip and she thought Sluggo had a nice ironic sound to it, me being such a tiny little preemie and all. Said she thought if I ended up being a little guy, my name would make me sound tough and no one would pick on me."

"How'd that work for you?" asked Jane.

"Well, for a little guy with a peanut allergy, I did all right. My dad decided I needed to take karate to go with the stupid name, so I held my own with the twerps who thought it would be funny to slip a peanut butter cookie into my stack of homemade oatmeal raisins." Slug smiled at the memory. "And hell, I'm a teamster, so what do you think, honey?"

Did everyone in Lucky's entourage call women "honey"?

"I think you've made a great recovery and you'll be back to work in no time," Jane said in what she hoped was efficient and businesslike Lucky production speak.

"Yeah, I'm just peachy. But you tell that bastard that the next time I, or one of my pals, reach for my EpiPen and find the case has been tampered with, we're going to have a little heart-to-heart."

"Why would you think Lucky is responsible?" Jane knew Detective Oh would advise her to just smile and nod and to let Sluggo keep threatening and showing his hand, but Jane Wheel, curious bystander, merged with Jane Wheel, girl detective, and a million questions popped into her head.

Sluggo pointed to the case. On the nightstand next to it sat a tiny laminated three-leaf clover.

"Who the hell would put that in there? And it's not even a lucky four-leaf clover, so what the hell does that tell you?

"Brenda didn't get a chance to fill you in on all your duties, did she? Let's just put it this way, I might have been able to tell Lucky and Brenda what it's like to have a full-blown attack, but perhaps I didn't convey how goddamned scary it is to not be able to breathe. Perhaps I'll give him a more detailed explanation by putting my thumb on his windpipe if he ever goes near my stuff again. And that goes for his pretty new assistant, too. Got it?" Jane nodded. "Besides," he added, "Lucky's responsible for everything, right? It's his shindig, yeah?"

She thought about offering him a ride, but by the way he looked over her shoulder at every footstep in the hallway and his glances at the clock on the opposite wall, she knew he was already expecting someone.

Jane did however plaster on a secretarial smile and ask what she hoped sounded like an innocent question prompted by curiosity, rather than an investigative follow-up.

"You said someone tampered with your case, but was your EpiPen actually touched? Because if it was, that would be . . ."

"Yeah, it would, wouldn't it?" said Sluggo. "Let me guess, Lucky hired you for your brains, right?"

Jane managed to keep her smile intact until she turned away. His answer might have been an nonanswer, but one thing that it clarified? Sluggo Mettleman's personality would attract more enemies than friends.

In the elevator and through the corridor on the way to her car, Jane kept an eye out for anyone in a Lucky cap or a Lucky jacket but she didn't see anyone making their way up to Sluggo's room. Then again, she wasn't sure the teamsters, the drivers, and caterers, and other members of the production all wore the heavily logoed apparel that she now kept seeing everywhere around town. Slipping behind the wheel, she peeked into the mirror on her visor. How would she look in a Lucky baseball cap?

The large brick building on Water Street was always referred to by people who lived in Kankakee as the old brick factory, as opposed to the old paint factory or the old hosiery factory or the old battery factory. Whenever Jane asked her father about any building in Kankakee, he seemed to know its history, when it opened, when it closed, what was made, who worked there. But this old building, long closed and vacant, was simply the old factory on Water. No one ever offered what kind of factory it had been. It was across the street from a small park that had a playground, a concrete slab with a basketball hoop, a few picnic tables and benches, and a sloping bank that slid down into the Kankakee River. It wasn't a particularly scenic park, filled with old growth trees and flower gardens and the old stone picnic shelter like Cobb Park, Jane's childhood haven, but it was a nice little green space off of a busy street. *A pocket park* is how Jane always thought of it. This small patch of green space was always a convenient spot for the neighboring residents to bring their kids for a swing and a teeter-totter, or for someone to simply take a seat on the bench and stare at the river.

Jane couldn't remember ever seeing anyone using the basketball hoop until today. Jane had to park all the way down on Hawkins Street and walk to the factory where trucks were parked nose to tail around the entire two-block area. The basketball hoop was being used by four young men, all wearing LUCKY 4 YOU PRODUCTIONS T-shirts. Jane stopped to watch. They were enthusiastic amateurs, talking trash and giving attitude, but sinking very few shots, Jane noticed. She laughed when one of them yelled out that the player who had just missed what looked to be an easy unguarded lay-up shot like a writer. Must be the Hollywood version of shooting like a girl.

"Wanna play?" asked one of the guys and Jane had to turn and look around to make sure he was addressing her.

"No, thanks," said Jane. "I probably shoot like a writer, too."

"I had you figured for hair and makeup," said the guy.

Jane, ready to bristle at what was surely going to be a sexist remark asked why.

"All you stylists are so pretty you don't wear any makeup, then you come in and work magic on mooks like Lucky and them. Also," he added, pointing to the giant leather tote bag, her daytime just-in-case, "you all carry a pretty big bag of tricks."

Jane smiled and waved, continuing on to the heavy double doors at the factory's entrance. Tim Lowry was standing, pointing to his nonexistent watch and shaking his head.

"If you don't wear a watch, you can't tell me I'm late," said Jane. "Besides, I—"

A yell came from the basketball court followed by a string of expletives Jane would put up against anything she had ever heard from an EZ Way Inn customer. The player who had been accused of shooting like a writer had gone down hard, crashing all on his own, twisting his ankle. He sat on the court, rocking back and forth, insisting on an ambulance.

"I don't want you guys carrying me," he said, his voice wavering. "It's too painful."

"Jeez, Tommy, that's what you get when you try to play like a driver instead of the writer that you are," said another one of the four.

"Very funny, you asshole," said Tommy. "Get me to a doctor."

The player who had invited Jane into the game came over to her. "Don't worry about Tommy. He gets injured all the time. He'll be okay. I'm Sal." He put out his hand. Jane nodded and introduced herself and Tim.

"You're the new set stylist," he said to Tim, "I heard your name from Maurice. Doing the table setting for the roast, right?"

Tim nodded and began, "And Jane Wheel here is going to be my—"

"I'm filling in for Brenda as Lucky's personal assistant."

"Welcome aboard, Tim, and to you, Jane Wheel, I offer my condolences," said Sal, bowing his head.

A young woman ran out of the factory and over to Sal, crying. She laid a hand on his arm and tried to catch her breath.

"Slow down, Fran. Tommy just has another sprained

ankle. Won't put us behind schedule or anything. You bean counters can get pretty emotional over—"

"It's not Tommy. It's . . ."

Jane dug into her bag and found tissues, and offered the woman the whole package.

"Thanks," she said, mopping her face and wiping her nose. "I'm really doing the big ugly here, aren't I, but it's just that he was such a jerk sometimes and still when something like this happens you feel like maybe you liked someone more than you thought you did, you know?"

"No idea, honey," said Sal. "What the hell you talking about?"

"Lucky just got a call. And I—"

"Will someone get me to a doctor, for Christ's sake? Sal? Some help here? Just because your boyfriend dumped you again, Fran, is no reason to—"

"Shut up, you baby. He's dead and you've got your fifth sprained ankle of the year. Big whoop."

"Who's dead?" asked Jane. When the girl looked at Jane and shook her head, still wiping her eyes, Jane added," Jane Wheel, just coming to meet with Lucky about a temp job filling in for Brenda."

"You don't know him, then," said Fran. "He's one of the drivers."

"Oh shit," said Sal. "Oh no."

"Sluggo Mettleman," said Fran. "We just got a call. Sluggo Mettleman died."

10

Screaming Tommy quieted down when he heard about Sluggo and allowed himself to be half carried inside the factory to get his ankle taped. Fran, the messenger, stopped weeping long enough to explain that Sluggo had signed himself out and come down to the street entrance to the hospital to wait for one of the drivers to pick him up. When Mickey got there, Slug got in the car and something happened to him, he started choking like he did at the Steak and Brew and Mickey turned the car around and headed back to the hospital. By the time they got there, Slug, according to Fran, was already gone.

Jane and Tim had followed the basketball players and Fran into the factory, but because of the hustle and bustle inside, found themselves on their own just inside the building.

"Feels weird, huh, to be here in the middle of all this, just when this guy we don't even know died," said Tim, running his hand over the vintage Steelcase chairs in the waiting room. "Think these were here when they took over the place?"

"I knew him," said Jane, looking around at the narrow space. Jane could see that at one time there were offices that ran the length of this side of the building, but more recently, the walls had been taken down and the space resembled an art gallery. High windows fronted the street side, but the back wall was all a soft yellow brick. Jane pictured paintings hanging the length of that wall, illuminated by unobtrusive track lighting. In the center of that wall was a large arched doorway that led to the main body of the old factory. Since no one was sitting at the front desk, a heavy oak relic of the twenties, Jane sat in the wooden swivel chair. She reached into her bag and pulled out a notebook and started writing down everything she could remember from her conversation with Sluggo Mettleman.

"Seeing the guy on the floor at the Steak and Brew doesn't mean you knew him, Jane," said Tim. "And what's this about you filling in as Lucky's assistant?"

"Sorry, seems like everybody wants me for an assistant these days . . . you, Lucky, Don and Nellie . . ." said Jane. "And I did know Sluggo. I visited him at the hospital."

Jane sent a quick e-mail to Detective Oh with a few questions. She was managing the tiny keyboard better these days, but she'd never be Nick, whose thumbs could fly across the tiny face of the phone. Looking up at Tim who was trying to decide whether or not she was serious, she nodded.

"I'll tell you all about it later. Right now, we need to go get started on our new jobs. And Timmy, be careful who you pal around with here."

Tim raised his eyebrows into question marks. Jane started walking through the doors to the main factory floor and, without fully turning around, quietly told Tim over her shoulder, savoring the opportunity to utter the phrase, "Might be a killer loose."

* * *

Lucky was on the phone when Jane found him on the "set." Basically the building was one giant factory floor. It had been meticulously cleaned and the wide wooden floor planks glowed. Although she could eyeball how perfectly a Pembroke table could fit in front of someone's dining room window, Jane wasn't great with large area measurements. Jane did know, however, that the factory building with its brick walls and six large skylights covered at least half of a city block. Cables and lighting subdivided the space further, defining the actual taped off set located in the rear of the building. Two wooden tables were pushed together, set up with a dozen or so chairs. A large-scale monitor hung behind the tables. A few nooks and crannies along the side walls were set up as mini-offices and Jane saw at least two makeup and hair stations. They had turned the old factory into a working studio. Who would have guessed? *It's amazing what a little hard work and thousands of dollars can do,* thought Jane.

"Sweetheart, hand me a pen and paper from over there, huh?" said Lucky, from one of the larger alcoves along the side of the main room. He gestured to her with his cell phone, waiting for someone to get back to him. "When I hired you, I had no idea how much I was going to need you around here, I just . . . yeah, I'm here, shoot. Okay, got it and send a shitload of flowers, okay? Oh, they don't? Find out what the kid's family wants, and send it. Yeah. Oh yeah, she's here. I'll tell her." Lucky hung up the phone and nodded to Jane.

"Brenda says she's available if any questions come up, you can call her. She also said to tell you not to be too good at your job, since she plans on being back next week."

While Lucky was finishing up his call with Brenda, Jane

had scanned the large folding table that appeared to be serving as a second desk. Loose script pages and DVDs were piled on top of food wrappers. Several dirty coffee cups were stacked in one corner. Two laptops were open on the table, their cords crisscrossing over the rest of the debris. When did Brenda leave? How could Lucky have trashed his office space this quickly?

"What exactly do you need me to do?" asked Jane. "I'm not totally sure I'm the assistant type, but I do have some questions for—"

"You're my girl, all right," said Lucky. "Nellie's daughter is exactly who I want working for me."

Jane had remained standing, wanting desperately to close a door so she could talk privately with Lucky. She had to settle for pulling the makeshift curtain that surrounded the table and chairs as if it were a hospital bed in a double room. She supposed it was set up for the time this area would become a dressing room.

"What? Time for my sponge bath?" said Lucky, unlit cigar firmly planted between his teeth.

"Time for some honest answers," said Jane, thinking a beat too late that if she wanted to be considered as a writer for this show, she could have said *time to come clean.*

Lucky's eyes, for just a moment, Jane noticed, seemed to dart around the space, Looking for an escape? Trying to come up with a quip or a lewd remark that would get him out of any serious answers? To Jane's surprise, he removed the cigar, took a long drink from a water bottle, which Jane hoped contained water, not vodka, and leaned back in his chair.

"Okay. Just so you know, I just had a driver die over at the hospital. He and I share the same affliction—allergy to pea-nuts. So you got me in a serious mood. Let's be serious."

Jane flipped through all of her questions. *Why Kankakee? What was the point of this special? Why would Sluggo Mettleman say someone, probably Lucky, was trying to kill him? Why was Nellie so suspicious of him? Where did the money come for this "special"?* Jane flipped over all the cards.

"Who's Boing Boing?"

"Right for the jugular, just like your mother," said Lucky. He actually smiled and dropped his voice low. When he wasn't talking with a cigar in his mouth, his usual growl turned into a normal speaking voice. He pushed some loose script pages off a book on his makeshift desk. Sliding the book over to Jane, he said, "That's what you and me and the author of this book are going to figure out."

RECOVERING LOST MEMORIES . . . *recreate the journey and recapture your life.*

Jane glanced at the book, but quickly looked back at Lucky's face to see if this was some kind of joke.

"I've had every kind of addiction in the world, Jane Wheel—you name it. I've had problems with drugs and gam-bling and alcohol. Sex," he paused and sighed, before continu-ing, "although I'm not sure I'd call that the worst addiction. I've been agoraphobic, had panic attacks, anxiety issues. I've broken out in rashes. Lost my voice once for five months. People say I'm a hypochondriac, but that's just because the docs can't find out what's wrong with me. I'm a fucking mess, Jane, but you know what? I'm getting close to getting better because I finally found someone who knows what's wrong. My therapist wrote that book." He pointed to the volume in front of Jane. "She thinks I got some things I repressed from my childhood that are haunting me. I got whole chunks of time I just can't remember, see? And she thinks if I can figure them out"—Lucky paused and took another long pull of water—"I'll be right as rain."

Fran, her eyes still red, announced herself with a verbal *knock-knock*, and pulled the curtain back slightly.

"Lucky? Got a minute?" Fran nodded to Jane, looking a little curious about the new girl, but too busy to study her further. "I talked to the hospital and Sluggo signed himself out against their wishes. They wanted him to stay another day. They said he was already compromised, and it could have been a candy wrapper in Mickey's car that set off the reaction and he couldn't get to his pen. Mickey's a mess. Blaming himself. He says he should quit."

Lucky shrugged. "If he wants to go, let him, it's got to be hard . . . watching someone . . ."

Lucky broke off his sentence and stared down at the table. Looking back up at Fran, he waved her away. "Let him go if he wants, cut him a check for two weeks' pay or whatever the hell the union makes us do. Tell him it isn't his fault, pat him on the back. Do what you gotta do. I'll talk to him before he leaves, but get lost for a little while, okay?"

Fran left without seeming to take offense at Lucky's brusqueness.

Jane watched him write something in a small blue notebook and slip it back into his pocket.

"Had a little flash of something when Fran was talking,"

said Lucky. "Something felt weird. Maybe about Boing Boing? Who knows?" Lucky put the cigar back into his mouth. "Read that book, Jane, and you'll see. It's amazing."

"Any reason someone might want to kill Sluggo Mettleman?"

Lucky shrugged. "Probably. He was a mean little shit, always trying to start fights is what Sal told me. Sal's the, I don't know, crew chief, I guess. Been around the longest. My driver. Doesn't everybody always want to kill somebody?"

"I'm serious, Lucky," said Jane. "If I'm going to help you find out who's messing with your four-leaf clovers, I have to know what else is going on here."

Lucky dropped his voice a few notches, to what, for him, probably passed for a whisper. "Sluggo told me that somebody messed with his stuff, too. He told me that after he and Brenda talked about him having a peanut allergy, she wanted to know exactly what his reactions were like. He was a mess, that kid. He was allergic to a boatload of stuff. Anyway, he came storming in here a couple days ago and said he had left his kit out on the writer's table when he was demonstrating some tai fung fu shit to the other drivers and when he came back he thought it had been moved or something. Threw a fit and said nobody should ever touch his medicine."

Lucky unwrapped two sticks of gum, unplugged his cigar, and stuffed them both in his mouth and began chewing.

"What did the bag look like?" said Jane.

"Like mine," said Lucky, chomping on the gum and replacing the cigar. He gestured with his thumb and Jane saw a red kit identical to the one she had figured for a Dopp kit in Sluggo's hospital room.

Jane noticed Lucky look at his watch, swipe one finger over the face, look again and wipe it again. He repeated the gesture seven times before looking up and saying, "I got to be at some park in a few minutes; can we be done for now?"

Jane looked around Lucky's curtained-off space.

"Just tell me where you keep your lucky stuff?" Jane almost laughed. She sounded like she was shaking down a leprechaun.

Lucky gestured to a trunk that was covered with a few pillows. It appeared it was being used for extra seating. "Here's a key I had made for you. Don't let it out of your sight," said Lucky. "I've been collecting those things for years. You can't imagine what it's like to feel like you're losing all your favorite stuff."

Jane toyed with giving Lucky Miller a rough inventory of exactly what she had lost in the past twenty-four hours, but decided against it.

"Any other real assistant duties I should know about?"

Lucky shook his head. "You'll catch on. You just need to walk around with a clipboard and keep track of my schedule. Brenda left everything right there. When you're here, you can answer that landline, but I got my cell and anybody who's supposed to be calling me will probably do it directly. We do most of the rehearsal stuff in the morning and remotes, like at your folks' tavern, in the afternoon or evening. We'll begin taping next week."

"Who's paying for this? I mean producing this?" asked Jane.

"My company. I'm rich, baby. You'd be surprised how much being a second banana comic pays over the long haul. No ex-wives, no alimony, and no extravagances except the usual, so

I got a nest egg. Besides, you'd be surprised how cheap everything is here. We got the building in a swap for a fix-up and cleanup and the food and motels are pretty damn cheap compared to anything out west.

"I also helped a few members of the Rat Pack bury some bodies, so they took care of me, if you know what I mean?" said Lucky, raising his eyebrows.

Jane opened her mouth and was trying to decide exactly what to ask, when he held up his hand palm up, then pulled back the curtain. "Kidding baby, kidding. I just want the roast enough to produce it myself. It's like being at your own funeral and getting to hear all the best jokes. Now you be a good girl and read that book. You'll get me. Belinda's notes about my case are tucked into the front of chapters and you can read them, too. You'll see. Belinda says as long as I can afford to do this, I got to do it. And I need all the help I can get."

Belinda? Couldn't be. Then again, why not. Jane flipped over the book to the back where the familiar photo of a wise-looking woman with startling green eyes stared back at her, an almost smile playing around her lips. Belinda St. Germaine had been an organizer and decluttering guru, who had been featured on Oprah and whose book, *Overstuffed*, had nearly dismantled Jane's psyche when she decided to give Belinda's suggestions a whirl. The author had moved into the life-coaching business in California, authoring a best-selling book about navigating Hollywood that Tim and Jane had mistakenly tried to follow when in California on business and now, apparently, in her most recent incarnation, Belinda St. Germaine was a therapist specializing in the recovery of lost memories. Jane shook her head as she read one of the blurbs praising

St. Germain. *Remembering what caused our fears is what allows us to face them. St. Germaine might not be the first to claim this, but she says it in language we can all understand.* Wouldn't Jane be better off if she could repress some of her Nellie memories?

Lucky gave her a nod as he stepped outside his quasi-private space, parting the curtain with one hand and holding a bulging briefcase in the other.

"Hey," he said, dropping the curtain and holding it back with his shoulder. "You said you talked to Mettleman? Where the hell did you see him?"

"Hospital visiting a friend and I saw his Lucky hat and popped my head in, that's all. Figured it was what Brenda would do."

Lucky took out his cigar and pointed it at her, as if he were bestowing his own form of knighthood.

"You got some Nellie in you, all right." Jane saw the light in his eyes flash again and he whipped out his small notebook and scribbled something. "It's coming back, baby. After the writers' meeting, I'll have a bunch of new pages to go over. You can put them all in one of those binders in the morning. All the numbers to reach me or Brenda or any of these chumps are in the front of that binder. Meantime, just give me a buzz if anything new comes up on the schedule, *comprendez-vous?*"

Scanning the schedule Lucky had shuffled over to her, Jane saw it was dated at the top with today's date and a time of nine A.M. It appeared that it was e-mailed or delivered in person daily to the principals involved and Jane saw a folder where the previous schedules were all filed. She picked this up along with Brenda's notes and dropped them into her bag.

Jane also dropped the weighty *Recovering Lost Memories*

and Finding Yourself into her tote bag and picked up the key Lucky had placed in the table. Before sinking into Belinda St. Germaine's prose of self-help, she would help herself by unlocking the kind of closed doors she preferred.

Jane removed the chain from around her neck that she wore with a few of her own totems. She had two small open-work iron keys, a Yellowstone Park souvenir silver medal with a deer on it and a tiny gold baby ring she had found in the bottom of a battered jewelry box, otherwise filled with knotted chains and orphaned screwback earrings she had picked up for a dollar at a rummage sale. Jane added Lucky's trunk key to her necklace, then knelt in front of the box and pushed aside the cushions on the trunk's lid. Putting the key into the lock and turning it, Jane recovered a few memories of her own. As soon as she figured out what was going on here and who was tampering with Lucky's lucky stuff, she would get on the case of her own lost memories, boxed and crated, now cruising somewhere through Nebraska or wherever in the back of a moving truck. Between Jane and Tim, they had taken on so many part-time jobs, she realized she had let some of her own household responsibilities slip. *Like getting back my household,* she thought.

"There should be music," said Jane, turning the key and feeling the satisfaction of the tumbler sliding back. She lifted the top of the trunk. "And light pouring forth."

No music, though, and no light. Inside the trunk were several small boxes and bottles. Jane settled herself cross-legged on the ground to open them one by one. Four-leaf clovers, rabbits' feet, stickpins crafted into horseshoes, and a large vintage celluloid box apparently devoted to lucky tokens and coins that had been advertising pieces from various shoe stores, bars, and amusement parks made up most of the contents. There was a small jar of beach glass, another one that held smooth round beach stones. Jane picked up a small silk drawstring pouch and shook the contents into her hand. Petrified wood? No, these were teeth, large and pointed. From a shark? No, not angular enough. An elk, a buffalo? Were teeth considered lucky? Not for the elk, of course. A felt jewelry bag held a lop-sided blue marble and two wrinkled buckeyes. Jane smiled at the buckeyes, which were her personal favorite lucky pieces. In addition, of course, to Nellie's four-leaf clovers, now that she knew Nellie had the "gift."

There was also a buttery soft leather lidded box shaped like a fortune cookie that held, naturally, fortunes. There were hundreds of scraps of paper, most with dates printed neatly on the back. Apparently Lucky not only noted memories in his little book, he also kept track of any ancient Chinese wisdom that accompanied his mu shu pork. One of the fortunes had been separated from the pack and was tucked into a tiny clear Ziploc, the kind Jane used for special buttons in her collection. Carefully separating the sealed top, Jane pulled out the paper and read:

I KNOW WHAT YOU DID

There was no writing on the back of this one. Either Lucky had been so unnerved by this ominous message he had neglected to date it, *or*, thought Jane, *Lucky hasn't seen this one yet.* This might be one of those tweaks to his collection that had prompted him to hire her. Jane put it back in the box, planning to ask Lucky about it later. She opened a few more small cardboard boxes. There was a bottle filled with holy water from Lourdes. Jane resisted the urge to open it and dab it on her pulse points. After all, who was she to deny powers? There was an empty Skippy's glass jar with wooden disks printed with LUCKY signs on one side and DON'T TAKE ANY WOODEN NICKELS on the other. Two identical charms, mustard seeds encased in small glass orbs, hung from a silver chain.

Jane heard Fran's voice just on the other side of the curtain and closed and locked the trunk, listening and tugging to make sure the lock caught. She slipped her own necklace back around her neck, thinking about how lucky she was that she had already been wearing keys, so one more would never be noticed.

"Knock-knock," said Fran, parting the curtain as Jane was fluffing the pillows and staring at her phone. She hoped she looked like she was just tidying up the office space. And although Jane had warmed slowly to the idea of these phones too smart for their own good, she now appreciated that anytime she wanted to look busy or distracted, all she had to do was pull out her phone and stare at it intently.

"Lucky told me to give you this list of everyone working here, although I can't understand why you'd need it, filling in for Bren just a few days, not like you'll actually see half these people." Fran clenched one fist then unclenched it, as if she were working one of those hand-exercisers or squeezing a rubber ball. "Half the people on the payroll are the rubes who live in this town who he's paying to make their places look like he remembers them. Easy money for people to use for remodeling, if you ask me."

Jane gave her what she hoped was the encouraging

un-rube-like smile of a coconspirator. "He's paying towns-people to upgrade their businesses?"

Fran shrugged. "Paid a guy to reopen his grandfather's diner and paid to upgrade parking lots at a few bars and restaurants. Paying for extra security at every place scheduled for a visit. Oh, and all those banners and signs and stuff? You think that the town has money to pay for that kind of blitz? Lucky's a man who likes buzz and he who buzzes loudest gets the most buzz back—that's his motto. I know I sound like a crank, but I'm his personal accountant, too, and the man's bleeding money for this project and who knows if it'll even see the light of . . ." Fran broke off to take a phone call and handed Jane a sheaf of papers.

Jane slipped those papers into her tote bag with all of the other Lucky Miller material she had gathered. She checked her own phone for the time. She was going to have to remember to always wear her wristwatch now that she was a working girl. She couldn't keep depending on her phone as a clock, having to pull it out every time she checked to see how late she was for her next appointment.

This time, though, there was a message on the screen. She hadn't felt the vibration, so missed seeing Nick's message when it came in thirty minutes earlier.

just kicked butt in our soccer game against St. Rs— nobdy expects math and science geeks to be jocks, but a few of us know what we're doing. Love you.

Jane put down her bag and using both thumbs to type, managed a *hooray for the nerds—love you back*. Getting an onscreen message was definitely not even close to Nick bursting in the kitchen door, spreading peanut butter on five slices of bread and stacking them to stuff into his mouth while he told her of some goal kicked or blocked, but it was something. No amount of sadness or loneliness washing over her could dim the equally potent wash of relief that Nick was so happy. He was some-place he belonged. Now it was up to Jane to find her perfect fit. And if Jane didn't quite belong in Lucky Miller's entourage, she at least felt comfortable in this factory-turned-studio. She loved this building—the old stone factory. She hoped they had man-ufactured something good here at one time.

"Hate to find out they made shopping cart parts or something," Jane muttered, gathering up her bag filled with pages and lists and clipboards and Belinda St. Germaine's gi-ant book. She touched her necklace, fingering each key and counting, realizing she had just given herself a new supersti-tious tic.

"Timmy," she called, as she walked over to where Tim was bent over a place setting, studying the patterns in two different napkins. "I have to go back to the tavern and work for a while so Don and Nellie can have a rest and go see Carl."

Jane stopped, realizing she hadn't told Tim about Carl. He shook his head and placed a hand over hers. "I stopped at the tavern before I came here to see if you wanted to ride with me. Don filled me in. I'm sorry, Jane, I know he's family."

"Yeah, for a family tree as dysfunctional as ours, it's amaz-ing we still have so many branches," said Jane. "I've got to go to Evanston and sweep the house clean of stuff I want. Can you come with me tomorrow?"

"I'd like to, but I doubt I can. They want to film some of the roast stuff early next week, so the table stuff has to be done. Speaking of stuff, I got a message from the movers," said Tim.

Jane waited.

"Might be a while," said Tim. "They got another gig somewhere in Western Colorado and they think they might have to retrace one stop because one of your crates might have been dropped off in Iowa by mistake."

"I'm never seeing this stuff again, am I?" said Jane.

"Don't be absurd, Janie. Of course everything will come back—and think of the money you're saving in storage. Did I tell you? They're not charging for your stuff on the truck. Isn't that great?" Tim looked back down at the fabric arrayed before him. Jane wasn't sure whether he was compelled by the designs or simply couldn't meet her eyes.

"Peachy," said Jane.

Walking to her car, almost dragging the impossibly heavy bag, Jane was startled and relieved when someone approached from behind and lifted her bag, taking the load off her arm and shoulder.

"Not stealing it, it's way too heavy," said Sal, the driver who apparently was headed in the same direction.

"Aren't you Lucky's driver and isn't he . . . ?"

"Wow, you are stepping in to fill Brenda's shoes. I better warn her you're after her job full-time. And no, to answer your question, I have not finished off Lucky and dumped his body somewhere even though half the people on the crew would give me a medal. He's meeting with the writers over at the diner and sent me back for a few things," he said, holding up a leather portfolio. "I'm heading back there now. Lucky's car is parked over there."

Jane nodded. "I'm a few cars down."

"Want to come with me to the diner? I could buy you a milk shake."

At just the mention of the milk shake, Jane wanted one. Badly. But she knew Don and Nellie would be getting antsy to get back to the hospital. She shook her head.

"Rain check?"

Sal nodded, dumping her bag into her trunk as she popped it open for him. Jane thanked him for the assist.

"How about tonight?"

"What about it?" asked Jane, confused.

"The rain check. How about dinner or a movie or something? Who knows what they do in this town for fun?"

Jane looked at Sal a little closer. He was almost her age, maybe a couple years younger. Handsome, too. Good smile. Intriguing. But, Jane told herself, also impossible. If timing was everything, then the timing of dating anyone who was only in Kankakee on what might be compared to a temporary work visa, when Jane was here sans home, sans stuff, sans everything was totally impossible.

"I used to know. I'm a townie, so watch what you say," said Jane. "I'm afraid I have a million things to do while I'm here, but maybe after the weekend."

"I'm a patient man," he said, and as he walked forward to Lucky's car, he tapped on the hood, the way New Yorkers did when they wanted to tell a cabbie he was clear.

At least that's what Jane always thought they meant when they pounded on a car.

*　*　*

When Jane got to the EZ Way Inn, only a few regulars sat at the bar. The mood was gloomy and despite the ballgame on in the background and cold beers sitting in front of everyone, no one looked happy.

Don did his best to give Jane a smile and asked her how it went with Lucky. Jane gave him the shortest easiest answer she could, then asked about Carl.

"I went up there for a few minutes after lunch, then when I got back, I had Francis drive your mother up. They should be back pretty soon."

"Dad, you look so tired. How about a rest in the back room while I tend bar? Better yet, you could go home for a while."

Don shook his head. "I'll just sit for a while," he said, situating himself on the first bar stool on the other side of the bar entrance. "I just need to rest my feet."

Jane's phone buzzed and she gave her dad an apologetic look. "I have to check, Dad, although I won't when I tend bar by myself. It's just that Lucky . . ."

Don waved away her concerns and she looked at the text, which came through in three parts. Lucky wouldn't need her tomorrow because he was going to lock himself in with the writers. If she wanted to nose around the studio, it would be fine. Since she said she had to go to Chicago for the weekend, maybe she could go tomorrow? After tomorrow, they would really need her around.

Since she had her phone out, Jane checked e-mail and saw that Melinda had written to tell her that the buyers offered to pay a premium for the quick move which should cover any furniture she wanted moved out of the house. They were hoping they could keep most of it. Really liked her taste.

Well, I don't get that every day, thought Jane. *I hope I get to meet these people.*

Melinda also told her that they had a quickie inspection and all seemed fine. The sooner she could get up there the better.

"Dad, how about I go up to Evanston tomorrow to do my house walk-through and sign the papers? It's fast, but it'll be like pulling off a Band Aid if I just get it done. Then I can be here for you guys if anything happens over the weekend."

Don nodded and Jane e-mailed Melissa that she would be at the house by ten.

Jane slipped her phone back into her pocket and grabbed a bar rag. Time for some on-the-job training.

"What'll it be?" asked Jane, doing her best Nellie impression, barking out of the side of her mouth and standing in front of Don with her arms folded.

Don smiled and asked for a draft. Miracle of miracles. Jane held the glass, pulled down on the lever and drew a perfect glass of beer. Half inch of foam and no spillover. She grabbed a Lucky Duck paper coaster and slipped it under the glass as she set it in front of her dad.

"Beautiful," said Don. "Now bring me a whisky and water."

Jane lifted one eyebrow at her father. It had been a hard day, but it still seemed a little early for Don to be hitting the hard stuff.

"What kind of whiskey? Water on the side?"

"Nah, I don't want a drink, I just wanted to see what you'd

say. You asked the right questions, but the dirty look you gave me was your mother through and through."

"What the hell's that supposed to mean," said Nellie, walking in from the kitchen. Neither Jane nor her father had heard the back door to the tavern open and close. Since it was a slamming, banging screen door, that meant Nellie had held on to it, closed it silently and come in quietly. Since she usually made a dramatic entrance at the tavern and saved her sneak-up-from-behinds for Jane at home, both Don and Jane turned to look at her.

Nellie's face was as hard to fathom as her moods. She clearly had been a pretty young woman, perhaps a beautiful one. Her eyes were sometimes gray, sometimes green, and piercing and she always looked right at you, sometimes until you flinched and looked away. Her hair had gray in it, but you wouldn't call her gray-haired. Enough color remained to confuse any carnival age-guesser. The thing about her face, though, is that it was almost always in motion. She grimaced, she grinned, she chortled, she raised her eyebrows, and she sneered. She was an itchy, twitchy woman who was in constant fidget mode and her facial features were equally mobile.

That is why, when Jane looked at her mother, she felt a chill. Her mother's face was completely still. And Jane realized, when Nellie's face was not in motion, she simultaneously looked ten years old and she looked one hundred years old. Every minute she had lived was apparent in her eyes, in the set of her mouth and every bit of childlike innocence and vulnerability that remains in all of us was present in the curve of her cheek and the stillness of her head.

"He died," she said.

Don stood and put his arms around his wife. Nellie allowed it, but over his shoulder she stared straight ahead. When she moved away, Don sat back down heavily, his head in his hands.

"I read all of his wishes and he wanted to be cremated so I okayed that," said Nellie. "We'll have a memorial service in a week or so, when everyone's heard about it. He wanted it to be here."

Jane saw that Don was crying, tears streaming down his cheeks, but Nellie remained dry-eyed. If she had cried, it was in private, away from all of them.

"You call Salt and Pepper, and the newspaper, and the rest of these guys'll do the rest, right? You all tell everything you know anyway, so you can spread the news, okay?" Nellie asked, looking around at the two customers who remained on the other side of the bar. Jane knew one was named Gil, but didn't recognize the other man.

"Now finish your drinks. We're closing up now," said Nellie.

And for the first time in the long history of the EZ Way Inn, the closed sign went up on the door at five o'clock on a sunny weekday afternoon.

11

"And you believe him?" asked Nellie, using the back of a fork to crushed canned tuna into a fine pâté.

Jane had just explained to her mother that Lucky Miller did not remember his Kankakee childhood or at least not much of it. She was trying to plow through Belinda St. Germaine's book, but the going was heavy.

"I think I do," said Jane. "He's struggling with something, anyway. And I can't believe anyone would carry this book around with him if he didn't think he could learn something from it. It's so much mumbo-jumbo. I mean, I believe there can be repressed memories, but this is like reading the back of a cereal box . . . if the cereal was all-natural granola with a kombucha glaze."

"What's she talking about?" Nellie asked Don, who was chopping onions for her. "Make them finer. And chop a little celery, too."

"New-age claptrap? That what you're saying, Janie?"

Between the phone calls Don and Nellie had to make about Carl and the many more phone calls they received with condolences, there hadn't been time to make a real dinner.

Now Nellie insisted on taking the phone off the hook and making tuna salad, so they could all sit down and eat something in peace and quiet. Jane was doing her best to entertain and distract.

"Yeah, it's new age and shamanistic with a little Ouija board thrown in for good measure. But it's also an expensive way to self-help. She recommends total recreations of one's past. A kind of spare-no-expense tableau. Says you can't truly know your history unless you *actively* remember, which will make you truly recover the past. Belinda's a cross between Dr. Phil, a Magic 8 Ball, and a battalion of Civil War reenactors."

Jane stood up and snatched a piece of celery from the counter.

"Mom," said Jane, "who *was* Boing Boing? I think your mention of him was what made Lucky want to hire me, made him want me close since he thinks that's some kind of memory trigger for him."

"Ought to be," said Nellie.

Since Nellie said no more and seemed terribly busy looking for mayonnaise, Jane looked at her father.

"Boing Boing?"

Don shrugged. "You know I didn't grow up in town. Until high school, I lived out past Herscher on my stepdad's farm, so all of these names your mother drags out . . . if I don't know them now, I have no idea who they are. Maybe she's making them up. Instead of those repressed memories, maybe your mother's got the opposite. Maybe she's got brand-new invented memories."

Jane wondered if this teasing was such a good idea on

such an emotional day, but as soon as Nellie closed the refrigerator, Jane saw that once again, Don proved that he knew Nellie better than anyone. And knew how to get her to talk.

"Oh yeah? You think I made it up that Dickie Boynton burned down his own garage and then ran away. They dragged the river for weeks before they found him. Only kid I ever knew who got a nickname after he was dead. Shorty Phillips, when they told us kids at school that Dickie was dead, started crying and said, 'poor old Boing Boing' and from that day on, that's what everybody called him. Whole school went to the funeral. You'd think he was everybody's best friend. Boing Boing this and Boing Boing that."

"Was he your friend?" asked Jane.

Nellie shook her head. "Not really. We were all poor at St. Stan's. All of us Lithuanian kids and Polish kids, we were all dirt poor. But our houses were clean and our mothers always made sure our clothes were mended. That's just the way it was. No money didn't mean you had to be a bum. But Dickie, he was always dirty and raggedy. Most kids made fun of him right to his face.

"Tell you the truth, I think that's why everybody got so nice to him after he showed up dead. Gave him a nickname and pretended he was one of the gang. That way nobody had to feel guilty."

"Why would Lucky figure in to any of this?" asked Jane.

"You saw the way he looked when I mentioned Dickie Boynton. He looked guilty as hell."

"That's not an answer. Why did you mention Dickie Boynton at all?"

Nellie took out a spoon and tasted the tuna. The taste sent her to the refrigerator for mustard. Adding a small amount and mixing it in, she looked at Jane.

"You'll laugh at me," said Nellie.

Jane and Don both looked at Nellie. When had Nellie ever cared about such a thing?

"When those TV people told me to make up a bit, I planned on talking about Hermie's nickname. Some of the kids called him Muley and he hated it. It's really all I remembered. He didn't make much of an impression. He had a little more money than us and was only at our school for a year and a half. I couldn't remember who his friends were or anything. Then when he came in and was mouthing off at the tavern, the memory of Dickie Boynton came to me. And that nickname, Boing Boing. So maybe you're thinking now, maybe I got those impressed memories."

"Repressed," said Jane.

"Except for one thing," said Nellie, setting the bowl of tuna and a gigantic bag of potato chips on the table. She opened a loaf of bread and looked down at Rita, who had begun to whimper at her feet.

"Oh hell, I didn't save any for you without the onions and mayonnaise, did I, girl? I know all that stuff in it can't be good for you," Nellie walked over to the cabinet and pulled out a new can of tuna and reached for the opener.

"No, Mom, her dog food's enough for now. I have a little treat for her from the studio. I picked up a sandwich on the buffet and saved some roast beef for her. Just finish what you were saying."

"What was I saying?"

"Except for something," said Don. "Something about your memories."

"Oh yeah. My memories about Boing Boing weren't repressed. I just forgot them," Nellie said, and put her hands on her hips as if she had proven her point.

"Run it by me one more time, Mom," said Jane. "Not following."

"Memories are just things you forget then remember, right? That's what makes them memories. So I hadn't thought about Boing Boing in a long time, but when I saw Hermie Mullet acting like Lucky Miller with that stupid cigar and everything, I remembered Boing Boing, because the two of them were friends. At least they used to hang around together on the playground. I can remember that now clear as day," said Nellie. "And if Lucky can't remember, like how he acted when I brought it up, like he didn't remember anything about Dickie, he's either lying or if he's having those repressive memories, he's feeling guilty about something. So, I got to thinking maybe he knows something about why Dickie drowned in the river."

"Do you remember how Lucky reacted when they found Dickie?" asked Jane, taking a piece of bread and starting to make a sandwich. It was almost seven o'clock and they were all starving. These European dinnertimes were killing them.

"Nope," said Nellie. "Lucky was gone. His family moved right around then, right after Boing Boing's garage burned down. I think police thought Dickie's dad had done something to him at first. Old man Boynton was a drunk with a temper. Heard he got sober and respectable afterward, went into the family restaurant business and all, but it was too late to help out Dickie."

Don stood up to get the pitcher of iced tea from the counter. "I'm putting the phone back on the hook, Nellie. We should be available for people if they want to call about Carl," said Don, hanging up the phone. It rang immediately and he answered, taking it with him into the living room, so Jane and Nellie could eat in peace.

"Maybe he should just talk to them on his portable cell phone," said Nellie, eyeing Jane.

"You know Dad has a cell phone?" asked Jane.

"Apparently he told you even if I had to find out for myself. Who do you think hangs up his pants and jacket every night when he leaves it on the chair? That man couldn't keep a secret from me if he locked it in a briefcase."

"He got you one, too," said Jane, whispering.

"Yeah, I know. I know my number, too. I've been reading the instruction book and I'm going to text him as soon as I figure it out. Scare the hell out of him and it'll serve him right."

Jane and Nellie ate their sandwiches and crunched their chips. Had there ever been a more satisfying meal? Sandwiches, chips, and iced tea, and Nellie had brought home a whole strawberry rhubarb pie from the tavern. Don and Nellie planned on staying closed for much of the weekend. Lucky Miller Productions was staging some kind of casserole-tasting out at the fairgrounds and on Saturday afternoon, there was the big bowling tournament. There was also a rumor that some guest stars for the roast were arriving over the weekend, so business was going to be even slower than usual anyway.

"By the way, I don't think that's true about the guest stars arriving. Nothing on any of the schedules about it," said Jane.

"Nobody's coming because this thing isn't ever going to

happen," said Nellie with a shrug. "Who the hell cares enough about Lucky Miller to insult him on television?"

Jane could see that her mother looked tired. This might be the only weekend they had ever taken off since they started in the tavern business fifty years earlier. Fifty years? Was that possible? They should be retired, her father playing golf whenever he wanted, her mother . . . What would Nellie do if they retired? Maybe that's why they weren't.

Don came in from the living room and hung up the phone. He told them it had been Wally calling and that he and Pepper would come in on Monday to discuss a memorial. Wally reminded Don that he had given them the key to Carl's apartment and they should come over any time to look at the stuff there. Wally didn't want to seem pushy, Don said, but he wanted to be able to rent out the apartment the following month if possible.

"Can't blame him," said Don. "Not enough money in the saloon business, might as well be in the landlord business.

After pie was consumed and dishes were washed, Jane excused herself. She planned to leave for Evanston early in the morning and hoped to be back by dinner. She took Belinda's opus with her to her room and crawled into bed. She hoped she could stay awake long enough to get through a large enough chunk so she could discuss it with Lucky. The sooner his "repressed memories" came back, the sooner Jane could put a stop to Nellie's suspicions that Lucky was up to something. Unless of course, Lucky *was* up to something. Hadn't Slug Mettleman implied that he was? Even playing back what had happened in Slug's hospital room didn't help Jane fight the wave of fatigue that rolled in. She began nodding after two pages.

Jane's phone rang and she clicked it on forgetting to check who was calling. She twisted it in her hand and held it out, tried to make out the number before saying hello.

"Mrs. Wheel?"

"Oh? Hello, I mean . . ." Jane fought to sound alert and not just awakened at nine o'clock at night.

"Yes, it is. I am so sorry to have wakened you."

"Detective Oh, I didn't expect to hear from you. In fact, I didn't, I mean I wasn't sleeping, I just couldn't locate my phone at first, I couldn't . . . okay. I was asleep. I'm trying to read an enormous book on repressed memories and I'm sorry to say it's putting me right to sleep."

"Mrs. Wheel, you are a woman who makes her living by experiencing the memories of others as well as your own. Surely you aren't concerned about repressed memories?"

Jane explained Lucky's phobias as briefly as she could. Earlier, she had phoned Oh to ask if he could locate a Dickie Boynton, since she had Googled when she stopped in at a copy shop that had free wireless, hoping for a Kankakee address and phone number, but found nothing. She had also asked him to find out what he could about the early life of Herman Mullet and his family without mentioning anything about that being Lucky's real name. Might as well double-check Lucky and his repressed memories and his biographer Malcolm and his false memories and find out whatever facts existed about Lucky Miller's early ties to Kankakee.

"Mrs. Wheel, I'm sorry about the news I have. You didn't tell me why you were interested so I don't know the connections, but sadly, there is no good news about either individual."

"Yes," said Jane, sitting up straighter in bed, fully awake now.

"Richard Boynton went missing when he was thirteen years old. Several days later his body was found. He drowned in the Kankakee River."

"What's the bad news about Herman Mullet?" Jane asked.

Herman Mullett also went missing at thirteen years old. His body was never found."

12

Too wide awake now to go back to sleep, Jane pulled out her laptop. Only after she powered up, did she remember that at Don and Nellie's, she had no wireless.

"What would I look for anyway?" she said. Rita, lying at her feet, raised her head briefly, then, seeming to know that no answer was required of her, resettled herself and went back to sleep.

When Jane had quizzed Oh about Boynton's death, his information had more or less meshed with Nellie's memory. The boy's body was found three weeks after he had been accused of starting a fire in which a garage and shed had burned to the ground. According to Mr. and Mrs. Boynton, their son Dickie ran away after the fire. He had a history of "staying away from home" as they had put it at the time, and they waited four days before reporting his disappearance to the police. Three weeks later, his body was recovered from the Kankakee River. The parents said he often camped out by the river and one night, after a particularly heavy rain, police felt he could have slipped in and perhaps been caught by a current. He was not, Dickie's sister had reported, a strong swimmer.

The more puzzling announcement—that Herman Mullett had also disappeared at thirteen—was a little murkier. According to what Oh had found out about Herman and his family, they left Kankakee right around the time of the fire. *So far, so good*, Jane thought. However, the Mulletts reported their son missing immediately after they moved to Louisville, Kentucky. No neighbors had ever seen them with a boy. Police at first thought Herman Junior had run away, back to his old home in Kankakee, but no one there saw him. The boy had disappeared. One account said that the parents claimed that he was fascinated by the water and might have drowned. No one really knew the Mullets in their new home, so no one knew what Herman looked like. There were only old school photos that were briefly circulated. No one ever saw a young boy with Mr. and Mrs. Mullet before or after his reported disappearance. A few years later, Herman Mullet Senior was accused and convicted of fraud involving a Ponzi-like bond scheme and he died in prison. Mrs. Mullet remarried and relocated to Canada with her new husband.

"But Lucky Miller *is* Herman Mullet. Neither he nor anyone else disputes that," said Jane, although even as she said it, she wondered who would dispute it and why?

"Interesting," said Detective Oh. "Lucky Miller took that name legally when he was eighteen years old. The name he changed it from," said Oh, pausing for a moment and Jane could hear him turn a page in his notebook, "was Herman Muller."

"Mullet and Muller are practically the same name," said Jane. Maybe he faked whatever he showed to change his name . . . birth certificate or whatever."

"Possible. Records were typed and filed then, rather than

saved on a computer so of course, a mistake or a forgery might be more possible."

"Were his parents suspected of foul play? I mean, when a child goes missing, aren't the parents always investigated?"

"Yes, sadly the parents are always under suspicion, correctly or incorrectly. But this was the era before twenty-four-hour cable news. With no zealous anchorwoman or anchorman trying the case in front of the public, the story probably just faded. The Mullets were new and unconnected in the community. No family, no friends. No advocate to keep the boy's disappearance in the news. The parents held a small memorial service for him. They did produce a birth certificate so there was no reason to believe they had made up a child. It appears that the boy's death was accepted and ruled an accidental death."

"Do you believe that?" asked Jane.

"Mrs. Wheel, you know that speculation and assumptions are the mark of the amateur . . ." said Oh. Jane sighed, feeling like she should apologize first for interrupting and, secondly, for forgetting everything he had taught her. Then Oh added, "Instinct, however, is invaluable. And my instinct, I believe, is in agreement with yours. I think that although my research turned up this news about Herman Mullet Junior, I feel the reports of his death might have been greatly exaggerated."

"Especially since I work for him now. He better be alive and kicking. Ghosts can't sign a paycheck," said Jane.

"Mrs. Wheel, I understand you are helping out your parents now, but you've also taken a job with Mr. Lucky Miller? Must I change the sign on the door to our office?"

Bruce Oh so rarely made a joke that Jane thought for a moment that he had, indeed, put a sign on the office door. Oh and Wheel? Jane liked it. But she caught his throat-clearing, which she realized was his nod to a chuckle and assured him that she was immersed in many part-time jobs, none of which added up to a full-time anything.

"I am, though, between places of residence, it seems," said Jane, filling Oh in on the house sale, the quick move, and the endless merry-go-round that her worldly goods seemed to be riding.

"You sound more sanguine about this than I might have imagined, Mrs. Wheel," said Oh.

"Yes," said Jane. "I know. I haven't quite figured this out yet. Losing my stuff. Either I'm in denial or I have come to a curious crossroads. I think I'll know more after I make the sweep through my house tomorrow."

"Perhaps you have been seduced by the idea of a clean slate, Mrs. Wheel."

"Go on," said Jane, sitting up straighter in bed.

"There are those who sell many of their belongings and start over just to have a tangible new beginning. My wife, Claire, tells me stories about many of her Chicago clients who do this with their condos and their lakeside cottages. This adds greatly to Claire's business. But I think on a deeper level than home furnishings, sometimes people just need to rid themselves of everything familiar and breathe new air, don't you?"

"Breathe new air," said Jane aloud. The house was quiet when she woke up, dressed, and made coffee and toast. It wasn't like her parents to sleep in, but Carl's death had shaken their world. Jane leaned over the sink and peered into the African violet plants on the window sill and pressed her nose up against the screen, repeating, "Breathe new air."

"Who you talking to, honey?"

Don padded into the kitchen, wearing a robe and slippers. He reached over for a mug from the maple cup tree on the counter and held it out for Jane to fill.

"I can't remember the last time I was dressed before you, Dad," said Jane, filling his cup to the tiptop. Don had trained her to pour a full cup. As someone who never messed with cream or sugar, he liked to know he was getting his money's worth.

"I can't remember the last time we didn't open up on a Friday," said Don.

"I can't remember any time that mom slept this late," said Jane.

"She's not sleeping," said Don.

Jane's dad pointed out the kitchen window that faced the side yard. "She's out there pulling weeds. Nope, she's out there . . . well, I'll be damned."

Don had seen his wife bending over and, accustomed to seeing her doing one chore or another, initially assumed she was tracking an errant dandelion making a late fall appearance. Jane joined her dad at the window and echoed, "I'll be damned."

Nellie had found a tennis ball somewhere and was throwing it for Rita. Bending over to pick up the ball, Nellie paused for a moment, plucked out something from the grass, then threw the ball again. Rita ran out for the long one and jumped and caught it. Nellie waved her in with one hand, staring down at whatever she had found on the lawn.

Jane and Don stared at each other. Nellie, their Nellie, playing fetch with the dog? Don nodded as if agreeing with an offstage voice and when Jane gave him her what-gives expression, he laughed. "I guess you can teach one old dog new tricks."

"What's so damn funny?" said Nellie, coming into the kitchen to wash her hands.

"What did you find on the grass?" asked Jane, covering for her dad.

Nellie unclenched her left fist and dropped a four-leaf clover on the counter. "I told you I find them all the time. Even in that little patch of weeds behind the tavern."

Nellie elbowed Jane away from the toaster, removed two slices, buttered them, and had two more toasting before Jane could protest. Since she knew she wouldn't get near the counter again, Jane gave up and sat down, spreading her toast with peanut butter and strawberry jam.

"Since you and Rita are getting along so well, can I leave her here while I drive up to Evanston? I'm walking through the house and tagging stuff for the movers. I left a message for Tim and he's picking me up in the van so I can bring a few boxes, but there's not much . . ."

"No, he's not," said Nellie. "He left the van in the driveway for you an hour ago."

"Oh no," said Jane.

"Here," said Nellie, handing her a note that had obviously been folded, unfolded, and refolded.

"Want to just give me the gist?" said Jane.

"Moby or somebody wants him to work today on the place settings for the roast. Lucky and his writers are going into an all-day meeting, so they can have the studio space to themselves and Tim's sorry, but he's sure you'll be fine. Then he apologizes again for the movers he got you the first time. Says your stuff is now heading back to Iowa or someplace."

Jane had already taken a large bite of her toast. She now reminded herself to chew it and swallow carefully. Nellie was peering at her, waiting for her to say something. Nellie had chastised and scolded and tsked-tsked and shaken her head over each new object she had seen Jane unpack—either here in Kankakee or on the rare occasions when Nellie had visited Jane and Charley's house in Evanston. Nellie didn't approve of clutter or unnecessary dust catchers. Whenever Jane protested that the objects she found told her stories of the people who had left them behind, Nellie snorted. "Why the hell you need somebody else's story?" she'd ask. And Jane, never coming up with a satisfactory answer, would simply shrug.

"Yup," said Jane, after she swallowed. "It appears that my stuff has truly taken off without me."

"Lowry," said Nellie shaking her head.

Jane was surprised that Tim was taking the heat—not that he didn't deserve it—and that Nellie wasn't saying "good riddance" and telling her how she should thank her lucky stars.

"I'm sorry to hear that, honey," said her dad. "I'm sure you'll get everything back."

Jane took a sip of coffee. Her father had a scratch pad in front of him and was making a list. At the top, he had titled it CARL, printed in all capital blocky letters. She felt a breeze coming in through the window over the sink and stood, deciding to grab a sweater to bring with her to Evanston. Jane reminded herself that she now had one cardigan, not a closet from which to choose.

"No, Dad, I probably won't get it back," said Jane. "It doesn't matter, though," she whispered, laying her hand on her dad's shoulder. "It's only stuff."

A few minutes later when Jane was ready to leave for Evanston, her father was on the phone, fielding another call from a customer, answering questions about Carl and the CLOSED sign on the EZ Way Inn. Jane blew him a kiss and picked up the keys to Tim's van. Rita was curled up under the kitchen table, and she began to disentangle herself to come with Jane, but Jane held up her hand the way Officer Mile had taught her when Rita had first wandered into Jane's life. "Stay," said Jane. "Stay with your buddies, Don and Nellie. I'll be home before you know I'm gone." Jane knelt down and gave Rita a good ear rub, then headed for the garage door.

Jane had thrown a few essentials into her just-in-case for her trip to Evanston, but realized as she chose a pen and notebook, her cell phone, and the digital camera Tim insisted she use instead of the one in her phone so she could document what was left in the house, that she was traveling ultra-light. No extra sweaters, notebooks, earrings, scarves, books; no roll of duct tape, no bungee cords, no folded up canvas bags, or envelopes packed with clippings of wish-list objects. Her bag looked curiously squashed in the middle. Was it time for a smaller just-in-case? Just in case?

As Jane was musing about the pared-down life and the odd feeling of lightness it bestowed upon her, she realized that one item that she carried everywhere with her as personal baggage had not been lost in the move. It occupied its own corner of the front seat of Tim's van.

"Mom, get out of the truck," said Jane.

"Number one, you shouldn't be driving through Chicago alone," said Nellie, scrunching her already small form into a tiny woman in the shape of a fist in the front seat. "Number two, you don't want to go through your house for the last time by yourself. Number three, you need somebody to make sure that real estate woman isn't out to screw you. Number four . . ." Nellie hesitated, looking down at the ring finger of her left hand. The only jewelry Nellie wore was a thin gold band. She pointed to it now as she finished. "Number four, I can't be in the house all day alone with your dad. He'll be calling people and people will be calling us and I just can't think about Carl all day long like your dad can. He's good at all this and I'm not."

That might not have been Nellie's longest speech, but it was close. And it was certainly one of the more revealing. Carl's death had made everyone look in some kind of a crazy funhouse mirror, but instead of delivering distortion, it made things crystal clear.

"So my pathetic homelessness is your distraction for the day?" asked Jane.

"Yup," said Nellie, opening a brown paper bag on her lap. "And I brought snacks."

"Number one, I drive in Chicago by myself all the time. Number two," said Jane, starting the truck, "Melinda will be there and possibly the new buyer, so I won't be alone to collapse in a sobbing heap on the floor." Jane continued, backing out of the driveway, "Number three, if Melinda was screwing me, she's already done it since I've signed and agreed to the offer, and number four? You're good at so many things, Mom, I think you can let Dad handle this one."

"And he can call me on this damn cell-phone thing when-ever he has a question," said Nellie, pulling a phone equipped with the largest keypad Jane had ever seen out of the paper bag. "I texted him we were on our way to Chicago, so let's see how long it takes him to figure that one out."

Jane had forgotten that Nellie, who never liked to talk or answer personal questions, became a complete chatterbox once they were in the car driving down a highway. As long as Jane drove silently, Nellie played navigator and entertainer.

"Look at the way that woman drives, will you. What the hell does that billboard mean anyway? That woman's hardly got any clothes on, how's that supposed to sell scotch whiskey? Watch out, that guy's going to change lanes, I can tell the way he's bobbing and weaving in his seat, see? I told you. Want a Fig Newton? I don't give a damn what you say, this is the best cookie in a package. They never get stale, you notice that? What the hell they put in these things anyway, they never get stale?"

"So, Mom, since we're on the road and you need to keep me company, tell me more about Herman Mullet."

"What the hell is guar gum?" asked Nellie.

"I'll tell you if you tell me more about the whole Boing Boing episode. Lucky Miller claims not to remember anything about that time and he's here trying to get the whole story back, so maybe you can help."

"Yeah, I brought that book with us," said Nellie, pulling Belinda St. Germaine's heavy volume out of her bottomless paper bag.

Had Nellie taken on the role of overpacking a just-in-case?

"Have you read any of it?" asked Jane, knowing her

mother's answer. Since Jane was a child, Nellie had railed against reading as the tool of the devil. "It's laziness pure and simple," Nellie would shout when she caught Jane holed up in her room, hiding out with the latest Nancy Drew mystery.

"Yeah, I read the first chapter or so," said Nellie. "Clap-trap."

Jane held her hand out for another Fig Newton and made her own childhood memories promise to shut the hell up for a while.

"They way I see it," said Nellie, "if a memory isn't pressed in good enough, you lose it or if something bad happened, you just don't want to remember it. But this idea that you have to go back to where you lost it? If you can't remember it, how do you know you're in that right spot? Lucky Miller changed his name, which says to me that he didn't want to be who he was as a kid. That says to me he did something bad. What happened bad while he was here? Dickie Boynton burned down his garage, ran off, and got himself drowned. Herman might want to forget that since Boing Boing was his friend, but . . ."

"But Herman's family moved away right after the fire, before he knew Dickie drowned," said Jane, exiting the highway. "Did you ever hear any news about Herman after he moved away?"

"Slow down," said Nellie, sliding over in the seat.

"Sorry," said Jane. "We're almost home . . . I mean, we're almost at the house."

"No, I mean slow down on Herman and Dickie. Before we had these things," Nellie said, holding up her cell phone, "people wrote letters and postcards and such. Maybe Herman wrote to

Dickie and . . ." Nellie stopped. "What the hell am I saying? Two guys who hung around on the playground wouldn't become pen pals all of a sudden. That isn't how things worked."

"No," said Jane. "But maybe Mr. or Mrs. Mullet kept in touch with somebody . . . or . . . hey wait. We keep trying to come up with stuff Lucky forgot, which is impossible because we can't know for sure what he's blocking. But what about the stuff he remembers? The places he's trying to recreate like Mack's? And didn't he get the bowling alley all fixed up for a shoot? Seems like somebody or something from what he remembers might lead us to what he doesn't remember."

"Just as good an idea as what's in that book," said Nellie, dropping it on the floor next to her feet.

"Okay, we'll save this discussion for the way back. Now it's time to switch gears," said Jane, pulling up to her house, looking not quite familiar with its giant FOR SALE sign, already with a large UNDER CONTRACT banner running across its face, planted firmly in the front yard.

Nellie was opening the door before Jane could get her seat belt unfastened. Melinda stood on the porch with a giant convenience-store drink cup in her hand. Over her shoulder, Nellie cautioned Jane. "You just let me do the talking."

13

Jane expected the walk through the house to be strange. After all, she had lived on Hartzell Street with Charley for almost twenty years, raised Nick there. In fact, she had been anxious about Nick's reaction to this. It was one thing to tell him the good news about a quick sale, but to tell him she'd be walking through their home for the last time? She had called him yesterday, trying to reassure herself that he wasn't just saying that he was pleased about the sale. He was such a good kid, Jane reasoned, that he just might be suppressing his own feelings about the house to make life easier for her.

"Mom, I am so okay with this. Please. I loved the house. I loved being there with you and Dad. But now, I'll just love being with you and Dad wherever you both are, okay? Honest. You're the one who likes the walls and floors, Mom." Jane could almost hear the smile in her son's voice. "You like having a place to put things or hang things. Me, I'd rather be in a tent. Or maybe once in a while in a classroom." Jane could hear boys yelling in the background. "I got to go. Soccer practice. I love you, Mom, and I'm happy about the house. So's Dad. I told him last night in an e-mail and he said he's happy we're all moving forward."

Nick's happy. Charley's happy. And the really odd thing, the strange part about walking through the house? Jane realized she was happy.

It was so unlike her.

"Beatrice is meeting us here in a half hour or so if that's okay with you," said Melinda, staring at her phone. "I'm supposed to text her either way."

"Beatrice who?" asked Nellie, opening up the bottom doors of the built-in corner hutch.

"The buyer, Mom," said Jane. "Tell her it's fine. Weird, but fine."

Jane was using the paper and masking tape that Melinda had provided to make a sign for the built-in book case in the hall. With smaller items, like books, Jane was leaving notes that said she was okay with leaving whatever remained on the shelves. Melinda was following her listing figures that Jane threw out so they could negotiate a final price for the contents. Melinda had two large cartons for smaller items Jane wanted to subtract from the contents. Jane removed eleven books from the shelf, signed first editions that she cared about. Seven of them had been gifts from Charley and four of them had been scavenged from estates, missed by the book guys and discovered by Jane. She was relieved that she hadn't boxed them up for the movers, but surprised that there were only eleven that she wanted.

"Take that one," said Nellie, pointing out a hardcover on the top shelf that Nellie herself couldn't reach.

"No book jacket, Mom, so its value isn't really that great," said Jane, squinting at it to read the title. "Oh my god, you're right," said Jane.

It was a gift edition of *Little Women*. It had come with a

cover and cardboard slipcase that Jane had mislaid long ago. It wasn't a valuable book, but when Jane opened the cover she saw the note from her grandmother. *For Jane on her eighth birthday.* Below it, Jane had written her name in shaky cursive.

"How did you spot that?" asked Jane, placing the book in the box.

Nellie shrugged. "Just thought twelve was a luckier number than eleven."

Jane looked at her mother, already sprinting ahead into the kitchen. She barely made it to five feet and her eyes were thirty plus years older than Jane's. Had she spotted the title, thought of its sentimental value, or just wanted Jane to go out with a dozen books? Nellie was superstitious and had an internal divining rod for four-leaf clovers, but Jane hadn't really seen Nellie using her powers out in the wild.

"Hey, I forgot to tell you. Bruce called this morning while you were in the shower and I told him he could meet us here," said Nellie, shaking her head at the sorry state of Jane's pots and pans.

"What?" asked Jane. "Stop calling him Bruce, Mom."

"It's his name, ain't it?" asked Nellie. "What do you call him? There is nothing in this kitchen that you want, right?"

Jane shook her head. She had packed up all of her vintage tablecloths, her fiesta ware and Hall china, her Hazel Atlas juice glasses, her Heisy pitchers and punchbowl, and all of the other brightly colored kitchenalia that she had accumulated over the last twenty or so years and it was gone, either stuck in the back of a truck or moldering in the back of a stranger's storage locker. The pots and pans and detritus of twenty years of failed attempts at cooking and binders filled with take-out menus could easily be left behind. Her red formica kitchen set was a good one, but did she really want it to define her new kitchen, wherever her new kitchen happened to be?

"We can take the table and chairs," said Nellie. "I'll put them in the basement and Dad and I'll keep them if you can't use them."

"Do you really want them?" asked Jane.

"Nope," said Nellie.

Jane was touched. Her mother was really trying to help.

"We'll let them go," said Jane. "For now, anyway. We'll put a good price on them and see what happens when we add everything together."

Melinda nodded at the figure thrown out by Jane.

"Wise, dear," said a familiar voice. "These retro kitchen sets have remained fairly desirable, but I'll be able to find you another," said Claire Oh, preceding her husband into the kitchen.

Jane was always startled by Claire's low throaty voice. It seemed to come from somewhere other than this impeccably groomed stately woman. When she described the high-end antiques and objets' d'art that she dealt with in her business, Claire always made the items sound provocative, dangerous, like something it might be naughty to own.

"This Capodimonte porcelain stallion? Perfect for the master bedroom," Claire would croon and the North Shore matrons would eat it up. Jane hardly believed Claire would stoop to scavenge for a fifties dinette set.

"Claire thought she might be of some help, Mrs. Wheel," said Detective Oh, slightly bowing toward Nellie, who was shaking her head at Claire's pronouncement.

"We already got Lowry to look for more junk. We're here to get rid of crap," said Nellie.

"Not that I agree with your mother's assessment," said Oh, "but it appears that many things have already disappeared."

"Disappeared is exactly what they've done," said Jane, with a smile.

Why did she feel so calm? Breathing new air? Was it the clean slate that Oh had described?

Jane had a few large pieces of luggage that she filled with some clothes from her dresser. There really weren't many things she wanted to take, but the clothes needed to be either packed or donated. Melinda had some large heavy trash bags Jane filled with over a dozen worn black turtlenecks. Why did she own so many? All black? If Tim were here, he would analyze her dour fashion choices as the selections of a depressed woman, who thought she was dressing boho but instead was sporting hobo. Just the fact that Jane knew that was what Tim would say made her hear his voice in her ear. *Time for a new look. Time for some color. Time for . . .*

"Beatrice would like to meet you, Jane," said Melinda, from the door to the bedroom.

"I would like to meet her as well," said Jane, turning to face the soon to be new mistress of the castle.

Beatrice had a wide open smile to which Jane immediately responded. How can you not like someone who likes your stuff? Beatrice came forward and shook Jane's hand.

"I am so pleased that this is working out," she said. Her voice was musical, with a clear bell tone. She had the slightest hint of an English accent. Jane, from her former career selecting commercial actors and actresses and voice-over talent, could detect accents, even those long tucked away in childhood.

"I am, too, of course," said Jane. "I'm not sure how I got so lucky."

Melinda shook her head slightly.

"It's a beautiful home and I can tell you've cared for it lovingly," said Beatrice and behind her, Melinda nodded. Jane realized she wasn't supposed to act lucky, she was supposed to act businesslike.

"My realtor said he would try to be here, but wasn't sure he could come over. He was shocked that you agreed I could be here while you walked through. I half think he didn't believe you'd show up," said Beatrice. She gestured to a large shopping bag and basket. "I stopped at the charming little purveyor on Central Street and brought a picnic lunch. I think I have enough for everyone."

Nellie entered the bedroom in time to hear the last statement. She hefted the trash bag filled with Jane's castoffs to take out to the car and said she'd bring in the pie she had brought from Kankakee.

This was turning into quite the party.

Jane gave Beatrice the list of items she would be taking. Two antique Persian carpets, three lamps, the elegant partner desk she had purchased from the Kendall estate in Kankakee and the leather chair and ottoman from the den. Although Jane had found most of the furniture piece by treasured piece, she now looked at each item with a different eye. If she wanted to replace it all, she could do it easily, probably with better pieces now that she really knew what she was doing. Her real treasures had flown the coop, so what was left, the remains, were mostly expendable. If she did move into a loft or a condo or a barn or a houseboat, the desk and the leather chair would keep her happy.

Beatrice had thought of everything for their picnic. She had brought paper plates and napkins and explained while laying everything out and opening containers of curried chicken salad and green beans vinaigrette and roasted vegetables and pesto pasta that she had been a transient for so long with her husband on the move for his job that she was over the moon about settling down on such a lovely block, in such a lovely neighborhood.

Claire asked her about her plans for the house and Beatrice began explaining that she had apprenticed to a decorator in London years earlier and was anxious to try her hand at bringing the house back to a kind of authentic twenties to thirties late-Arts-and-Craft style. Jane knew Arts and Crafts was not Claire Oh's cup of tea, but that did not stop Claire from oohing and aahing over Beatrice's ideas, handing over her business card and offering to find her any piece she might need.

"I have a matched set of bookcases that look like they were torn from this very house," said Claire. "I do love uniting pieces, bringing together objects and places that belong together."

Had Claire developed a slight British accent as well?

Detective Oh wandered into the living room as coffee and tea were being made in the kitchen and Jane followed.

"I apologize. Claire sensed a business opportunity and would not take no for an answer. I hope this isn't too unpleasant for you," said Oh.

"Not at all," said Jane. "I cannot for the life of me figure out why, but I am totally fine with all of it. I feel no attachment here.

Maybe if Nick were with me, or if my special stuff was here. But the house is so showcase-ready, it doesn't feel like mine anymore. I actually feel sort of lighthearted ... or maybe it's light-headed ... but I like feeling nonattached. I don't know if it will last, but ..."

"It's still my daughter's house you know, so ..."

Nellie had raised her voice and Jane looked at Oh, her new lightness rapidly replaced by the weighty realization of uh-oh-did-I-just-leave-Nellie-in-a-room-full-of-take-charge-women-who-don't-know-she's-the-boss?

Jane hurried into the kitchen, but by the time she got there, all were smiling with large slices of pie in front of them. Apparently Nellie didn't like the way Beatrice was dishing out portions and took over. Now she was putting lids on containers and washing the counter.

"We tried to tell your mother to relax, that we'd clean up, but it wasn't well received," said Beatrice.

Melinda and Jane slipped off to look over the values Jane had assigned to the property and the sum came to well below what the buyers had offered for "contents."

"Should we tell her she doesn't have to pay as much?" said Jane.

Melinda patted Jane's shoulder and shook her head. She made a quick call to a mover, who would pick up the desk and chair and lamps along with a few pieces of art that Jane wanted to keep. "Do they take it to your storage locker in Kankakee?" asked Melinda.

"No such thing," said Jane. She gave Melinda her parents' address. One side of their immaculate garage could house these few pieces until Jane decided where she would light.

Nellie had cleaned up the kitchen and was already making her second trip to Tim's van with Jane's suitcase. Oh had carried out the box that held books, Jane's printer from the den, and a small portable file box which had Nick's school and medical records, birth certificate, and last year's tax returns. Jane looked over a few more papers that Melinda needed signed and gave her all the bank information needed for a wire transfer of the money.

"I just want you to know how pleased I am that my children will be going to school here and enjoying this neighborhood as your children did," said Beatrice. "It's a wonderful house. I can feel the warmth here, the—"

Jane gently cut her off. She still had no regrets, but she wasn't sure how long she wanted this love fest with the Hartzell Street house to continue. "There's plenty of life and love left in this house. I think you and your family are a great match for the place," said Jane.

"You're getting yourself a good deal," said Nellie. "I told her to hold out and not take the first—"

Jane's cell phone began to vibrate and as she reached for her pocket, she gave Melinda the eye and nodded toward Nellie. Melinda interrupted and began to point out that most of the older windows on the first floor had been replaced recently with a quality product.

The phone number of the caller was unfamiliar to Jane.

"Where the hell are you, Jane Wheel? Don't you work for me anymore?"

"Lucky, I told you I'd be out of town today. I'm in—"

"Jeez, you townies think you can get away with murder. When you coming back?"

"I'll be back in town in about two to three hours or so, depending on traffic, but you said you'd—"

"You got to come here, you got to come back," said Lucky.

Was the man crying?

"Somebody's messing with my stuff. Messing with me. Somebody's messing with me real bad."

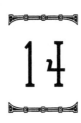

14

Jane shook hands with Beatrice, who looked as if she was about to cry.

"I feel you in this house, your touch," she said. "I wish I could have the house and you." Beatrice then pulled her in for a tight hug.

When Jane and Nellie got into Tim's van, Nellie reached over and manually locked her door. "I don't want that woman throwing herself in here and riding home with us. What the hell is her deal? Jeez."

Jane began laughing, then quickly looked out the windows and checked the mirrors. "You didn't know I had such a magnetic attraction, did you?" she said as she pulled away from the curb and headed west to the highway.

"She's a nut job," said Nellie.

"But she's a nut job with money, good taste, and a cash offer. In three days, my bank account will be huge," said Jane. "I'll be, well, I'll be very comfortable, which is good since I don't really have any . . ."

"Nobody has any retirement or pension anymore," said Nellie.

"How'd you know what I was going to say?"

"I'm a genius. Jane, everybody's worried about the same thing," said Nellie. "Why the hell you think Dad and I keep working?"

"Because you love the EZ Way Inn? Because the regulars wouldn't have any other place to go? Because you like ordering pies every day? Because you and Dad would drive each other crazy at home? Because you and Dad would kill each other?"

"We might, but nope. We can't afford to retire, that's all. Dad put money away, but he had it in some fund or something and I don't know what the hell happened, but he asked me if we could go a few more years and I said what the hell, so . . ." Nellie stopped to count on her fingers. "That was about five years ago."

"How old are you, Mom?"

"Old enough," said Nellie. "You hungry? I took all the leftover food." Nellie opened her large purse to show Jane all the foil packets and plastic containers. "You know how much that chicken salad cost? Jeez, I serve that at the EZ Way and try to get those prices, people would string me up."

"Where's the folder that Detective Oh gave me?"

Nellie jerked her thumb to indicate the one seat that wasn't folded down to accommodate the boxes they were taking back to Kankakee. Without undoing her seatbelt, Nellie squirmed and turned, grabbing the file and opened it up.

"What do you want to know?"

"Put it away, Mom. I just wanted to make sure I had it. Detective Oh got a little more information for me. Let's talk more about a retirement plan for you."

"I told you something wasn't right with Lucky," said Nellie, scanning the page.

"Something's sure not right today. He sounded pretty anxious on the phone."

"He's a nut job, too," said Nellie. "Sometimes I think we're the only non-nut jobs left. Want a pickle?"

"Wasn't that from Melinda's sandwich?" asked Jane.

"She didn't touch it. I watched," said Nellie.

Nellie crunched the pickle while continuing to read the contents of the folder Oh had given Jane. He had told her that he had found more information, but he couldn't verify all of its accuracy since some of the hospital and medical records were for Herman Mullet and some for Herman Muller.

"Someone either mixed up the name and Herman Mullet took advantage of the change or he himself adopted the alternative spelling," said Oh.

"How were you able to get this information? This is from Canada," said Jane. Oh had obviously gone beyond a Google search for these copies.

"Much of my father's family emigrated to Canada and I have several cousins there, two of whom happened to be well placed to obtain this type of personal information," said Oh. "As I said, though, some of this is a little confusing, although I've gone over it a few times and the ages work and the times of hospitalization."

It was at that point that Beatrice had asked Jane about the brass horse head hook that Jane had wanted to remove from Nick's old bedroom, asking if it were an authentic Arts-and-Crafts piece that had been in the house when they bought it. Jane told her that it was not, it was something they found at a flea market in South Dakota on vacation and Jane just wanted to give it to Nick as a souvenir of his old room.

It was only a half lie and Jane only felt half guilty about telling it. They had taken a vacation in South Dakota. Besides, she was leaving Beatrice the hand-forged fireplace damper handle that had taken Jane two years to find.

When Nellie and Jane arrived home in Kankakee, Don was sitting on the driveway in a folding lawn chair. He was staring down at his hands.

"What the hell's wrong with him?" said Nellie, opening the car door before Jane had fully stopped the van.

Jane hurried out of the van herself, leaving the unloading of boxes for later.

When she got closer, she saw Don was staring not at his hands, but at his new cell phone. Nellie was trying to look tough and inscrutable, but she began her sideways laughing when Don looked up at her with a lost puppy face.

"How the hell did you do this?" *On R way home* read the small screen. "I've been trying to write you back for an hour," said Don. "Every time I type in *Where* I hit the wrong letter and the word *were or here* or some other damn thing comes up on the screen and then I try to erase it and I lose the whole damn thing. Something's wrong with this thing."

"Mom's got smaller fingers and a natural penchant for misspelling. It's easier for her to figure out texting, Dad," said Jane. She wasn't happy to see him frustrated, but the distraction from all things Carl and the decision to close the tavern for the day was a blessing in disguise.

"Thought I was too dumb for one of these things, didn't you? There's a book with it, you know. And even though you and Jane don't believe it, I can read," said Nellie. "Want some chicken salad?"

Don got up, slipped the phone into his pocket and followed them both inside.

Jane washed her hands and face and decided to call Tim before rushing to Lucky's side. She needed to know if he wanted her to drive the van over and it wouldn't hurt to find out if Tim knew what had happened that had so unnerved Lucky since Miller, nee Mullet or Muller, had refused to give Jane any details over the phone.

"Don't know anything about Lucky, Jane . . . haven't seen him all day. The writers were holed up somewhere and I heard that Lucky and Malcolm came in here around lunchtime but I didn't really see them," said Tim. "Wait. What? Oh, Maurice just said that Lucky was upset about the horseshoes in his office. Don't know what that means, but apparently Lucky was screaming about his luck running out." Tim paused before adding, "Sorry I couldn't help at the house. Are you okay?"

"I'm great. I'm breathing new air."

"Yeah, okay. Did you bring back a lot of your stuff?"

"Nope, hardly anything," said Jane. "Do you need me to drive your van over?"

"Who is this and what have you done with Jane Wheel?" said Tim. "Nah, don't need the van until tomorrow. In fact . . . what?" Jane could hear Tim talking to someone, laughing at something. "Apparently I have a date tonight," he said. He sounded happy and a little bewildered.

"It's been a while, hasn't it, Tim?" asked Jane. She realized her mother had gotten the name wrong earlier. Not Maureen. Maurice.

"Talking about me or you, kitten?" said Tim.

"Okay, I've got to find Lucky. Maybe I'll see you over

there and if not, have fun. Don't rush into anything, Timmy, those Hollywood type heartbreakers can—"

"Gotta go, Janie. I've got a date to rush into something."

Jane shook her head. Maybe Tim had the right idea. Maybe she should find that teamster, Sal, and rush into something herself. Jane walked into her old bedroom to change clothes before heading out to find Lucky, but when she remembered that her wardrobe wasn't exactly unlimited, she decided her jeans and sweater were perfect. Maybe she'd snag a Lucky Productions windbreaker over at the studio.

Jane grabbed the folder with Oh's information. If she couldn't find Lucky right away, she could do a little homework. Don and Nellie were at the kitchen table and Rita was hovering, hoping for more of what Nellie had in the foil packet.

"This roast beef is pretty good. I didn't even see it when that nutty woman put the food out. I wonder if she meant for us to have it for lunch?"

"Mom! Did you go into the refrigerator and just take everything she brought? That was probably tonight's dinner for her family. They're staying at some apartment hotel!"

"It was in your refrigerator. You own it until Monday, right?" said Nellie, feeding Rita another slice of rare roast beef, which Jane knew cost double digits a pound.

Jane looked at her dad for support but he was lost in the manual for his cell phone. Next to the phone on the table was a list of people and phone numbers. Jane picked it up and read over the names. "Friends of Carl?" asked Jane.

Don nodded. The memorial was set for next Friday. One week would give everyone time to plan. A few old friends of the EZ Way Inn had retired and moved out of town, but Don said almost everyone he called was planning on making the trip back to pay their respects. There wouldn't be an official funeral, since Carl had left instructions that he wanted to be cremated.

"Me, too," said Nellie. "I want to be cremated. Nobody gets to look at me when I can't look back." She bent down to pet Rita and whisper roast beef promises for later.

"Right," said Don, not looking up from his instruction book, giving his usual response. "We'll wait until after you're gone, though, okay?"

Jane was halfway out the door when Don called to her.

"When you get a chance, honey, Salt and Pepper really want you to get into Carl's apartment and take his stuff out or help decide what to do with it. Keys to the place are right there."

One more part-time job. Jane picked up the plain silver key ring, admired the fact that it was sterling, and left it next to the flowerpot on the counter. One more part-time job.

Lucky wasn't answering his cell phone. Tim had said he wasn't at the studio, so Jane headed over to Mack's Café. That seemed to be a favorite meeting spot for the writers. The sign in the window said OPEN, but only a few Lucky crew members sat in a back booth. Jane took a seat at the counter. The perky waitress wasn't on duty, but Sam was behind the counter.

"Back for a burger?" asked Sam. Everything's finally cleaned up in the kitchen."

"One of those perfect milk shakes, please. Chocolate."

Sam nodded and reached into the two-door stainless steel freezer with a large metal ice cream scoop. Jane recognized the piece of restaurant equipment. Don and Nellie used to have one in their back room, back in their busy days of serving lunch to the Roper Stove crowd. It held two giant five-gallon tubs of ice cream, one under each heavy lift-up door. Nellie offered a choice of vanilla and fudge ripple. When Jane was around eight, Nellie caught her kneeling on a chair she had pushed up against the freezer, tunneling out the fudge with a spoon, eating it directly from the container. Nellie had laughed and told her that Don didn't need to know about it. When she was older, Jane remembered Don handing her a coffee mug and asking her to put a spoonful of vanilla into it. When she brought it back, he'd pour hot coffee over it and say, "Wonder what the poor people are drinking tonight?"

It took Jane a while to realize that this was Don's standing joke about just how rich he felt. Every Sunday when Nellie put the pot roast on the table and slammed down a pitcher of silky brown gravy that Don poured over his plate heaped with meat and potatoes and onions and carrots, he would tuck his napkin into his belt, and look at Jane and Michael and Nellie and muse, "Wonder what the poor people are eating tonight."

Eventually, Jane and Michael learned to answer him with whatever they were having for dinner, whatever Don was about to tuck into, and he would nod approvingly, agreeing with them.

Jane knew, though, that even though Don and Nellie weren't rich, Don had been a shrewd businessman and that he and Nellie had been tireless workers, remained tireless workers. They owned their own house, they'd always paid cash for a car. There had been no hesitation about paying college tuition for both of his children—as long as they went to school in state, of course. Don hadn't even wanted to get a credit card until one of the Roper office workers whom he trusted persuaded him that he might be in a situation where he couldn't use cash somewhere.

"What planet would that be on?" Don asked. "Planet Kankakee will always take cash."

There had been a few medical scares and some tests and hospital stays. Everything had always turned out all right and Jane knew that Don and Nellie paid for health insurance over and above the Medicare they now qualified for. What else, though . . . what else had Nellie been talking about when she said they had to keep working? Had Don trusted their savings to a retirement fund that had tanked with so many others? Jane's brother, Michael, was a lawyer in California and did well, but he had two young children. Jane was now divorced and hadn't had what Don and Nellie would think of as a "real" job for several years. Her parents were thinking about their ages and long-term care and their children and their grand-children, just like everyone else these days.

"Too much whipped cream?"

Jane hadn't noticed the picture-perfect milk shake that had been placed in front of her.

"It's fine. I just got really lost in your ice cream cooler."

"Beauty isn't it? When we came in to spruce up the place for this . . . what—reopening—so much of the equipment in here hadn't been touched in decades. Then we cleaned it all up and sure enough, when we plugged stuff in? Everything started working again. Apparently Lucky was willing to replace a lot of this stuff to make the place authentic, but we hardly had to use any of our budget."

"Is that how it worked? Lucky Productions came in with a check and asked you to make it like it was?" asked Jane, suck-ing hard on the straw, then giving up and going for the spoon.

"Pretty much. Everybody said Lucky Productions was

cutting checks left and right. They told me I could make it like it was in my grandpa's day. There were certain things I could change—like the curtains and the table arrangements and stuff. But there were some details that Lucky insisted on. He wanted the blackboard menu the same. They brought in a sketch to show me what the board had looked like, but no need. It was still here. And Lucky remembered the ice cream cooler, too. I thought it would take me months to find a vintage one still running, but it was right here, just needed a little cleaning and polishing."

Jane nodded and opened the folder with Oh's information. Mr. Mullet's occupation was listed as salesman, although his line seemed to vary from month to month and town to town. Most often he was listed generically, his line not described, but in some of the places he lived, Jane noted he had sold pots and pans, brushes and cleaning supplies, and baby-bottle sterilizers. Every new town seemed to mean a new job, a new product line. Times were tough for Mr. Mullet. Just like now. Jane looked up from her reading to see Sam looking at her thoughtfully. *Probably hoping I'm a paying customer today*, thought Jane.

"Will you make money on all this?" Jane asked, gesturing around the café with all of its new/old improvements.

"Of course. This place has been sitting closed for decades. When my grandma died, we put it up for sale. It's been over four years now. Most of the commercial property around here's been just sitting on the market. Hell, your folks' place has been on for five years. Although I hear that's because your mom keeps raising the price," Sam said with a laugh.

"No, that can't be . . ." began Jane.

"Yup, raising it. I know people are supposed to lower the

price, but not Nellie. Anyone talks about coming to look at the property and the price goes up."

"No, I mean the EZ Way's not for sale."

"Sure it is. Everything's for sale, Jane," said Sam, his posture defensive, his voice sharper. Once again, Jane reminded herself that her good fortune in the real estate market was an aberration and the economic suffering around her was the norm.

Jane tried Lucky's number again. Odd that he didn't pick up his cell phone. From what Jane had observed, all of the production people spent most of their time either talking on their phones or staring at the screens, their thumbs flying over the keyboards. The two crew members left in the dining room stood to leave and Jane rose to meet them at the door. She introduced herself as Lucky's fill-in assistant and explained that she just returned to town and couldn't locate her boss.

"Is it unusual that he isn't picking up his phone?" asked Jane.

The taller of the two men looked over Jane's head and pointed. She turned and saw that he was gesturing to the large advertising clock hanging over the door.

"Yes," said Jane. "A little after five. So . . . ?"

"Any time after three in the afternoon, our boy Lucky starts getting restless."

"Restless is a kind word for it," said his friend.

Jane shook her head and held up her hands in surrender.

"Three o'clock means it's cocktail hour somewhere," he explained.

Jane caught on, but must have not shown it in her face since both men made drinking gestures, tipping their hands toward their mouths. The tall one advised her to travel up and down the street, checking out the taverns. "And listen for Malcolm holding court," he advised. "He's usually Lucky's tour guide through his 'tastings.'"

Jane finished up her shake and told Sam she was official, she could sign for it as one of the Lucky staff. Sam handed her the notebook. Jane signed and glanced over some of the other signatures. She saw two names printed on one line—MICKEY and SAL—but in the signature box, only Sal had signed.

Jane asked Sam if he remembered the two of them in earlier.

"Yeah, I've talked to them both. I deliver all the food over to the studio and sometimes, Sal comes over and drives me and the food there. I come to set it up. Then Mickey or Sal run me back here."

"I thought Mickey was going to quit after what happened," said Jane, more to herself than Sam.

Sam shrugged and shook his head, either not knowing or not caring what she was talking about. He closed the notebook and brought it back to the cash register area. Jane left Sam a generous tip, since she didn't think tipping would be a part of the "book" system and headed for the door.

Stopping again at the table with the two Lucky staff members, Jane tried to give them her most fetching and befuddled smile.

"Guys, could you tell me when payday is? I forgot to ask Lucky if we get a check once a week or every other or . . ."

"Honey, said the tall man, setting down his glass, "you tell us. There's been a jam-up on the writing of staff paychecks.

That's what Brenda went to take care of. Don't know about tech and the drivers, but cash flow is a trickle around here."

"I told Brenda before she left if my next check—supposed to come every two weeks, by the way—was even a day late, I was walking and calling the union."

Jane thanked the pair and decided to follow the tavern trail down Station Street and pop her head in at each saloon as she made her way west. She began at the Pizza Slice. She had never really known anyone who went there for pizza. She continued down the street, popping her head in and scanning at the Shot Glass, the Wild Hare, and Frosty's. As she was about to enter Rusty's, her phone buzzed and she saw Lucky's number on the screen.

"Jane Wheel, I need you to meet me right now at the corner of North Seventh and what the hell is this? I passed a shut-down video store on my way. Do you know where that is? There's a street named Seneca that I passed."

"I think I know the general area," said Jane. "Why?" she asked, already turning her car around.

Lucky had already hung up.

15

Lucky was standing on the corner, looking first right, then left, then spinning around like a weather vane. He wore loose fitting jeans, a Lucky Production windbreaker, a baseball cap, and he carried a small notebook and pen. And although the sun was descending in the west, he still wore enormous sunglasses. If someone was trying not to be noticed, the sunglasses would have the opposite effect.

Jane pulled up at the curb and rolled down the window, calling to Lucky. She also turned off the car and hopped out. Lucky did not look her way, although he began talking as soon as she had closed the car door behind her.

"First it was a lucky charm or two moved or taken and replaced with something else. That was all. Pranks. Head games. That's not what it is anymore, Jane. Somebody wants something bad to happen to me."

Jane went to his side and took his arm. He seemed a little unsteady on his feet and allowed her to walk him to her car, but he refused to get in.

"Now somebody wants me to know my luck's run out."

"Did someone threaten you?" said Jane. "Maybe it's time to call the police."

"No police. Not until I remember what happened. I mean, if we call the police and they find out something I don't even remember . . ." Lucky's voice drifted off.

Jane tried to keep her voice as neutral as possible. "What happened today, Lucky? What happened just before you called me?"

Still not looking at her, Lucky explained in a shaky voice that Malcolm wanted a file that was in Lucky's desk back at the factory. The two of them decided to run over at lunch and then head back to the writers' meeting. When they got to the office, all the horseshoes that Lucky kept in his trunk were out and hung up on the wall. Seven of them.

"Is it possible that someone on your staff was just trying to decorate the place? Put some personal touches up in the office?"

"No one who knows me would have done what they did, what he did, what this devil . . ."

Jane shook her head and although she didn't think Lucky was looking at her, he apparently was keeping a lookout behind the dark glasses. Now as he took the glasses off and stared at Jane through red-rimmed eyes, Jane realized he had been hiding behind the shades not as an affectation but because he had been crying.

"The horseshoes were all hung curving downward. Everybody knows you have to hang a horseshoe with the open end up. Otherwise the luck runs out."

Jane patted his arm. She could feel him trembling under the windbreaker.

"And that's what the note on my desk said. " 'Your luck is running out.' It was signed 'H. M.' "

Jane opened the passenger door and half guided, half pushed Lucky into the car. It seemed like the kind of thing a good assistant would do, especially since they had been standing one someone's lawn and Jane could see a woman peeking out from behind the blinds. It didn't seem like a good idea to have this strange and shaky Lucky questioned by the police for trespassing.

"Who's H. M.?" asked Lucky. "Why is he doing this to me?"

"Can I see the note?" asked Jane.

Lucky fished the note out of the large kangaroo pocket of his windbreaker. The words were exactly as Lucky described. Jane noticed one detail that Lucky had not mentioned. Before she could question him further, Lucky pointed at the corner house where the woman still stood, keeping an eye on them.

"That woman, I've seen her watching me before. She was younger. It was a girl, really. A girl was watching me," said Lucky.

Jane studied Lucky, who was staring out the car window. When he spoke, his voice came from far away.

"When was that?" Jane asked, speaking softly. She decided to treat him as if he were a sleepwalker. Instinct told her it would be best if she didn't wake him.

"That day, you know," said Lucky. His voice even sounded younger. His cocky old comic swagger was replaced with the voice of a Midwestern child.

"I didn't see her, didn't see anybody. Then after, I remember she was looking out the window. I told somebody . . . I told . . ." Lucky opened and closed his mouth. He removed his sunglasses again and wiped them. When he spoke again, he was back. He was the gravelly voiced comic who may or may not have visited a few bars before ending up on this street corner in an area of Kankakee called "white city," by longtime residents. "I think I told my old man," said Lucky, shaking his head. "It's funny, I can't remember anything about him, but I think I told him about a girl watching me through the window. It must have been him."

"Where exactly were you just now, Lucky? I mean, where were you in your past?"

"Here. Right here," said Lucky. He searched his pocket for his cigar and jammed it into the corner of his mouth. "I live here," he said. "Lived. I mean, I lived here. I think this was my house."

"I can check. My mom grew up about eight blocks from here, so it would make sense if you went to the same school. This could have been her parish."

"Or that one," said Lucky, pointing a few houses down. "Maybe I lived there."

"Don't you have the address written down? I mean . . . you know you lived in Kankakee. That's why you brought the show here, right? You must have some documents with the address. Shouldn't you be shooting something at your old house? I mean, you're visiting the bars and you've got the diner and bowling alley all tricked out. Shouldn't you visit your old house?"

"I just knew the street name. I didn't live with my parents after Kankakee, so I never talked to them much. I lived with my aunt in Canada. I . . . this is the part I don't remember very well. I mean, I remember my aunt and moving in with her, but there are just whole chunks of time missing. Like on a film reel, you know? Somebody unspooled the damn thing and snipped out a few inches here, a few inches there.

"Malcolm said we should come here, back to the old neighborhood, and wander around. He thought there ought to be a shoot here, too, and I . . ."

"Where is Malcolm?" asked Jane.

"He stayed to take care of the tab. I thought I should walk around and clear my head." Lucky explained that their visit to the old neighborhood meant a trip to a tavern next to the railroad tracks. It had been Lucky's idea to walk around and he said he'd send for the car for a ride back after he found what he was looking for.

"But you called me," said Jane, "which is fine, but where's Malcolm and the car? How long have you been wandering around?"

Lucky looked down at his phone.

"I guess I've been gone for five missed calls," said Lucky, "however long that is."

Lucky handed Jane his phone and Jane called Malcolm back. She reassured him that she would drive Lucky back to the studio, then back to his hotel if necessary. Malcolm was screeching into the phone that he had been seconds away from an APB or whatever it was that the Yanks called it.

Lucky snorted. "He gets his Limey knickers in a twist when he has a snootful, doesn't he? Notice how that accent gets really thick? I hired the guy to class up the writing room, but he's just as much a lowlife as the rest of them," said Lucky. "Guy can spin a yarn, though. He really can write."

Jane noted the address of the corner house where the woman had finally left the window. Jane hoped it wasn't to call the police and report a Peeping Tom. She asked Lucky to point out again the house he thought he might have lived in. Jane wrote down that address, too.

If Lucky had been inebriated when he wandered away from Malcolm, his recovered memory, even though it was just a sliver, a hint of a memory, sobered him. He even managed to ask Jane a question that didn't revolve around himself.

"So you had a trip up to your house today. How was that? You recover any memories?" asked Lucky.

"Nope. Not really. Keep in mind, though, that I haven't really lost any, just all my stuff, not my . . ."

Jane remembered her earlier conversation with her mother.

"Of course, how would I know if they're lost? Nellie says memories are just things you forgot that come back to you, so how do you know they were missing until they come back?" As Jane said it, she thought about how convoluted it sounded. It was like Nick trying to explain the time travel in one of the novels he read. Jane tried to understand the concept, but kept running up against the fact that you really couldn't meet yourself, could you? How would that work?

"Nellie's right, in a way. I can go along for days, then something comes through my mind. It's like a wisp of smoke or something. Like a word that's on the tip of your tongue or just out of reach or something. That's when I know I'm missing something. Belinda says in her book that you got to knit those wisps, those ghost thoughts together in order to 'read the fabric of your lost memory' or something like that. She's got a way with words, that woman," said Lucky.

Jane thought her prose, if accurately recounted, a little overwrought. It would probably be more accurate to say that

Belinda had a way with bestsellers. She jumped around like a literary jackrabbit in the self-help market mining the readers and *needers*, who were desperate for answers. Of course, Belinda's advice to re-create the time and place where the memory was lost didn't seem like that bad of an idea. Wasn't that what Jane always said about her stuff, her found treasures? *It's the stuff that's left behind by others that tells their story* she had always insisted to Charley and Nick. And isn't that how she had earned her keep as Oh's junior partner? It was the stuff, the objects that helped her separate the innocent from the guilty.

So maybe she and Belinda could both help out old Lucky Miller nee Herman Mullet. And that thought reminded Jane of what she wanted to point out to Lucky earlier. Jane parked her car in the reserved spot behind the factory studio. Lucky shook his head.

"Not sure I want to go back in there," said Lucky.

Jane had a few superstitions herself, but she realized hers were fairly mild compared to Lucky's real fears about reentering his office.

"We'll fix the luck," said Jane. "I have Nellie's four-leaf clover with me." She slipped it out of her wallet and flashed it in front of Lucky. "Nothing can mess with Nellie's lucky charms." Even though Jane thought she had made her mother sound like a cross between the Godfather and a leprechaun, Lucky seemed to be mollified.

Lucky waved her over to a side door right off the parking lot she hadn't noticed before. Jane realized if one had a key to this entrance, no one in front of the building, no crew members playing basketball, none of the staff using the office space that faced the park and the river, would see you going in or out.

"Do you always use this door?" asked Jane.

Lucky shrugged. If he got dropped off in front, he used the front door. If he parked in back and the crew was moving anything in through the garage doors, he came in the back. If he or whoever he was with parked in the side lot, they used the side door. "Good thing about this door, I can slip right into my office space without running by all the riffraff working in the studio. Some of those townies are always wanting to ask me questions about my experiences, other celebrities, you know," said Lucky. He had recovered his sense of self, Jane noted, and she wondered exactly who working in the studio really stopped him to ask for show-biz lore. Tim was the only townie she had seen there yesterday and he was more interested in the designers working on the set.

The side door opened into an area directly between two curtained-off spaces. Lucky's private "office" was to the left and off to the right was a space that could be sectioned off as a meeting room with a conference table and eight chairs. If one continued straight into the heart of the factory/studio, he or she would be in the area where the catering tables were set up. A hard right to the other end of the huge space was the set, crisscrossed by cables and taped off by the stage manager and his assistants. Jane peered around the curtains to look at the set area and saw Tim standing next to another man, slightly taller, who stooped slightly to hear something Tim was saying as he gestured toward one end of the long table set up for the roast. Jane hadn't watched a lot of the comedy roasts, but knowing Tim, she had a feeling this set was much more elegant than most. In fact, she thought it resembled some kind of old master's painting of a feast, with the platters piled with fruit, the small low vases filled with flowers and the tapestry table runners. It really reminded Jane of something, but she couldn't quite grasp it. She trusted that the "lost memory" would return to her soon enough.

While Jane was looking around to see if anyone else was still working this late in the day, Lucky was waiting for her outside his curtained-off doorway.

"After you," he offered in a shaky voice. "Who knows what might be in here now?"

Jane saw immediately what had so disturbed Lucky. The exposed brick wall was covered with horseshoes, all mounted so their opened ends were down, spilling all the good luck. It seemed silly, Jane knew, and it was silly, but it did mean that someone was unlocking Lucky's trunk and messing about with his things. That was, at the least, mischievous. And in the case of a neurotic like Lucky, Jane understood how ominous it seemed. Jane went over to the wall to see how the horseshoes had been affixed to the wall. It had been announced on the schedule that Lucky would be out of the studio all day, so who-ever had done this either knew that he or she or why not *they* had plenty of time to redecorate Lucky's office.

"Open the trunk, Lucky, and see if these are the horseshoes that were in there or if somebody brought their own," said Jane. "Everyone knows about your attachment to your good luck charms. And if someone wanted to threaten you or scare you, they might just bring in something to spook you. Might not necessarily be someone with a key."

The horseshoes had been hung on little hooks that were attached to what looked like adhesive tape. The tape and hook were a sandy brown color that blended in with the bricks, mak-ing them almost invisible. Jane had seen these hooks before in white. They were the kind of hangers that students used so they wouldn't damage their dorm walls. Jane had used them herself last month to hang Nick's framed posters in his new residence hall room. A dab of glue might have been used on these to bolster the adhesive since the horseshoes were fairly substantial. Jane tugged hard at one of the taped hooks until it finally peeled off. She set down the horseshoe, but stuck the hook into her pocket. She continued removing the horseshoes and asked Lucky if he knew if they used those kind of hooks here in the studio. They seemed flimsy to her, but maybe they had to be careful on the brick walls?

"How the hell would I know the answer to a question like that?" asked Lucky. His obnoxious bravado came back stronger with every unlucky horseshoe that Jane removed. She toyed with leaving at least one of them up.

"You were right," said Lucky. "Those aren't my lucky horseshoes." Lucky leaned back, away from the open trunk and Jane could see the shoes still stacked on one side. "How'd you know this prank was a BYOH?"

"If I were going to do something like this, I'd want to slap the hooks up on the wall fast. That way, in case someone came in or I got interrupted, you probably wouldn't even notice these hooks by themselves. I'd stick the hooks up, maybe even the day before, then when I got a chance and knew nobody was around, I could come in with the horseshoes in a box or a bag and hang them up in less than a minute, drop the note on your desk . . . Is that where it was? On your desk?"

"No, it was taped to the horseshoe right next to the door, so as soon as I sat in my desk chair I could see it. Malcolm took it out and read it to me, then I . . ." Lucky slapped his pockets. "What did I do with it?"

Jane took it out of her pocket. She remembered that she wanted to point out something Lucky had misread on the note.

"Who's H. M.?" asked Lucky. "It was signed H. M."

"No," said Jane, spreading the note out flat in front of Lucky. "You missed the comma."

YOUR LUCK IS RUNNING OUT, H. M.

"It's not a signature. It's a form of address. To you. You're H. M. Herman Mullet," said Jane.

"So what? So I changed my name. It's in my bio. Anybody who bothers to read that piece of crap Malcolm wrote for my press packet and for the publicity for this roast could know my name."

Jane asked Lucky if anyone called him Herman.

"Not if they still want to work for me. I always hated that name. I would have changed it even if . . . even if . . ."

Lucky sat down with the same glazed look in his eyes Jane had seen while he was standing on the corner.

"Take your time," said Jane. "Why did you change your name?"

"I wanted to live," said Lucky, in a voice that sounded like it came from another planet.

Jane resisted asking another question. She watched and waited. Detective Oh would be proud, thought Jane, allowing ten long silent seconds to pass. When she was about to touch

Lucky's arm, to bring him back from wherever he was, he opened his mouth and nodded before he spoke.

"Yes. I changed my name because Herman Mullet was dead."

16

If a young man found out that his parents had sent him out of the country to live with an aunt and then claimed he had disappeared, it would certainly send that young man to a therapist's couch. *Wouldn't it?* Jane asked herself. Nellie had gotten rid of her favorite teddy bear and all of her toys when they moved and it had sent Jane on a lifelong quest of rescuing discarded or lost objects. *Hadn't it?* Jane asked herself. Jane had uncovered secrets her mother kept about her own past and about relatives Jane never knew. Nellie's secretiveness accounted for Jane's own foibles and tics and mistrust. *Didn't it?* Jane asked herself.

Jane did, however, remember everything. Perhaps a little too clearly? Nothing had been so traumatic that her memory was erased. Was that even possible? Jane knew that the idea of repressed memories was controversial. She remembered the outrage when a psychologist came forward and suggested that the epidemic of patients with repressed memories was caused by their own therapists, planting memories of abuse and trauma. The doctor wasn't suggesting that abuse and trauma did not exist, just that the overwhelming numbers of those who were "recovering" memories had been manipulated by unscrupulous therapists.

Lucky was not suffering from memories falsely planted. He seemed to have genuine gaps in his own history. Jane knew, with some of the information from Oh, she could fill in a few of the erasures, but what about the initial trip to Canada to stay with an aunt. According to the information from Oh, the Mullets left town and Herman was never seen with them in their new location in Louisville. They reported his disappearance and mentioned that he might have drowned. Had Herman really run away? Was he taken? Did his parents simply tell him they were getting rid of him? Did they explain why? Was money too tight? Was someone ill? Did they simply send him off to spend time with his aunt, then "forget" to pick him up? Although Lucky told Jane he knew his aunt had raised him from around the age of thirteen, he could not remember why he had been sent there. He remembered one town before Kankakee, a little farming community in Indiana. Then, in Kankakee, he remembered certain places of business, his neighborhood, attending school, riding a bike, bowling, drinking a milk shake, but there was a kind of fuzziness around it all. Then, when he tried to recall leaving Kankakee with his parents, everything was blank.

"Herman Mullet was dead," Lucky repeated several times, before Jane touched his arm and patted it.

"What does that mean, Lucky?" asked Jane, unsure about what Lucky actually knew and what she should reveal while he was in this state.

"I don't know," said Lucky

"Would you like me to find you a cup of coffee? Tea?" asked Jane.

"There's a crystal decanter on the table of the set. It has real whiskey in it. Bring that back," said Lucky. "I should . . ." He stopped and cast around for a task. "I should check my messages."

Lucky seemed to be on his way back from wherever he went. If he was faking this memory loss, he was a much better actor than anyone ever gave him credit for. Jane wasn't ready to end the conversation about Herman Mullet's demise, since she needed to know what he knew before blurting out anything she and Oh had uncovered and she could see he needed to return fully to earth. Recalling things seemed to take its toll. Belinda St. Germaine had a chapter in her book entitled, "The Exhaustive Work of Remembering." Jane had skimmed it and the actual fatigue on Lucky's face could have been an illustration from the book.

Tim and the man Jane had seen before were packing up to leave. Jane could tell by the smile on Tim's face, by the easy conversation between them, that this man was Tim's date for the evening. Jane put on her best big-sister-best-friend-protector-of-her-fragile-friend's-scarred-heart face and approached the two.

"Jane, Maurice. Maurice, Jane," said Tim. No cute remarks, no scintillating repartee, no cracks about Jane's wardrobe. Jane could tell right away this was important.

"Hello, Maurice," said Jane. "It's a pleasure."

"The pleasure is mine. Truly. Every other word out of this guy's mouth is about you, a quote from you, or a funny story about the two of you. I feel like I'm meeting the family," said Maurice with a warm and firm handshake instead of the air kisses Jane had seen flying around this studio the day before.

"You are," said Tim. His smile made Jane's own heart do

a flip. Tim looked happy. Not I-just-found-a-signed-Kalo-silver-pitcher-in-a-throwaway-box-of-old-plate happy, but innocently and truly happy. Jane thought there might be just a dash of tentative can-this-be-happening hovering around his grin, and that, she decided was really a good thing. It meant that he really wasn't rushing forward like a fool, he was falling at a normal human rate. Jane felt a heady mixture of joy and wonder and celebratory glee that her friend had found something sweet here. This was tempered by a modicum of uh-oh-if-Tim-is-finding-love-what-will-happen-to-me envy, but that, she knew, was also a normal human reaction and if this was real and right, Tim would make room for her. That's what she and Tim did—they expanded their hearts when others moved in. They built on rooms and knocked out walls. Jane's relationship with Tim had not changed substantively during her marriage or her motherhood, nor had it changed when Tim was in a long-term relationship with Phillip years earlier. And, if this relationship with Maurice flowered, Jane knew that there would be place for her at the holiday table—the elegantly set, meticulously designed, and deliciously prepared table.

"This looks amazing," said Jane, noting all the wonderful details up close. The gleaming modern silver, the cut crystal wineglasses, everything turned just so to catch the light. "It reminds me of something. It's a good thing, but I can't put my finger on it."

Tim and Maurice both laughed. "We know what it is, but I won't give it away," said Tim. "We're a little worried about it actually. It's because of the drapes in back mostly, but still . . ."

"Would you like to join us for dinner?" asked Maurice.

Tim continued to smile, but Jane thought she saw a glimmer of hope in his eyes, hope that she would refuse.

She shook her head. "I'm still on duty with Lucky right now." Jane looked back at the table. She was so close to getting it.

"Jane," yelled Lucky. "My life is in danger!"

If someone is really dying or something is happening, do they phrase it as *my life is in danger?*

Jane shook her head, but hurried back toward Lucky's office without the decanter.

"We'll hang around to make sure he's okay," said Maurice. "I've heard him yell stuff like that before to Brenda and it's never anything, but you never know."

"I'm coming," said Jane.

Lucky waved a letter written on Lucky Productions stationary. He didn't appear to be in imminent danger, but he was definitely pale. "I'm being blackmailed."

"For what?" asked Jane, approaching the desk.

"I don't know. I can't remember," said Lucky.

Jane read the note, typed, not printed out from a computer, on an old machine.

```
$ will buy silence. I know what you did,
I can prove it, and there's no statute
of limitations. You'll die in prison
too.
```

"What's next?" said Lucky. "A body falling out of a closet?"

"Stop!" screamed Jane. She threw herself on top of the

desk toward Lucky and slapped the half sandwich he was about to bite into. She nearly impaled herself on the fountain pens Lucky had lined up in a wooden rack. The sandwich half lay on the floor and she could hear Tim and Maurice running toward them.

"What the f . . . ?" said Lucky, looking from Jane to the sandwich and back to Jane.

"Did you take a bite?" said Jane, out of breath. "Peanut butter, peanut butter, I smell peanut butter. Call 911, Tim!"

"Hold the phone," said Lucky. "I am impressed, Jane Wheel, but no need to panic. Watch this."

Before Jane realized what he was doing, Lucky snatched up the other half of the sandwich off the paper plate and took an enormous bite. He dropped the sandwich on the plate, chewed slowly, and held up his hands, palms up, in a what-are-you-gonna-do gesture. He then wiped his mouth with a cloth napkin he pulled from a desk drawer.

"What the hell?" said Tim.

Maurice shook his head. "I heard the stories, but I didn't believe even you would be that deceitful, Lucky."

"Who are you again?" said Lucky.

"Your set designer. I have a contract and I'm union. You can't fire me, so don't even start . . ." said Maurice, without raising his voice. His tone was evenly balanced between disgust and amusement.

"You're not allergic to peanuts," said Jane.

Lucky shook his head, taking another bite of the sandwich.

"So what about the show at the EZ Way Inn?" asked Tim. "He had a reaction there, right? After Nellie's Lucky Duck?"

"Did you taste that shit?" asked Lucky. "Anybody'd have a reaction. Draino with a dash of soy sauce."

"I give up," said Tim.

"Well," said Maurice," the rumor is that Lucky fakes his allergies and a lot of other ailments because he likes the extra attention, is a bit of a hypochondriac, and he wants a convenient way to get out of uncomfortable or boring situations. Am I close?"

"You're wasting your time as a set designer, Maurice, I ought to promote you to writer."

"I make more than your writers, Lucky," said Maurice, with a smile. "And since I'm with the production company you partnered with, you can't fire me, remember?"

"Anybody else in the building?" asked Lucky.

Maurice and Tim both shook their heads. "We're the last ones here."

"Okay, you're partly right, Necktie," said Lucky. Maurice stopped him from christening him with a new nickname and reminded Lucky who he was. "Okay, Maurice, here's the real story. I do need an excuse to get out of places sometimes. I have panic attacks, okay? Nobody wants to hire a comic or an actor who has panic attacks because they look a lot like stage fright. So once when I froze up backstage at some shithole club in Delaware, Brenda comes up with the peanut allergy. Starts screaming about somebody eating peanuts backstage. She whips out a fountain pen and pretends to give me a shot, then has somebody help me back into the dressing room. She shuts the door, finds me a Xanax, hands me a shot of Jack Daniel's to wash it down, and we're all good to go. I realize this peanut allergy is a good gig. Gets me out of things fast and who's going to ask questions?"

"Do you make it a habit to hire people who have peanut allergies?" said Jane.

"No," said Lucky. "You're thinking about that kid. I asked him about it, what his reactions were like. And he gave me the fish-eye and asked me if I was concerned or if I was doing research. I told him a little bit of both. I wanted to make sure I didn't do anything stupid."

"Your medical kit?" asked Jane, beginning to pace back and forth. "Real EpiPens and fake shots? Or fake EpiPens and fake shots?"

"Real EpiPens that we just empty. And then a fake shot. Brenda's the only one who would ever touch the kit. I don't have a "reaction" unless Brenda's around. I wouldn't have sprung it on you, Jane. Although you have proven your worth as a temp, that's for sure."

"You're wrong," said Jane, shaking her head.

"Nah, you were good. I think you would have saved me," said Lucky, stuffing the last corner of the sandwich into his mouth.

"You're wrong about your kit. Somebody touched it. Or they thought they did. Somebody picked up Sluggo Mettleman's kit and stuck a three-leaf clover in it because he or she thought it was your kit. And if somebody had the kit and thought it was yours, maybe they messed with the EpiPen, too. If Brenda's the only one who touches your pens—she'd know your kit from Slug's even if they looked alike. So, whoever did it was either trying to embarrass you by proving you didn't have an allergy, showing somebody that you didn't really need the medication or," said Jane, "somebody believed you did have an allergy and was trying to kill you."

Lucky swallowed hard and Jane believed it was more than the peanut butter that stuck in his throat.

"So, Slug was murdered?" asked Maurice.

Jane shook her head again. "Not exactly murder, but if Slug's EpiPen was tampered with because someone thought it was Lucky's . . . it was malicious mischief to say the least. I mean he did recover from what happened in the Steak and Brew, so even if the pen didn't do the trick, the paramedics got there in time. I heard that they found the peanut candy wrapper in his friend's car and that caused the reaction that killed him. But if Slug hadn't already been compromised, if he hadn't left the hospital early," said Jane, "who knows?"

"Somebody wanted to murder me," said Lucky.

"Everybody wants to murder you, Lucky," said Maurice.

"I think attempted murder by EpiPen or lack thereof is a pretty imprecise way of going after someone if you really want to kill them. I think it's more likely that the person who was messing with your lucky stuff was trying to figure out some way to embarrass you or scare you. Whoever it was figured out that messing with the horseshoes and talking about you running out of luck was a better way to get to you."

"Does everybody really know the rumor that Lucky fakes the allergies?" Tim asked Maurice, who nodded.

"Everybody I know around here. Malcolm takes credit for scripting Lucky's life and after he has a few drinks, he likes to tell the tales."

"Okay, somebody's trying to mess with you, scare you a little with the superstitions, and maybe embarrass or expose you as a liar. Or somebody is playing a more serious game and tried to *murder* you or at least let you die? And now what, blackmail you? Same somebody? Two different people?" asked Jane, not expecting an answer. The threats against Lucky seemed curiously out of order.

"You boys got something more to do before we lock up?" said Lucky.

Tim and Maurice, taking the hint, headed back to the set to finish photographing the arrangement before leaving for the night.

Lucky didn't try to answer Jane's question. Jane could see Lucky looked exhausted. No amount of Botox could keep his face from sagging into a well-lined map. Jane stood and announced they should all call it a night.

"We need to call the police, Lucky," said Jane. "At the very least, this is blackmail and blackmail is a crime."

"Not yet," said Lucky.

"You're not thinking of paying any money?"

"Haven't got much left. Besides, I don't want to pay for what I can't remember. But something else," said Lucky. "I don't want police involved for the same reason. What if I did something terrible? The note says 'statute of limitations,' which means I might have broken the law. I might go to jail for something. I can't call cops in until I know what I did."

"Or what somebody is trying to make you think you did," said Jane. "How many people know you can't remember most of your childhood?"

Lucky shrugged. "My therapist, you know, Belinda. And my assistant Brenda knows everything. Malcolm knows, too, and from what I gather tonight, that means anybody might know."

"Do you have a security guard on tonight?" asked Jane. Lucky shook his head.

Was he kidding? This was a guy who was so afraid of being swarmed by fans he faked a food allergy, but he didn't hire security at the studio with all of this equipment, with access to his office?

"Tomorrow we hire someone. Either someone from your crew goes on all-night duty or we get someone from town. I'm thinking maybe someone from here; no ties to your production company might be the best idea."

Lucky agreed that they would hire someone in the morning. In the meantime, Jane went around flicking on lights in various spots and turning on a radio that someone had at their desk. Might as well make the place look like someone was there 24/7. Jane also found switches for outside lights at the rear of the building and turned them on. No harm making the place look lived-in and watched.

Maurice and Tim were also parked in the side lot, so the four of them made a final sweep of the space, then left together, locking up after themselves.

Later, after driving Lucky back to the hotel, making him promise to stay put, carefully handling the blackmail letter with a handkerchief and slipping it into an envelope, Jane returned to her parents' house and called Oh. Explaining everything that had happened since they had said good-bye in front of the Evanston house earlier in the day, Jane repeated her questions.

"Same somebody? Two different people?" she asked, hesitating just long enough for Oh to clear his throat. "But," added Jane, before her partner had the chance to speak, "why would someone try to kill Lucky, then blackmail him? I mean you can't blackmail a dead man, so if the object was blackmail money all along, it was someone who knew he wasn't allergic.

"And," she continued, "there are so many people who might want to murder Lucky. He is not beloved by his staff or by anyone else as far as I can tell. And as far as blackmailing him? I'm not sure he really cares who knows he's got a made-up story. Wouldn't he have fired Malcolm a long time ago? Malcolm tells everything he knows to just about everyone he meets."

"Mrs. Wheel, I believe you just said something that is true and not true at the same time," said Oh.

"You can't blackmail a dead man? That's true," said Jane. "So what's not . . . oh. Unless the dead man is Herman Mullet. This is about something Lucky did as Herman Mullet."

"Have you read the book by the memory expert yet? The one Mr. Miller is so fond of?"

"I've just skimmed parts of it," said Jane. "Lucky has visited her as a therapist so he quotes her a lot and I have read her other books. . . ."

"I'm not trying to make you feel guilty," Mrs. Wheel. "I'm just curious about what she says in terms of fact-finding. I have good resources at my disposal, but Lucky Miller seems to have money and could hire someone who also has resources to investigate his past."

Jane agreed and after hanging up, she remembered that Lucky made a big deal of wanting to find out what Nellie knew. Why not just look up a few records? Jane flipped through the numbers in her phone until she got to W.

"And this is why you don't ever push DELETE," said Jane out loud, clicking on the number for Mary Wainwright.

"Jane Wheel?" Mary answered the phone by reading her caller ID. "What a great surprise! Are you in town for the community theater auditions? *Music Man!* Can you believe it? Do you think I'm too old for Marian? Chuck isn't even trying out for Harold Hill, he's going right for the mayor which I think is a shame, since he has a lovely voice and you don't really need to dance if you're Harold, I mean, you just sort of have to march and prance . . . oh and maybe he's in the 'Shipoopi' number, do you remember? Because then I guess you'd have to be able to learn some steps and between you and me, he has two left feet. What's up?"

Jane had no idea how to answer Mary, an old high school friend who was now the only real estate broker she knew in Kankakee. They had had an odd, and according to Mary, "curiously bonding" experience in a recent community theater production, but Jane wasn't eager to reprise. She decided to come right to the point, since she guessed that Mary wasn't really all that interested in her take on who should play Marian the Librarian.

"Mary, can you look up a few houses in Kankakee and tell me the history of their ownership?"

"Sure," said Mary, switching to a much more professional voice just in case Jane happened to be a client. "Addresses?"

Jane gave her the addresses of the houses Lucky had pointed out as the ones he might have lived in. She was able to convey a certain amount of urgency and that got her out of a longer conversation. She did promise to have coffee with Mary soon, but conveniently did not mention she was in town indefinitely. If Mary thought Jane still lived in Evanston? All the better.

"I knew you'd come back. Everyone comes back," said Mary right before she hung up.

Jane could hear Don and Nellie's voices coming from their bedroom. Since they had never been the kind of parents who discussed things out of her earshot or her brother, Michael's, Jane was surprised to hear the low gravelly mutter of voices discussing something privately. Although Nellie never gave up any secrets of her own, she wasn't shy about saying anything that popped into her mind—unfiltered and uncut—in front of her children. She was especially free with opinions and advice, most often negative and uninvited.

Jane left the bedroom hallway and quietly entered the dark kitchen. Switching on the light, she began rummaging for anything fast and filling. When had she last eaten? She saw the containers in the refrigerator from Beatrice's fancy picnic neatly lined up on the shelf. Right, she had lunch in Evanston but it was hours and hours ago. She removed all of the cartons and started opening them, adding bread and cheese to her buffet. She poured iced tea and once again noted there was a bottle of expensive champagne looking like a stranger in a strange land on the top shelf. She picked it up and this time, saw the tag attached to the neck of the bottle. *Happy Anniversary* read the tag. And it was signed *Carl*. It was September. Her parents' wedding anniversary was in the spring. Jane had sent a card and flowers, hadn't she? Had the bottle been here the last time she had scrounged in this refrigerator? Hard to believe she'd miss seeing a giant bottle of Veuve Clicquot.

"Why do you keep staring at the bottle?" asked Nellie.

Jane shook her head and replaced it.

"Are you and Dad hungry? I assume you had dinner," began Jane.

"When you assume you make an 'ass out of u and me,'" said Nellie.

Jane stared at her mother. Where the hell had she picked up that one?

"We've eaten," said Don, following Nellie into the kitchen, "but I'll have some ice cream. Nellie?" he asked as he headed for the freezer.

Nellie shook her head. "That's expensive champagne."

"Yup," said Jane. "I used to give it to my creative team at the agency as the holiday gift."

"You think Carl won it on a punchboard or something?" Nellie asked Don.

"I think he bought it for us. A nice gesture," said Don. "Carl could be like that."

"What anniversary?" asked Jane, spreading mustard on roast beef.

"EZ Way Inn," said Don. "This month. Forty-five years in business."

"Wow," said Jane, wishing she could think of a more profound remark, something that didn't sound like the realization that her parents were really getting older. Too old to run a tavern and work twelve hours a day.

"We've been talking, Jane," said Don. "And I'm just going to say this and you don't have to answer or say anything yet. Just think about it. Your mom told me about your stuff going missing and how the house deal has gone through and we know Nick's in school out of Evanston and happy there and Charley, well, you know about Charley, and like you said, you used to have that good job at the agency and everything, but now, you're . . ."—Don searched for the unfamiliar word—"freestyle."

"Freelance?" Jane asked.

"Freelance," repeated Don. "Your mother and I have been talking and we were thinking if you wanted to move home for a while, we could fix up the basement so you could have some privacy down there . . . You could do it up however you wanted. We don't usually use that door that leads in directly, but we could unboard it and fix it up as a better entrance so you could come and go. . . ."

Jane went over and hugged her father. She buried her face in his shoulder, knowing he would think she was crying. She didn't want him to see that she was smiling. She had been touched enough to cry at this sincere and heartfelt offer, but the thought of Jane having privacy in Nellie's basement was hilarious.

"Thank you, Dad," said Jane. She looked over at Nellie, who stood in front of the sink with her arms crossed and her lips pursed. "But, no."

"I told you," said Nellie. "She doesn't want to live here with us. My idea's better."

Don and Nellie had a plan B?

"Carl's apartment over Wally's tavern," said Nellie.

Jane couldn't think of a response fast enough. She had been a successful advertising executive, a happily married woman with a wonderful son, and a PPI, picker and private investigator, with a fairly successful record . . . and why was it again her parents thought she might want to live over a bar in Kankakee?

"You look lonely," said Nellie. "And we thought while you got on your feet, you might want to be around here for a while. That Lowry would be close by and you could work at the EZ Way every now and then if you needed spending money."

Jane was about to have more money deposited in her checking account than she had ever imagined having all at once. Even after putting aside the money for Nick's high school and college tuition, she would be in fine shape. The insurance on all of her lost items was excessive, Tim had seen to that, and the replacement value check would be more than generous. But instead of laughing about how rich she was, she tried, unsuccessfully, to hug Nellie.

"Thank you," said Jane. "I'll think it all over."

Don and Nellie both nodded. Jane was surprised that Nellie didn't agitate for more of a commitment. Nellie had always preferred the fast yes or no to the slow maybe. Jane realized that those bedroom mutterings she overheard were about her. Don had told Nellie that they'd present their offers and suggestions and then just leave it up to Jane. Since Jane was a middle-aged woman who had faced down murderers, thieves, forgers, rabid scavengers, and pickers as well as the even larger specters of downsizing and divorce, she appreciated that now, at forty-something, fortyish, the new mid-thirties, Jane's parents were letting her make up her own mind. It touched Jane more than she could say that Nellie must have agreed, at least for now, to let Jane think for herself.

Nellie took Don's ice cream bowl from him as he scooped his last bite and his spoon as soon as it left his mouth. By the time he swallowed, Nellie had the bowl and spoon washed, rinsed, and in the drying rack. Her parents went to bed, leaving Jane at the kitchen table with Belinda St. Germaine's book on repressed memory and a roast beef sandwich.

Jane used her phone to e-mail Nick the good news about the house. She needed to fill him in on the details, emphasize their good fortune. She knew he would be relieved and grateful not to picture his mother there. It had already been planned that he would spend Thanksgiving with Jane and for his longer holiday vacation, fly to Honduras to be with Charley. Jane told Nick that she had a couple of ideas about where to live, but in the meantime, she would be in Kankakee. Don and Nellie needed her and she was happy to be there. She signed off, feeling guilty that she wasn't totally honest with her son. She knew that if she told Nick the whole truth, she would have to admit that, right now, she needed Don and Nellie as much, if not more, than they needed her.

Jane took a bite of her sandwich and opened Belinda's book to a chapter entitled, "Researching What Really Happened—Pros and Cons."

> *Why travel to your childhood home? Why walk the path that you trod so long ago? Why not simply look up the facts, interview the family, talk to friends? The answer is painfully simple. Your friends and families will not be the source of truth you seek.*
>
> *Even the best-intentioned family members will have faulty memories themselves. If you don't believe me, call your brother or sister and ask about the last holiday you spent together. Ask about the food served, the conversation at the table, who cleaned up, and who watched a football*

game in the den. Ask about who liked the pie and disparaged the green beans. I will bet you the price of this book that the answers you receive on everything, from the dinner menu to who complained, who argued, who bragged, will be different from what you expected. No two people have the same memories.

If you are trying to piece together what happened in your youth, you will not be well served by someone who was there with you. Why? Because they have their own struggles with their memories, their explanations for what happened in their lives, why they turned out to be who they are. You were not and are not their focus. Ask yourself this—do you remember everything about their days, their nights, their important moments? Then why should they remember yours? Even if they claim to know something about your childhood or have a vivid memory of an event that revolved around you? Their accounts will be heavily filtered by how the event affected them, what impressions were left on them. Only you remember you.

Okay. So you can't trust the truth and accuracy of the accounts of others. But what about facts? you ask. What about simply looking up dates on the calendar, addresses of the houses of friends or relatives, checking for photographs that might offer factual answers?

I will answer that with a story. Suppose you decide to walk through your old neighborhood, hoping to find the house of your old friend Bill. You know something happened in that house but your memory is blank, an erasure on the page. You walk up and down the block, searching for the house where it happened. What happened? IT happened, but you do not have a clue about what IT was. You walk up and down, back and forth. Did Bill's house have a red door? Did it have a red door or has it been painted? Was there a porch? With a swing? Do you remember a rosebush, a birdbath, a crooked chimney stack? Why not simply find a phone book from your childhood years and look up Bill's family's address? Once you've obtained the facts, the address, you can simply walk to the house and look at it and not waste all of your precious time pacing and speculating.

Precious time indeed! It is the time you spend walking up and down the block, searching literally as well as figuratively, that offers the rewards you seek. For every moment you spend speculating on whether or not you sat on that porch swing with Bill, you build another small piece of your bridge back in time. You build it intricately and carefully, engineered with your own memory of you. Perhaps that wasn't Bill's house, but you and Bill trick-or-treated there, sitting on the porch swing gazing at the scarecrow that was built in the yard. Perhaps it was there that you realized what had happened to you was not right. Perhaps that's where you began the process of forgetting. It is there, then, that you must rebuild the bridge of remembering. That bridge to another time cannot be made of pylons of disjointed facts—addresses and accounts of others—or you will be forced to leap across the span, from teetering column to teetering column. No. You must become a careful architect, engineer, and builder. All three of these jobs are yours—and no amount of facts will hasten the memories or the reconstruction of who you were and how that led to who you are.

Jane had to admit that Belinda St. Germaine could make a case. Of course, Jane might be able to poke some holes in her theories and make a case of her own for gathering some easily obtainable facts. But that bit about the architect and engineer and builder? Jane liked the idea that one had to multitask in order to grab hold of one's life. Maybe that's what Jane had been doing with all of her hunting and gathering. She searched out all sorts of memories from her childhood and beyond, surrounded herself with all sorts of items that were keepsakes, defining objects of the lives of others. Why in the world did she do that? She admired Art Deco design, loved the feel of worn wood and the patina of old silver, but all that stuff about the stories, about the caretaking of stuff. What was all that about? Jane built a bridge to the past, all right, but instead of her own past, she had constructed millions of those "teetering pylons" Belinda described and in Jane's case, where in the world did they lead? Whose past was illuminated?

Jane got up and rinsed all of her dishes and poured herself a glass of water. It was ten o'clock. She was tired enough to sleep, but it was always hard to go to bed without saying good night to someone. She had already e-mailed Nick. Tim was on a date and if she texted him good night, she would appear pathetic or nosy or both.

Jane turned out the kitchen lights, and looked for Rita. Where had she been all night? Listening at her parents' door, she could hear her dad's light snoring, her mother's breathing, shallow and impatient as if she resented having to sleep at all, and yup, the snuffling, sighing deep breaths of Rita, who had decided to sleep in with the 'rents.

Jane held her water in her left hand, Belinda's book under

her left arm, and her phone in her right hand. With her right thumb, she clumsily texted,

Read some Belinda and learned about her theories. Talk tomorrow. Good night.

Jane pushed SEND.

Settling into bed, heaping her covers around her chin, she listened for the late summer, early-fall cicada sounds, the Midwestern autumn song that had lulled her to sleep her entire life. A high-pitched trill joined the chorus and Jane picked up her phone to read the reply to her text.

Good night, Mrs. Wheel. Rest well. Oh.

17

Lucky Miller Productions was sponsoring a bowling tournament at the Flamingo Bowl beginning at three in the afternoon. Lucky had asked (demanded) all staff to participate (show up). There were teams of writers, drivers, designers, staffers, production assistants, and then there was Lucky's team. He had promised surprise guest stars and as far as Jane could tell, the townspeople in Kankakee had way too much faith in Lucky's "connections."

"According to an article in the *Journal* last night, some big TV stars are coming in on private planes," said Don, at breakfast.

"Dad, I saw the weekend schedule and unless there are changes, no one is coming in. I'm not even sure who the roasters are for the taping. I saw a list of names with no confirmation checks next to any of them, and to tell you the truth, I didn't recognize any of the names."

"You don't watch enough television," said Don.

Jane filled Rita's bowl, all the while telling her she had been quite the traitor, sleeping in Nellie's room. Rita paid no attention, wagged her tail in time to the music on the radio, and settled into her breakfast. The song ended and the local WKAN morning show host announced the various special events happening around town, ending with an exhortation to listeners to come over to the downtown farmer's market.

"Rumor has it that Lucky Miller might be dropping by the market with a few of his friends in town for the Lucky Miller roast. Come to the Gazebo at eleven when Lucky will draw a name for two tickets to the dress rehearsal!"

"What the hell?" asked Jane out loud, punching numbers into her phone. "Why don't I get any of these events on my schedule?"

"No problem, Jane. Malcolm can drive me over there," said Lucky, when he answered, sounding like he was in the middle of brushing his teeth.

"But, Lucky, if I'm your assistant, shouldn't I have these events on my schedule? I got it in my e-mail this morning, but I didn't see anything on there for you but the bowling today. Don't I need to know this stuff so I can . . . assist you?"

"Yeah, I guess. Trouble is, I've gotten kind of loose with the planning. I saw something in the *Journal* about the market and just decided it might be fun to take a stroll so I called up the radio station and told them I'd do it. Besides, all the shoppers and vegetables and stuff might give my memory a jog," Lucky said, between sips and swishes of water. "Belinda said that places with lots of people and colors and 'sensory triggers' are good places for breakthroughs. And what the hell, it seems like a nice thing to do on a Saturday morning."

Was it only Saturday? Was it Saturday already? *The rootless have no calendar,* thought Jane. She ticked off on her fingers the main events of the past few days. Drove down on Wednesday and got the offer on the house. Carl died on Thursday. Sluggo Mettleman died on Thursday. She became Lucky's assistant on Thursday. Walked through the Evanston house on Friday. Went to the studio with Lucky Friday night. Last night. So, yes, today would be Saturday. Yikes, Saturday. Soccer. Jane quickly texted Nick a good luck message. Then, with a second cup of coffee, she wrote a long and detailed e-mail to Charley about selling the house. The house was hers to sell, but she still thought twenty-some years of co-ownership gave Charley the right to know that the house was appreciated and passed on. She could also reassure him that the money would be most helpful with Nick's education, which might be important for any of Charley's future professional plans. He had made it clear he'd like to stay in Honduras working for the foundation there. Northwestern had been generous with extending his sabbatical—or rather, turning it into a leave of absence—but if they insisted he come back to hold his spot? Knowing Jane had money set aside for Nick might give Charley some breathing room. And breathing room was important. Breathing. Breathing room. Breathing new air. All important.

Jane took a deep breath herself. Writing that e-mail felt good. In the time since Charley had asked definitely for a divorce—no more extended work trips, or trial separations— but the call-a-spade-a-spade request for a divorce, Jane had felt mournful, frustrated, anxious, and angry with herself, but things were definitely changing. She noticed a few turning leaves on the trees in her parents' backyard, It was fall, her favorite season, and if Nellie had been right last night, that she was looking lonely, it was the right time for it. Jane loved the melancholy breeze of fall. Fall made sense to her in a way that the ripe hot summer never had. The dying days of autumn always lifted Jane to inexplicable heights.

Jane's phone vibrated signaling a new e-mail and she touched the screen, thinking Charley had answered back with an immediate "hurrah" for both of them, but it was a Lucky Productions e-mail with the "revised weekend schedule." Jane noted that the e-mail had been sent to the entire list of Lucky Production employees, the proprietors of the in-town locations for shoots, the caterers, the drivers, the support staff, all of the Kankakee contacts, people at the radio station and the *Daily Journal*. There was no need for Jane to feel like she had been the only one out of the loop with today's change. This time, the schedule included the walk through the farmer's market. Jane wondered just who Lucky had screamed at to make it happen so quickly. Where were all the people who scurried to do his bidding? So far, she had seen packs of writers, drivers, and a few production assistants like Fran who had delivered the tearful news about Sluggo, but no real secretaries and temps running around. Maybe e-mailed schedules and texting had eliminated the need for a full office staff. No need to have anyone copying pages and stapling and hand-delivering if everyone got every change pinged into their cell phone or laptop instantaneously. Jane repeated that thought aloud.

"Everyone gets every schedule change pinged into their cell phone or laptop," she said, scrolling back through the schedule and looking again at the list of recipients. She highlighted all the names and copied them into the body of a new e-mail, which she sent herself. It would be useful to see the names of everyone who knew and/or was kept apprised of Lucky's whereabouts. After all, if one knew Lucky was out of the factory studio and for how long, one knew if one had time to hang seven horseshoes upside down, didn't one?

"Come down here for a minute," yelled Nellie. Jane had noted her mother's absence in the kitchen, but figured she was out in the yard. Being summoned to the basement was unusual since Nellie did not trust Jane's laundry skills and when any extra pot or pan needed fetching from the cupboards below, Nellie was far too impatient to explain to anyone where the item could be found. Nellie was from the *forget-it-it's-easier-if-I-get-it-myself* school.

Jane descended into the basement and wondered just how long Nellie had been awake and busy in the basement. When her parents had purchased the house Jane's senior year in high school, the previous owners had left all of the "party room" furnishings. They had also left the '60s-style wet bar decorated with fishing nets and starfish and twinkle lights. Don and Nellie, with no need for an at-home bar had simply left it alone and had gotten used to the kitschy corner, no longer really seeing it on trips through the "finished" portion of the basement to the "unfinished" laundry area, much more beloved and utilized by Nellie.

Today Jane saw enormous changes before she even stepped away from the stairs. Nellie had stripped away all of the bar decorations and dusted and scrubbed. She had put a simple desk lamp on the bar, and slid a file cabinet next to the two tall high-backed stools, making the wooden bar resemble an old style accounting desk. With the addition of an eyeshade banded around her head, Jane and Bartleby the Scrivener might easily share the office space.

Nellie had also pushed aside an old EZ Way Inn table

and chairs that they had stored in the main area of the finished part of the basement. She had unrolled a colorful room-size braided rug made by Jane's grandmother in the center of the space, arranged the fold-out couch so that it faced away from the newly set up bar/office arrangement and pulled out two lamps that had been stored somewhere to warm up the space. It looked cozy and, Jane had to admit, apartmentlike.

"Just so you can picture it," Nellie said with a shrug.

Her mother had been cleaning and rearranging furniture for a couple of hours and it was barely eight A.M. Jane pictured it.

"I'm going to the farmer's market. Do you need . . ." Jane stopped and turned in a different direction. "Would you like to come with?"

Nellie shrugged again. Jane read it as a yes.

"How's it look down there?" asked Don, when Jane came upstairs, back into the kitchen. "Your mother wouldn't let me help."

Jane assured him it looked wonderful and she was continuing to think over their offer. She also promised, when he asked, that she would stop by Carl's apartment after the market. That would still leave her time to figure out what to do about Lucky's blackmail letter before the bowling extravaganza. Before discussing with Lucky, she really needed to talk more to Oh and, as much as she hated to admit it, read a bit more of Belinda St. Germaine's book. Nellie came out with a sweater in one hand and a canvas bag in the other.

"I can drop you back here," said Jane, with a wicked grin, knowing already her mother's reaction, "unless of course you want to come with me when I visit Carl's apartment."

Nellie snatched something from the depths of the canvas bag that she jingled in front of Jane. Carl's silver key ring. "How you going to get in without me?" she asked. "I got the keys."

"What's that noise?" asked Nellie, as they pulled into a parking space next to the downtown market. "Sounds like the big cooler at the EZ Way when the belt comes loose in the motor?"

Jane glanced at her mother whose ears seemed literally perked up, like a fox smelling a rabbit or hearing a hunter in the distance.

"My phone's on vibrate," said Jane. "I think it's a text."

Nellie reached into Jane's bag before Jane could take her hands off the wheel straightening the car in the space.

"Hmmm, Lowry's done it again."

"Give me," said Jane, turning off the engine and holding out her hand.

Nellie held the phone out of reach and looked her daughter in the eye.

"You think I don't care about the stuff you care about. You're wrong. I care about you and if that means all your damned doodads, I care about them, too. But the world's got plenty of stuff for you. Just remember that," said Nellie.

Nellie handed her the phone, undid her seat belt, and got out of the car, grabbing her canvas bag from the backseat.

No need to read the text. A message that prompted that response from Nellie meant only one thing. Her stuff was gone. It had been *gone* but now it was GONE. Fire, flood, famine, frogs, boils, some plague had descended on the movers who had taken Jane's stuff and Tim would now be able to file the insurance claim he had been reassuring her with. Jane almost felt relieved when she forced herself to look at the text.

> Truc impounded in CO. Driver arrested. Band equipment and remaining boxes destroyed in DUI accident. Company says to proceed with ins. clm. Sory for txt. Will explain later, but am filing claim today. I will make this up to you. so sorry.

Nellie had bounded ahead into the market crowd. Insurance claim. Jane's stuff had been precious to her, sure, but she had never thought about dollar value. Tim had, though, and set it so much higher than she would have imagined. Still, if all of the pieces were priced out, the replacement cost would be astronomical. Jane had been cash poor for so long, she wasn't prepared for the feeling that being "liquid" gave her. Before all this had happened, she would have said having cash would enable her to buy more stuff and that would be great. Now, having cash, Jane felt like she had to be so careful with spending. Being afraid to invest money in anything was one part of it, but her fear of once again investing her heart and soul into any one or one hundred objects was equally chilling.

Jane got out of the car, still staring at her phone, thinking about Tim's text. She could actually collect insurance money in exchange for the loss of her beloved objects. She felt a little strange about it. It was just stuff after all . . . it wasn't like anyone died and she was collecting life insurance which was another odd and uncomfortable concept. *Who, after all, was really comforted by a check after someone they loved died?* Jane stopped and moved aside for a young mother and father, each holding the hand of a little boy who walked between them. Jane smiled, watching the child bicycle his short legs in the air as his parents helped lift him through the air *Unless, of course,* Jane thought, *the person didn't die, just disappeared.* Then did the insurance company have to pay the claim? What if someone figured out how to have their cake and eat it, too?

The vendors were set up in the parking lot across from the new library, right in the heart of downtown Kankakee. What had been here before? Aldens department store? Was that it? Jane allowed herself a moment to remember walking into Aldens, turning to the right past the jewelry and cosmetics and purses, and being in the shoe department. Wasn't that where they had a big goose and if you bought the right kind of shoes, you got a prize that came in an egg? Wasn't that where Nellie would tell her that she needed to get shoes that fit, not look at some damn prize and pick the ones that pinched her toes? "If the shoes are made good enough and fit you right, they wouldn't need to give the damn prize," Nellie would always say. Despite Nellie's words of wisdom, Jane always opted for the toe pinchers and the prize. Maybe now was the time to invest in shoes that fit.

Jane saw two familiar figures across the lot, one of them hefting two vegetables as if weighing them against each other.

Jane quickly texted.

Forgive you only if you can find me the perfect eggplant and present it to me within 30 seconds.

Jane ducked behind a truck selling jars of amazing-looking pie fillings. She tried to read the flavors out of the corner of her eye while watching the two people across the lot. The tall, handsome sandy-haired man set down a full ripe eggplant and took his phone out of his pocket, He frowned at the text, then laughed. Picking up the eggplants and quickly paying for them both, he spoke to the equally handsome man at his side, then turned and began an almost robotic scan of the market, his head turning slowly from stand to stand. Just as he was about to turn in Jane's direction, she ducked behind the display of jars. There were only two strawberry-rhubarb left. Someone came up and bought one of them, toying with taking them both, Jane stayed crouched, but as soon as the customer left, she knew she was going to have to come out of hiding if she wanted that last jar. Paying for it, she felt the tap on her shoulder.

" "Two perfect eggplants in under fifteen seconds. You'll have to forgive me twice," said Tim.

Opening her canvas bag, she nodded as imperially as she could muster in the middle of the ghostly Aldens, now selling farm-fresh produce instead of Red Goose Mary Janes and hugged Tim, right in the middle of the shoe department, if her calculations were indeed correct.

"I'll help you replace everything . . . brand-new old stuff and better," whispered Tim.

"I'm fine. I am actually, really, truly better than fine," said Jane, meaning it and knowing it was true. Jane started to say something about finding her a place to live, but she saw Maurice approaching and right behind him, practically a puppy nipping at his heels, was Mary Wainwright.

"Tim told me what happened," said Maurice, shaking his head. "You're more generous with forgiveness than I might be."

Jane wished she could explain the whole sensation that led

her to this calm and Zen-like state, but she was having trouble understanding it herself. When she was packing the boxes for storage, she couldn't eliminate one collectible. Nothing ended up in the donations or throw away box—not even the torn old calendars and the books with crumbling bindings and foxed pages. But now, even when she could picture an object clearly in her mind, she found that when it wasn't touchable, when she couldn't hold it in her hands, she could say good-bye. So it wasn't out of sight out of mind exactly, since she could "see" it in her mind. It was just okay that it was all gone. Not good, not bad, but it was fine. She felt even. Balanced. Yikes. She might have to start attending a yoga class. What was wrong with her? Was this what some called happiness? Peace?

"You call that a fair price? That's robbing the people."

Peace was short-lived. As Mary began to greet Jane and flirt with Maurice simultaneously, Jane heard Nellie employing her bargaining techniques with a young couple selling tomatoes. They looked as if they were about to cry.

Jane fished out a twenty and asked Maurice to go over to the stand and start bagging up the best tomatoes he could find, right out from under Nellie's nose.

"It's a dangerous mission, but I have faith in you," said Jane.

"Don't do it, man, it's suicide," said Tim.

Maurice saluted them both and nodded, eschewing Jane's twenty-dollar bill. "Save it for some new old McCoy," Maurice whispered, with only a hint of a smile.

"You found a good one," said Jane, watching him stride over to the stand and position himself directly in Nellie's line of fire.

"Don't want to jinx it," said Tim, "but yeah, he's really special."

"Ooooh," said Mary, catching on. "Sorry, Tim, didn't mean to step on your toes."

Since Tim was immune to Mary's flirting techniques, he hadn't really noticed her trotting them out for Maurice. Glancing at Jane, seeing her shake her head and raise a subtle don't-even-go-there hand, Tim quickly told her there was no problem.

The morning was so crisp and bright and the stands were teeming with September's reddest, greenest, and the deepest yellow, orange and purple produce, herbs and flowers. Jane spied tables with craft displays—dried flower wreaths, baskets packed with homemade jams and pickles. What could be better than a morning filled with friends greeting each other and people planning the amazing dishes they would be cooking later that day?

"I got your info," said Mary, handing Jane a sheet of paper.

Jane tore herself away from looking at the people, her hometown neighbors meeting and greeting, and looked down at the sheet. She nodded. It was what she had guessed last night when she saw Lucky wandering the neighborhood.

"But you don't want these," said Mary.

Jane shook her head. Mary always conversed in a random way, answering unanswered questions and nodding in a knowing manner even when the person to whom she was talking had no way of knowing to what she referred.

"Chuck ran into Tim yesterday and Tim told him and he told me that you sold your house. With all that Evanston money, you can do better here than these dinky houses, Jane— you can live like a queen. Honestly, and I have some beautiful properties available right now and I shouldn't tell you this, but you can practically get them for nothing. Everything is so low and you could get one of those great old places on the river or a beautiful new construction in Bourbonnais or—"

"Mary, don't get your hopes up. If I decide to come here and I am not at all sure where I'm going to end up, I have a perfectly good apartment in my parents' basement," said Jane.

She tried so hard to say it with a straight face, but Mary had gone to high school with her. Mary knew Nellie. Hell, Mary had acted in a play with Nellie. The two women looked over at the Nellie in question, who, as soon as Maurice started buying up tomatoes without quibbling over price, started snatching up her own under his nose. The sellers who had looked dangerously close to weeping when Nellie was berating them for their high prices were now bringing out more tomatoes from the back of their truck, anticipating a sellout if business continued like this.

Mary handed Jane a folder with listings she had printed out and Jane silently accepted it, tucking it into her bag.

Jane watched Tim rescue Maurice before he backed up Tim's car to the stand to load tomatoes directly into the trunk. Jane watched the silent movie of him introducing Maurice to Nellie, and Nellie looking him up and down and giving him a grimace and handshake. Jane hoped Maurice understood that Nellie's grimace had nothing to do with homophobia and everything to do with misanthropy, but she could tell by Tim's look when he put his arm around Nellie and she accepted it for two seconds before ducking out of it, that Maurice, like Tim, could tell the difference between a hater and a scowler. No sign of Lucky at the market yet. Jane dialed his cell and got voice mail.

She suggested that he save time for a meeting before the bowling tournament and said she'd see him at the gazebo.

Her canvas bag, now filled with a large jar of strawberry-rhubarb pie filling, which Jane couldn't wait to stir into Greek yogurt for breakfast, two substantial eggplants, and a small wreath that Jane bought for Don and Nellie's front door, was just heavy enough to feel awkward. Jane decided to bring it back to the car, grab a second bag from her trunk, and join Nellie in the great tomato buy-out. At the car, she felt her phone buzz in her pocket and sat down on her trunk to have a conversation with Detective Oh.

Before Jane could begin telling Oh what she had found out from Mary Wainwright, Oh surprised her with news of his own.

"I spoke with Detective Ramey last night."

Jane, trying to remain in "Oh" mode, waited.

"Because what you described sounded like blackmail, a threat, to Mr. Miller, I thought it best to seek Detective Ramey's counsel, before . . ."—Oh hesitated for a second—"you find yourself meeting him under more stressful circumstances."

"But," Jane started to protest, then decided to trust her partner's rational nature. Oh knew that Lucky had not wanted to involve the police, fearing that he himself might have something to hide. "And what was Detective Ramey's response?" asked Jane.

"He agreed with you that murder by EpiPen or lack thereof did not sound like a very precise method. But he also agreed that if a wrongful death had occurred, if Mr. Mettleman died because his medical kit had been tampered with, this very well might be a police matter."

"You didn't tell him about the blackmail or alleged blackmail note?" asked Jane.

"As I said, Mrs. Wheel, I wanted to alert Detective Ramey that you were in town and might be turning up some matters that would be of interest to him. This way, we've come to the police before they come to us. I did not discuss the note. Mr. Miller's desire to remember what he might be being accused of before it's made public is a valid concern. If however that doesn't happen soon, and more notes arrive, or something more sinister happens, I know that you realize you won't be able to accommodate him."

Jane remained silent, thinking. She was sitting on the hood of her car and noted a rush of shoppers head toward the south end of the market. A large sedan, not, she was relieved to note, a limo, had just dropped Lucky Miller off and apparently was circling around to park. Lucky had planned his entrance at the spot farthest from the gazebo so he could saunter the length of the market. Maximum visibility and maximum schmoozing opportunity.

"Lucky just arrived," said Jane to Oh.

"You wouldn't believe the attention. This is a guy who invented his own celebrity, created his own backstory, and made up most of what he remembers about Kankakee, but everybody believes what they want to believe, I guess," said Jane.

"Remember, Mrs. Wheel, if another note arrives, one with instructions about the money or anything more threatening, you must—"

"Shooter?" asked Jane, raising her voice.

"What?" said Oh.

"I'll take one," said Jane.

"Mrs. Wheel, what is going on, please?"

"Sam is here from Mack's diner. He has these milk-shake shots that are amazing. He's wheeling around a cart and passing out samples in disposable shot glasses."

Jane signed off with Oh after agreeing to check in after her meeting with Lucky before the bowling gala. Jane followed Sam and his cart into the fray of the market.

"Fantastic idea," said Jane. "But I thought you were only opening for the Lucky Miller Roast and the café went back up for sale when the excitement died down. Why give out samples if you're not open to the public? Pretty cruel to get people hooked on the product." She held out her hand for another sample.

Sam nodded. "Getting people hooked is exactly the idea. We decided that it might be fun to run the place if we could drum up enough business. Terrible time to open or reopen anything, but if we keep our menu small and our overhead low . . . we've got the place all spiffed-up thanks to Lucky, so, if we can raise enough money, the family's going to give it a go."

Jane wished Sam good luck and watched him hand out his milk-shake shots. Nellie refused one and wagged her finger in Sam's face about something. He smiled and took whatever she was dishing out and continued on his way.

Jane wondered if Sam knew that Lucky didn't even remember the food he ate at his grandfather's diner. Did it matter? As long as Lucky endorsed the burgers and fries, that would give the place cachet for a while. At least Sam's food was excellent. That should help. Jane doubted that either Don's or Nellie's Lucky Ducks would have any kind of lasting influence on the EZ Way Inn's solvency.

Jane continued to watch her mother walk from vendor to vendor, keeping one of her eagle eyes on Lucky Miller as she walked and haggled. Jane decided to catch up to her before she reached Lucky. Isn't that the first rule of defensive driving? Avoid a head-on collision.

A pretty young woman in a brown checked shirt offered Lucky a carrot to replace his cigar and Lucky laughed, shaking his head. Jane could see from a distance that he was in fine performance mode, nodding and smiling at the crowd like some sort of show-biz royalty. Jane wondered if he really did have any celebrity guests coming into town. How disappointed would people be if the Lucky Miller Roast turned out to be all roasted with no roasters?

"Thinks he's something, doesn't he?" said Nellie who had double-backed and come around alongside of Jane, startling her as usual.

"He's not so bad," said Jane. "I kind of feel sorry for him." The words slipped out before she registered that she was speaking to Nellie.

"Feel sorry for him? With his money?" said Nellie. "There's a guy who has no talent, but managed to become famous and rich, and shows it all off. That's what they call being at the right place at the right time."

Jane didn't correct her mother. They were too close to Lucky to begin a cantankerous conversation about the man. But Jane, for once, had more information than Nellie, and knew that Lucky was not at the right place at the right time. In fact, the more Jane considered Lucky's struggle with what had happened to him, she thought the opposite was most certainly true. Wrong place at the wrong time described things pretty well.

"Ah, Nellie," said Lucky, "how are those Lucky Ducks selling at the bar?"

"Bar's closed for a few days," said Nellie.

Lucky was smiling at a teenager who had brought him a bouquet of flowers from her mother's stand. Lucky accepted them graciously, then looked back at Nellie. Jane saw that he was focusing on Nellie now. Was he remembering something?

"Why would you close this week? With all the . . ."—Lucky searched for the right word—"hoopla going on in town?"

"Death in the family," said Nellie.

Lucky opened his mouth but no words came out. Instead he handed Nellie the bouquet of flowers. Equally speechless at this gesture, both awkward and graceful, Nellie accepted them. Jane looked around for Tim and Maurice, caught Tim's eye, and pointed over Nellie's head—the universal gesture for "take care of Nellie and keep her busy."

Jane took Lucky's arm and began walking slowly with him toward the gazebo, speaking directly into his ear, hoping that she looked like an assistant giving him news of the day. She wasn't sure it would be good for anyone if Lucky had a breakthrough in the middle of the Kankakee Farmer's Market.

"Lucky, I know you're remembering something. Do you want to talk to me about it? We could grab a coffee and slip across the street and sit down as if we have business to discuss," said Jane.

"I'm okay, honey," said Lucky.

This time she didn't correct his form of address.

"What did you remember?"

"It's not something from the past that I've forgotten exactly. It's just my aunt's voice. Know how sometimes you hear something and it's said in exactly the way you heard it before so instead of being in this moment, you're in that moment?" Lucky didn't wait for Jane to nod or agree, but, instead went on as if he was afraid he wouldn't remember if he didn't get it all out fast, "When Nellie said 'death in the family,' it sounded just like my aunt, the one I lived with. I remember that I was sick or something for a long time. I remember coming home to my aunt's house and asking her why I couldn't go home to my mom and dad. Why can't I go back to Kankakee? I can remember asking it just that way, just that question. My aunt said, 'death in the family,' just like Nellie.

"I started crying and asked if my mother had died. She was always sick with headaches and stuff. Always lying down in her room with the door closed. And my aunt who was my mom's older sister, shook her head and then I asked, 'my dad?' He was the healthiest guy you can imagine, always talking and laughing and dancing around the house, you know, the fun parent, and my aunt shook her head. She just repeated 'death in the family,' then told me not to ask any more questions. She'd tell me all about it later."

"And did she?" asked Jane, gently, in what she hoped was the "guiding" tone advised by Belinda in the chapter on helping a loved one recover his or her memories.

Lucky whispered his response to Jane, but they had reached the gazebo and there were people waiting to meet and greet and introduce Lucky to the fans who had gathered to see him draw out the winner of tickets to the roast.

Jane leaned in and asked him to repeat his answer.

Lucky shook his head and patted Jane's cheek.

"We're meeting before the bowling tournament at the

studio, okay?" asked Jane. "How about two? That'll give us an hour and a half before the tournament begins."

Lucky nodded, chomped down hard on his cigar, and got himself back into character for greeting his fans.

"Are any celebrities coming in for the bowling tournament, Lucky?" shouted someone from the audience.

Lucky laughed on his way to the microphone. "Think I want the locals to mop up the bowling alley with those Hollywood types? We got too many Kankakee celebrities signed up!" The crowd applauded and cheered as Lucky ran down the list of local politicians and shop owners who were scheduled to participate.

"Knows how to milk the crowd," said Malcolm, coming up on Jane's left. Malcolm nodded, threw back his milk-shake shot with a vengeance. "And to think, I taught him everything he knows."

10

The Kankakee Library was no longer the old stone building on Indiana Avenue guarded by lions where Jane had spent her after-school hours. Sitting on one of those lions, waiting for Don and Nellie to pick her up when Carl came on duty was one of Jane's most vivid childhood memories. In the middle of the first decade of the twenty-first century, the Kankakee Library began its future. Because it had outgrown its 1899 building, the library moved to a downtown office building, becoming a modern state-of-the-art multistoried repository of books, information, media, computers, an auditorium, and community rooms. It was staffed by librarians who were a far cry from the stern bespectacled types portrayed in old movies as bun-wearing matrons whose fingers rested perpetually on their lips to shush patrons. Now, librarians were modern professionals who could teach someone to do online research, plan community programs, lead book groups, design teen study areas, and who only occasionally found themselves shushing patrons.

This was one of those occasions.

When Jane told Nellie she wanted to pop into the library, now located just across the street from the farmer's market,

Nellie had screwed up her face so tightly, Jane thought she was going to stamp her foot and throw a tantrum.

"What the hell you want to go into the library for?" she asked, not bothering to disguise her distaste.

Nellie disliked all public buildings. She was suspicious of courthouses, post offices, and police stations. Jane chalked up Nellie's mistrust of public spaces to her natural sense of anarchy and disdain for those in power, but Nellie reserved specific antipathy for the library.

"All they got in here is books," said Nellie, pushing open the glass door. "I don't get it."

"I'll just be a minute," said Jane. "You can go back to the gazebo and listen to Lucky and I'll come get you when I'm done."

"I can't abide that idiot talking to hear himself talk. I'll stay here and make sure you don't sneak off into a corner to read."

Nellie was staring around her in front of the main desk, doing a full circle of observation. "What the hell does anybody need with this many books?" she said loudly.

A young smiling librarian, long dark hair hanging loose, rushed over to Nellie and without an overt shushing, quietly asked if she might help her with something. Nellie jerked her thumb backwards and the woman looked at Jane, clearly hoping that she could control this woman who looked as if she wanted to dismantle the shelves and give the place a good scrubbing.

"Mom, I want you to sit over there with a cup of coffee and I'll be right back," said Jane. "Please."

"Okay, okay," said Nellie. "Coffee in a library? I never heard of such a thing." Nellie moved over to the table next to the coffee bar and Jane apologized to the librarian whose nametag read ALLISON.

"I need some early- to mid-twentieth-century telephone books or directories of local businesses. Are they all digitized or . . ."

Allison directed her to the glassed-off room, which was dedicated to genealogical research. Jane gazed around her at the shelves filled with ledgers and directories, yearbooks, newspapers, organizational minutes of meetings, old maps, church histories. Jane knew she could spend hours in this room, reading over names, looking at the old ads and graphics, and letting the history of her town wash over her in waves. Instead, picturing Nellie running from reader to reader trying to interest them in picking up a mop instead of a book, she quickly found telephone directories and instead of looking up the residential addresses, information she already had thanks to Mary Wainwright, she looked up businesses.

She had no trouble finding the business listing she was looking for: Herman Mullet, Suite 204, Arcade Building. Under his name, his title or his business? *Security Advisor.* What was a security advisor? Bodyguard? Someone who sold alarm systems? Someone who sold stocks and bonds?

"Excuse me," said Allison, poking her head into the room, "I'm sorry to interrupt, but . . ."

Jane jotted down the information. She wasn't sure if it was important, but it was something she could mention to Lucky. Maybe it would unlock a door.

"It's your mother . . ."

"On my way," said Jane, following Allison down to the main floor.

Jane understood why Allison and the other staff members might be getting anxious to say their good-byes to Nellie. She had helped herself to the rag next to the coffee urn and proceeded to circulate through the first floor, wiping down the study tables. Most readers simply lifted their books so she could swipe her rag beneath them, but a few patrons seemed dismayed to be interrupted and annoyed when Nellie commented on their choices of reading material.

"What are you reading a book on finding a job for? Just get out there and start going to places. Look for signs in the window. Pink's needs a dishwasher," said Nellie to a distinguished looking middle-aged man, who had been taking copious notes from a book on choosing graduate school programs.

Jane took her mother's arm and handed the dishrag to Allison, thanking her for her help.

As they exited, Jane saw a display from the old library, the one in which she spent her formative years. Front and center was a wooden card catalog. If it hadn't been out of reach, behind a velvet rope, Jane would have leaned over and caressed it. When Jane had first heard about the library move, she had mourned the change from the old building to the new in the way that many mourned the change from rotary phone to cell, from manual typewriter to laptop, from book to e-Reader. She was no longer sure that mourning was the right attitude—at least as far as the library was concerned. She liked this new space, the way it welcomed the entire community with different interests and needs. When she thought about it, she realized she also loved the smart phone that allowed her to wave good-bye to her son Nick and let him live apart from her, attending the school he loved and still stay in immediate touch. She loved the look of the old manual typewriters and their *tap-tap-tap*, but would she be able to work effectively with Tim or Oh if she didn't have online access to eBay or Google? *Trade-offs*, she thought with a sigh, and then wondered, if by any chance, the library could be persuaded to sell her the wooden card catalog.

Crossing the library parking lot, heading back toward the market and their car, Jane saw Mary Wainwright coming toward her, wagging a finger in her direction.

"I knew it, I knew you were up to something, Jane Wheel."

Jane had no idea what she was talking about and, uncharacteristically, Mary did not stop to elaborate. Instead, she walked past Jane and Nellie, shaking her head, intent on her own trip to the library.

"You said Herman Mullet had more money than the rest of the kids," said Jane. "How did you know that?"

Nellie shrugged. "Just knew. Better clothes, maybe. Not worn out. New shoes or something. I don't remember exactly how," said Nellie. "I wore my sister's clothes and she played ball all the time so everything had patches and mends where she had torn a hem or ripped a hole. I guess Herman just dressed nicer than the rest of us."

"That's because he didn't wear hand-me-downs," said Jane. "Herman Mullet was an only child so he got everything new and—"

"Yeah, that's probably why he still yaks so much, he was probably spoiled rotten," said Nellie, settling herself into the car.

"Because he was an only child? You think only children

are spoiled?" asked Jane, surprised at how much Nellie's opinions helped clarify her own thoughts on Herman's childhood experiences. Maybe it was Oh's "listening" techniques amped up to a whole new level. Jane had to admit that listening to her mother expound on almost anything did make one think.

"Spoiled probably, yeah," said Nellie. "But also, just alone, you know? In our house, my parents were both working their tails off. My mother took in laundry, Pa was working on the railroad. And all of us kids had jobs, too. Even if we ever had anything to say, there wouldn't be anybody around who had time to listen."

"So, one child meant that he got undivided attention?" said Jane, more to herself than to Nellie.

"Yeah, unless . . . hey, don't forget we're going to Carl's. Don't turn here," said Nellie.

Jane flicked off the left turn signal. "Unless what, Mom?"

"Unless they didn't like him. Maybe they had a kid and figured out they weren't cut out to have children. Maybe they didn't like kids that much."

"Come on, Mom," said Jane. She realized that her mother might be talking about her. Wasn't she the mother of an only child? "Nick's an only child and he isn't spoiled, and Charley and I love kids. Sometimes things just happen."

"Yup."

"Yup what?" asked Jane.

"Yup nothing. You're right. You and Charley are good parents. Nick's a great kid. And sometimes a cigar is just a cigar," said Nellie. "But not with Lucky Miller."

"Do you know what that means, Mom? A cigar is just a cigar?"

"Nah, but I hear people say it all the time. And if ever a cigar was more than a cigar, it would be with Lucky. He uses that thing as a weapon, for Christ's sake, stabbing at people with it all the time. And you mark my words, his parents either spoiled him or hated him, but it wasn't in between like it's supposed to be."

Jane pulled up in front of Wally's tavern and shut off the engine. "So I know you didn't spoil Michael and me, right?" said Jane.

"Nope," said Nellie.

"But you didn't hate us, either," said Jane.

"Nope," said Nellie. "I liked you fine. See, you just need to stay in between spoiling and hating with kids. That way nobody gets hurt."

Jane had no time to pursue any more of her mother's child-rearing theories, although she sensed a potential Belinda St. Germaine bestseller lurking in Nellie's words. Gears, however, needed to be changed for the visit to Carl's apartment. The entrance was next to the tavern doors and Nellie used the key marked "outer" to let them into a dimly lit foyer, barely large enough for the two of them to stand. The stairs were lit with two cheap fixtures, both fitted with low-wattage bulbs.

"Have you ever been here before?" asked Jane, climbing the stairs ahead of Nellie.

"Hell no. Carl didn't exactly do any entertaining at home. When he moved in here . . . it had to be over fifty years ago . . . he asked me where he should get furniture. I told him to go to Turk's and buy up everything new to fill up the place. Might be more money than he wanted to pay, but he'd get good stuff and it would last forever. He told me he went and bought what he needed. I remember somebody at the bar asked him what style he got." Nellie gave one of her rare short laughs. "He said, 'wood.'"

Although Nellie had opened the street level door herself, she passed the key to Jane to unlock the apartment. Jane usually loved opening the door to an unknown space. A kind of spinning reel began inside her head, all of her most coveted objects passing before her eyes. In a north shore suburb, she might walk in and find incredible art; in a small retirement apartment, there might be valuable first editions; in a stylish gated community, there might be weighty sterling serving pieces. Here, opening the door to Carl's apartment, where he had lived for nearly fifty years, over Wally's Tap, what could she possibly find besides the lonely furnishings of a lifelong bachelor bartender? Jane hesitated as she heard the tumblers in the lock click. She always played a game, imagining the first thing she'd see when she and Tim entered a house. It wouldn't be respectful if she didn't play it with Carl's place.

"What do you think we'll see as soon as we open the door?" Jane asked Nellie.

"A bottle of whiskey and a water glass he stole from the EZ Way Inn," said Nellie.

Her mother was good at this game.

"I think there'll be a plastic laundry basket on the floor in front of one chair that's positioned in front of the television," said Jane.

"Are the clothes clean or dirty?" asked Nellie.

She was really good at this game.

Jane opened the door and gasped. Even Nellie, standing next to her, took in a little puff of air.

"I'll be damned," said Nellie. "It's as neat as a pin."

Leave it to Nellie to note the cleanliness. Jane had her eye on something else. On everything else. The apartment opened into a living-dining area with a small galley kitchen off to one side of the dining area. There was a hall that led in the other direction, Jane assumed, to a bedroom and bath. There was a coat closet to their right and Jane could see a door off the kitchen that probably led to the rear stairs down to the alley.

"He was a clean man, he kept the bar clean and washed the glasses fine. I shouldn't be surprised at this, but I didn't expect it to look so . . ." Nellie stopped herself and looked at Jane. "What is this? What does this look like?"

"A bachelor pad from some early sixties movie with a B-list star?" said Jane.

"What the hell does that mean?" asked Nellie, stepping around the black leather ottoman that went with the impeccable black leather lounge chair, moving closer to the pale wooden table in the dining area surrounded by four matching chairs.

Jane didn't need to check any labels, although she would look later when she came back with Tim. For now, she was satisfied that the chair was an Eames lounger. The table and chairs were Heywood Wakefield, as was the matching credenza under the window that faced the side street. The bark cloth curtains were off the rack, in a great turquoise and black atomic print. Jane quickly walked down the hall and saw a double bed, neatly made with a plain tan corduroy bedspread smoothed over the top. The frame, end tables, and matching chest looked like Dunbar, but Jane wasn't ready to open drawers and start the label search. First, she wanted to marvel at the closet, with neatly hung pairs of pants, eight white shirts, and eight dark striped ties hung on a wooden rack. Two pairs of black shoes, polished, with wooden shoetrees in them, were on the closet floor.

There were two photographs on the wall, both of the EZ Way Inn. One was an exterior shot with the beer signs in the window and the tumble-down roof looking like it might fall at any minute and the other was a shot of the bar's interior with Don and Nellie smiling at the camera. Who had shot those eight-by-ten glossies?

"Uncle Chucky," said Nellie, behind Jane, looking at the photos, reading her mind.

"I have an Uncle Chucky?" asked Jane.

"No," Nellie growled. "Chuck had a studio where he took pictures of babies and kids and families and he called it Uncle Chucky's. He was a friend of your dad's and took those pictures. We had them hung up in the bar. Your dad took them down when we paneled the dining room twenty years ago and I never found them after that. Figured they got thrown out."

"Carl needed some family photos," said Jane.

"Yup," said Nellie, removing them from the wall. "Guess I can take them back now."

"So Turk's sold him some good stuff," said Jane, following her mother into the kitchen area.

"Yeah, he did okay," said Nellie, her head inside of a cabinet. "Wasn't much on the pots and pans."

Jane smiled. There was a teakettle and one sauce pan and a frying pan. Nothing looked like it had ever been used. In one of the upper cabinets, there was a set of turquoise and pink melamine dishes, service for six. Jane held up a plate and couldn't see one scratch made by a knife or fork.

"Here we go," said Nellie. "I win." The cabinet next to the stove had three bottles of whiskey in it with two EZ Way Inn glasses.

Jane and Nellie checked the other cabinets, finding them sparsely populated. A few cans of soup and an ancient box of saltines. There was a fancy jar of strawberry preserves that still had vestiges of a Christmas bow on the lid. Never opened. Jane held it up close and read the brand.

"I gave this to Carl last Christmas," said Jane. "In a basket with sausages and cheese and stuff. At least he ate the other stuff."

"Nope," said Nellie, opening the refrigerator.

Jane looked over her mother's shoulder and saw all of the fancy sausage and cheese and small jars of mustard set neatly on the second shelf. On the top shelf were two six-packs of beer.

"Why the beer?" said Jane. "Carl didn't like beer, did he?"

"He kept it for when he quit drinking," said Nellie, opening drawers and taking out a few old metal advertising trays that Jane was sure had come from the EZ Way Inn.

"What do you mean quit drinking? Beer's—"

"Maybe twice a year, Carl'd go on a bender and drink himself stupid. Then he'd sober up and quit drinking for a couple months. Then he'd get on an even keel and be okay for a while."

"I don't understand the beer," said Jane.

"It was for when Cark quit drinking," said Nellie, plainly annoyed that she had to repeat herself.

"But beer's—" began Jane.

"When you drink a quart of whiskey a day most all your life, switching to beer is quitting, okay?" said Nellie, on her knees looking in the drawer under the stove. "I don't know why anybody starts in the first place, but once you do, it's a slippery slope."

Jane had never heard her mother use the expression "slippery slope" before and was quite sure Nellie had no idea it signified anything other than a hill one shouldn't attempt to climb. No reason to get into a discussion on semantics with Nellie. It would be a slippery slope indeed.

Jane looked up at the clock above the sink and a small "oh" escaped when she registered what she was looking at. A George Nelson Petal Clock in those amazing four colors read 1:45. The clock looked so perfect in this kitchen that she hated to take it down. Pulling out a small step stool from the pantry cupboard, she did remove the clock. It was the bait she would use to have some fun with Tim before she reeled him in.

"Why don't you leave it up there?" asked Nellie. "You'll need a clock."

Jane shook her head. "I'm not moving in here, Mom."

Jane thought she saw Nellie's shoulders relax a little. "It's nicer than the basement and it's got all this good furniture in it from Turk's," said Nellie. "I wouldn't blame you."

"Nope," said Jane. "I've got an idea about a place to live, Mom, but it's not the basement or here. I'm still thinking about it."

Nellie shrugged. "Just as well. Your dad wouldn't like you living over a bar."

"And you?" asked Jane, with a smile.

"Up to you," said Nellie. "I don't interfere."

Jane had to meet Lucky Miller before the bowling tournament and in her big tote bag, she imagined that the Petal Clock was ticking. She dropped Nellie off back at home and ran inside to call Oh, pet Rita so that her dog might remember who she was, and see how her father was getting along on day two of the EZ Way Inn being closed.

"It's not bad, Jane, having a Saturday off," said Don. Quiet voices came from the television. Golfers were teeing up and someone was discussing the Leader Board. Don, however, had left his chair and was scouring out the coffeemaker with some kind of vinegar mixture. He also showed Nellie that he had cleaned out two junk drawers and looked through several old magazines for nonexpiring coupons.

"We'll save some money on groceries this week," he said proudly.

"What's got into you?" said Nellie, sniffing at the coffee-pot.

"We're always cleaning stuff up at the tavern, but we never have any time here. I thought maybe we should spruce the house up a little bit."

"Why? We putting it up for sale?" said Nellie. She had her back to her husband and was looking over the drawers that Don had organized. When Don didn't answer right away, she whipped around and faced him.

"You're not thinking about selling the house again, are you?"

Don shrugged.

"Again?" asked Jane, looking up from where she sat on the floor, rubbing Rita behind the ears. "When were you thinking about selling the house?"

"I'll tell you exactly when," said Nellie. "When Milt died. Every time somebody dies, your dad starts cleaning out drawers and closets and starts looking at brochures for places called 'communities' in Arizona."

"Not exactly true," said Don, looking at Jane. "But you know, a wake-up call now and then makes you think."

"Stop thinking," said Nellie. "We can't afford to retire and nobody's going to buy this house right now anyway. Remember your investment opportunity?"

Don shushed Nellie. Jane might be a grown-up with financial responsibilities of her own, but her father still didn't believe in discussing money in front of the children.

Jane pulled the petal clock out of her bag and set it on the kitchen table. "I have to go meet Lucky before the bowling tournament, but can we all talk about this later? I have an idea about me helping out at the EZ Way Inn while you guys get back on your feet. Then maybe I can help you plan ahead for retirement, okay? But can we talk about it later? No decisions right now? I'm already late," she said, pointing to the unplugged clock, positioned like a dinner plate on a woven placemat.

Don nodded. He gave Jane a hug and promised that no decisions would be made while she was out.

"We've been talking about this for ten years and haven't decided anything yet, so I guess we can wait another hour or two."

"Good," said Jane.

"Honey?" said Don, as Jane headed for the door. She turned back to face her dad, who pointed to the clock. "Wouldn't it be easier to wear a watch?"

19

Did the absence of ownership allow Jane to multitask more efficiently? On her way to Mack's Diner where she was due to meet Lucky, Jane placed her cell phone on her lap and her notebook and pen in the seat next to her. At a stoplight, she blatantly broke the law and clicked her e-mail so she could do a quick scroll-through, then placed the phone next to her notebook.

At the next stoplight, she phoned Tim. When he answered, she put the call on speaker.

"You won't believe where in Kankakee is a museum-worthy cache of midcentury modern," said Jane.

"I'm putting you on speaker. Maurice and I are driving over to the bowling alley."

"Hi, Maurice," said Jane. "Aren't you guys early? Not supposed to start for an hour."

"We've got the team shirts to deliver and the trophies," said Maurice. "Hi Jane."

"About that midcentury modern?" asked Tim.

"Ever been to Wally's Tap? They call it Salt and Pepper's, too," said Jane.

Before Tim could answer, Jane heard the beep that she was

getting another call. When she saw the caller was her brother, Michael, she promised Tim to call back soon and clicked onto the incoming. Before she could complete her enthusiastic hello, Michael was yelling. She hardly needed the speaker function.

"When was anyone going to call me about Carl? When did I stop being a member of this family?" shouted Michael.

Jane could think of no satisfactory explanation or decent enough apology. She just hadn't thought about it.

"How did you find out?" she asked quietly, hoping guilt and humility would soon make things right.

"The worst possible way, Jane. On fucking Facebook!"

Jane knew Michael must be in the car alone, on his way somewhere. He would never swear in front of her niece and nephew. Michael and Jane had both agreed that after growing up in a house and tavern where everyone swore early and often, they would not expose their children to the same language. Most of the time, they succeeded.

"Carl was on Facebook?" asked Jane. That couldn't be true.

"No, moron. I'm a friend of the *Kankakee Daily Journal* and they post the obits on Facebook. I had to find out that Carl was dead on Facebook!"

"Michael, I am so sorry. I don't know how I could have let this happen. . . ."

"Not just you. Mom and Dad should have called. He was part of our family, he was as much of an uncle as anyone of the family we ever saw once a year at Christmas. We saw Carl every day of our lives," said Michael.

Jane pulled the car over, and took Michael off speaker. She rolled down her window for a hit of September breeze and wished, just for a fleeting moment, that she could time travel back to her misspent youth and light up a Benson and Hedges, lean back, and have a long rambling conversation with her brother.

"It's been hectic here, but it's not an excuse. Carl's going to be cremated and there's going to be memorial at the EZ Way next weekend. He left everything to our family, I mean, it's really so strange here right now."

"I talked to Dad. I'm flying in. Q's having a fit that she can't come, but school just started."

"I'm so glad you're coming, but tell my Suzie I wish she was coming, too." Jane could picture her niece, hands on hips, furious about being left behind. "I can't believe I didn't think to call. I sold my house and all. . . ."

"Dad filled me in, with a little Nellie on the side. You're homeless, according to Mom who was shouting in the background. Dad talked about you moving in to the basement, then I heard Mom say you were moving into Carl's apartment above a bar. So what's the story, sis? Hunkering down in Kankakee for a while?"

"Sounds like a terrible idea, doesn't it?" said Jane. "Such a predictable story. Local girl makes good, gets fired, gets divorced, heads home with tail between legs, and—"

Jane sat up straighter in the seat and pitched her imaginary cigarette out the window.

"Gotta go. I'll call you back. Glad you're coming."

Jane tossed the phone on to the seat next to her. Whipping her car into a fast U-turn worthy of any TV private eye, she followed a blue sedan being driven by Lucky Miller. His arm hung out of the open window, unlit cigar dangling in his hand. He was driving a few miles over the city limit, with what Jane judged to be a great deal of confidence. No slowing down at intersections to read street signs, no hesitation about turning left or right. Even more interesting than the sureness of his driving? He was headed in the opposite direction of where she and Lucky were meeting, the opposite direction from the bowling alley.

It was only when she followed Lucky's car into a parking lot where he stopped abruptly, jerking the vehicle into a parking space, and she had to circle around and park a few spaces behind, that she realized he was not alone. Slumped into the front seat next to him was Malcolm, his head barely level with the headrest.

Jane picked up her phone and called Lucky. She watched him slap his shirt pocket and take out his phone, squint at the screen, then push a button. She started to talk before she heard him say hello, then watched as he put the phone back in his pocket. He had sent her directly to voice mail. She winced. So that's what it looked like when someone didn't judge you worthy of call acceptance?

Whatever Malcolm was saying must have been agreeable since Lucky was doing a lot of nodding. Either that or they were listening to a song, since Lucky was bobbing his head in a fairly rhythmic manner. Lucky suddenly jerked his hand holding the cigar, and pointed across the street to the river, where an old concrete slab angled down into the mighty Kankakee, just west of the dam.

This wasn't a riverside park or an area where picnickers or fishermen might gather. This was just a commercial intersection where there was an old access point to the river. Jane remembered when she was young that there had been a house there, next to the bridge, with a garage at the end of the sloped-down driveway. Jane always thought it seemed like a scary place to live, since waffling to the left or right as one drove down the concrete slab might take car and driver directly into the river. It didn't help that the stone garage had two windows in the door whose placement looked like large staring eyes. There was no house or garage there now, but the concrete drive remained.

Lucky got out of the car. Malcolm opened the passenger door and got out, looking like it was far too bright and early for him to be facing sunlight or fresh air. He shaded his eyes with one arm and shook his head. Jane could hear him say something that sounded like a question. *How would I know* or *how should I know* was what it sounded like, but Jane was too far away to be sure.

Lucky and Malcolm crossed the street and Jane saw them both head closer to the river. Her view was blocked after they started down the bank, so she eased her car forward into a parking place directly across from where the two men began their descent.

Without knowing exactly why she did it, Jane picked up her phone and snapped a photo of Lucky and Malcolm. It was only the backs of the men, but the ever-present cigar left no doubt that the larger man was Lucky Miller. Belinda St. Germaine's book was on the front seat and Jane rested one hand on it as she snapped another photo of Lucky pointing under the bridge. Jane rifled the pages of the book to see where Lucky had placed all of his bookmarks, remembering that she had seen some handwriting on some of the index cards. No. The only handwriting she could decipher looked like a list of errands. But the chapter where the card was stuck was titled, REVISITING THE SITES: SACRED AND PROFANE.

Jane was sure that's exactly what Lucky and Malcolm were doing. She called Oh and left a message with her location, the intersection where she was observing Lucky ramble on to a bored-looking Malcolm. Lucky had brought Malcolm here for a reason, he must be remembering something that had happened in that spot. Malcolm kept shrugging and shaking his head. Jane figured he was content to create the fictional life of Lucky Miller and wasn't that keen on doing the research into the life of Herman Mullet. Before Jane finished leaving her message, Detective Oh picked up the phone.

"I'm so sorry, Mrs. Wheel, I was in the garden and couldn't get to the phone quickly enough. How may I help you?"

"The information about Dickie Boynton's death? His body was found washed up from the river. Does the article you found say exactly where? Can you get that information?"

"It's here, Mrs. Wheel. I printed the article. His mother was quoted. 'Dickie liked to camp out by the river near his Uncle's house. He liked it because it wasn't a park and no people would come around. There was a garage where he could hide from the street, but he could get right onto an old concrete piling and be almost in the river.' The location is given as next to the bridge near the dam at the intersection of . . ."

Jane finished his sentence for him.

"I'm standing here right now," said Jane. She hung up after promising to call back as soon as she figured out what they were all doing there.

Belinda's book was still open to the first page in the chapter.

Revisiting the site where something traumatic occurred is, of course, important. Perhaps even more vital to the experience of "recapturing" is a reenactment of the event itself. You say you don't remember the event? You will be surprised what muscle memory can do. Once in the place, once in the mental space, you will know what to do. Embrace the pain, the rage, and the fear. Once you do, you will also embrace your past.

"Oh no," said Jane, rushing to get out of the car. If Herman Mullet had actually done something to Dickie Boynton, Lucky could be about to do the same to Malcolm. *What exactly did Lucky do to Boing Boing?*

Jane crossed the street, holding up a hand to stop the car bearing down on her. The driver laid on his horn, but Jane, paying no attention to the angry blast, just waved a thanks at him for stopping.

She skidded down the driveway and ducked right, where the bridge foundation hid people and activity from the busy street.

"What the bloody hell, man?" Malcolm was resisting Lucky's pull on his arm to get closer to the river. "Look at my shoes. I'm going to be sucked into mud up to my knees in a minute. Take your loony walk down memory lane with somebody else."

Jane could see that Lucky had that faraway look. He was

either remembering something or trying to remember something and he wasn't listening to any of the writer's protests.

"Malcolm, stay calm. He's in a kind of trance. Don't let him get closer to the water," said Jane, inching up behind Lucky.

"Don't let him? He's in charge here. What am I supposed to do?"

"He's not going to pull you into the water, he's just trying to figure things out. Stay calm. Lucky?"

Lucky Miller continued to stare out at the river.

"His childhood friend drowned and his body was found right here," said Jane softly to Malcolm. "Lucky's trying to figure out if he had anything to do with it, if he could have stopped it."

Malcolm's jaw went slack and he retracted his head, his beaky nose moving back and forth. "No, that didn't happen. Lucky had a happy childhood here in Kankakee. Drinking those milk shakes, and bowling, and whatever else you young Huckleberry Finns did in those days."

"That's the kind of stuff you write about Lucky, but that's not the way it was," said Jane. "He lived here about a year and a half. His friend's garage burned down and Lucky and his parents moved to Kentucky. Except Lucky never really made it there. He went to live with an aunt in Canada . . ."

"All wrong, Jane Wheel," said Malcolm. "I have it that his parents died and Lucky started working in theaters, doing whatever he could, filling in . . ."

"I read the biography," said Jane. "So has Lucky. Trying to live out the fake history while trying to figure out what really happened is what's making him crazy."

"Not crazy," said Lucky.

Lucky didn't stop staring out at the river, but he continued to talk to them as if they were sitting across the table.

"I told my dad that it should have been me. I should have drowned."

"Why? Dickie ran away because he burned down the garage and his dad was mad," said Jane. "Why should you be the one who drowned?"

"I did drown," said Lucky. "I did die."

Jane felt goose bumps on her arm and she saw Malcolm pale. Lucky's voice sounded like it came from outside of his body. No longer was this trancelike voice hesitant, speculative. Lucky was as sure of this as he was of anything.

"I died," he repeated. Lucky then shoved his cigar in his mouth and turned to face Jane and Malcolm. When he spoke it was present-day, fully inhabited Lucky Miller. "That's it, kids. I died."

"What the hell does that mean?" said Malcolm, beginning to extract his shoes from the mud.

"I can't say. I just know I died here. That's for you to figure out," said Lucky. "More precisely, you Jane Wheel, since that's the answer to this. I died," he repeated matter of factly. "I don't know what it means, but that's the answer. You figure it out and explain it to me, Jane."

"I think you already figured it out. You didn't need to come back to Kankakee because you lived here. You came back because you died here," said Jane.

"You're one hell of a fat foul ghost, Lucky," said Malcolm. Now that they were headed away from the river and back to the parking lot, Malcolm was recovering some of his bravado. Jane noted that the closer they got to the car, the louder he got.

"Or maybe you're one of those vampires that are so popular. They're all dead aren't they?"

"Or maybe I'm a fucking zombie who isn't going to sign your next paycheck," said Lucky. "Shut up and get into the car before I scramble your brains for my lunch."

Malcolm did as he was told. Lucky turned to Jane.

"It's the key to everything," said Lucky. "I just don't know where the lock is."

Jane noticed he was wearing a sterling silver four-leaf clover on a chain around his neck. Each of the leaves was inscribed with a name. James. Linda. Thomas. Elaine.

"Who are the people named here?" asked Jane.

Lucky shrugged. "I bought it at a thrift store somewhere. I can't resist a four-leaf clover or a horseshoe. My aunt's farm in Canada was called Lucky Acres and I . . ." Lucky broke off, then smiled at Jane. This smile was unlike the mugging he did on camera and in front of a crowd. "See? It's coming back. I haven't thought about that farm for years. And the name just came back to me. If I can hold out a few more days, it'll all come back," said Lucky.

The Lucky Miller Roast was scheduled to be taped at the end of the week. Jane reminded him that he had more than a few days.

"Yeah, well, we'll see," said Lucky. "Brenda's schmoozing some money in Las Vegas and if that goes as planned . . . well, we'll see."

"Have you heard anything more from the blackmailer? The one who left you that note?"

Lucky fished in his pocket with one hand and with the

other, rapped open-handed on the window as if slapping Malcolm in the face. Malcolm flinched and stopped staring at the two of them.

"Just because the bastard writes my life story doesn't mean he's got to know everything," said Lucky.

Lucky handed Jane a crumpled piece of paper.

I KNOW WHY YOU'RE HERE.
I KNOW WHAT YOU'RE HIDING.
MY SILENCE WILL COST MONEY.

"Maybe I ought to just let the guy tell me what I'm hiding and why I'm here," said Lucky. "Instead of paying for silence, I pay him to spill it to me. Whatever it costs, it's probably cheaper than throwing this damn shindig."

Jane thought Lucky might be right. If the blackmailer or whoever the mischief maker was—hard to call him a blackmailer when there weren't yet any demands to be met—would just meet with Lucky and tell him what he knew, Lucky would gladly pay for the information. If he was renting the old stone factory and paying for all the production costs involved in taping *Lucky Gets Roasted*, being blackmailed would be much more cost-efficient for Lucky Miller Productions.

"Got your bowling shoes, honey?" said Lucky, moving around to the driver's side of the car.

"We were going to meet, Lucky. Remember?"

"And so we did," said Lucky.

Jane remained sitting in her parked car after Lucky and Malcolm took off for the bowling alley. She called Oh and when she heard his voice-mail message, she said, "What kind of blackmailer leaves notes without asking for a specific amount of money? Without instructions? To call this man or woman an amateur is generous, right?"

Jane heard the beep and saw that Oh was calling her back. When they connected she repeated her question. "What kind of blackmailer never gets to the point?"

Before Oh could offer a suggestion, Jane answered her own question. "I'll tell you. It's somebody who's still deciding whether or not to do the deed. Someone trying to work up the courage to blackmail Lucky. Someone who was serious, even if he or she was an amateur, would ask for too much money. Or too little. Someone who wanted to chase Lucky away or drive him crazy would be specific and try to make Lucky crazy. Whoever is bothering to hang upside-down horseshoes and leave these vague notes is someone trying to work up the courage to actually commit a crime."

"A reluctant blackmailer?" offered Oh.

"Or," Jane continued, "someone who isn't sure of what he or she knows. Perhaps the would-be blackmailer is only a could-be?

"Perhaps someone is still gathering the facts?" said Oh.

"Like Lucky," said Jane.

20

Jane had to make two stops on the way to the bowling alley. First, she swung by her parents' house to take Rita for a short walk. Lately, she felt like she was ignoring her shaggy friend, or feeding her hollow round-the-block promises of longer walks to come. Rita looked at her with hope, as if she wanted to believe, but Jane knew by the droop of the tail that the dog was not buying the milk bones her mistress was selling.

Don and Nellie had gone over to the bowling alley already. The EZ Way Inn–sponsored team's shirts were delivered that morning and Nellie wanted to make sure each bowler had one of the red T-shirts with the EZ Way name emblazoned in black.

"If they look like a team, maybe they can keep the ball out of the gutter," said Nellie. She didn't say this with a great deal of hope. "I got too many XXL's in here," said Nellie. "The more XXL shirts you got, the less chance you got to win."

Jane poured a glass of ice water and flipped through her notebook. On the first pages, she had written all the information about her own missing stuff, the name of the insurance company Tim had used, the policy number Tim had given her. On another page, she had written down her brother Michael's flight information. In the middle of the notebook, she had devoted two pages to listing the furniture in Carl's apartment. That reminded her to take out her phone and send a few of the photos she had snapped there directly to Tim.

Finally, Jane got to the section of notes that concerned Lucky. She had been hired to be Lucky's assistant and to find out who was making mischief in the studio, who was tampering with his collection of Lucky tokens, who was leaving him those vague threatening notes, but her job had become more psychological detecting than the nuts and bolts of who was doing what. She had been spending most of her time trying to uncover what Lucky had forgotten from his childhood. So what was it she had become? An investigator of lost minds? There *had* been a death, and although everyone in authority agreed it had come about through natural causes, Jane had heard Sluggo talk about being murdered. She had written down what she overheard Sluggo Mettleman say in the hospital. Was that part of this? She opened the folder in her bag that had the addresses and e-mails of everyone connected to Lucky Productions. She ran her finger down the page until she saw the name she heard Fran and Lucky mention as Slug's ride from the hospital. There was, thankfully, only one Mickey listed among the crew members and without thinking through what she would say if and when he answered, Jane dialed the number.

"Yeah?"

"Is this Mickey McBride?" asked Jane.

"Yeah."

Jane fumbled through her name and her temporary title

as Lucky's assistant and without telling a direct lie, implied she was calling on official follow-up. As she spoke, she realized she didn't even know if he had decided to stay with the production or leave town after Sluggo died in the car he was driving. If she asked where he was, she would give away how little she knew and how tangential her employment with Lucky Productions was.

"We just wanted to check on you, see if you're doing okay," said Jane.

"Why wouldn't I be doing okay?" asked Mickey.

"Sometimes, when you've experienced an emotional or traumatic . . ." Jane desperately tried to conjure her inner Belinda St. Germaine.

"Look, I mean, thank you and all, but I'm okay," said Mickey. "It was an ugly sight, Sluggo gasping for air like a fish. I felt terrible there was nothing I could do. I got him right back to the hospital." Mickey paused and took a breath. "He wasn't exactly my friend. I mean we weren't buddies in the trenches or anything. Us guys were all playing basketball that day at lunch and I lost the coin toss to go pick him up at the hospital. I can still remember how the car keys felt in my hand when Sal threw them to me. Slug was a mean little shit, but just 'cause you're a jerk and nobody likes you, that doesn't mean you're supposed to die, does it?"

Jane was no Belinda St. Germaine and she was in over her head. She shouldn't have called and dragged all this up for Mickey.

"You did everything you could and we just wanted to make sure you were doing okay. I'm sorry. I didn't mean to make you talk about it all," said Jane, feeling less and less like the kind of ethical detective of whom Oh would be proud.

"It's okay. I'm supposed to talk about it. I been talking to a therapist Lucky set me up with and I'm supposed to tell the story, get it out, and make it part of my life's fabric."

Jane could guess the therapist.

"Mickey, you said Sal tossed you the car keys?" Jane was a beat late in hearing it, but once it registered, she had to ask. "Weren't you driving the car you always did?"

"I put on my sweats and didn't have the keys to the van with me, so Sal said I could take one of the better cars, the one he usually used to drive Lucky."

"But there was a peanut candy bar wrapper in the car?" asked Jane, more to herself than Mickey.

"I swear I didn't see that. It was stuffed in the pocket of the passenger side. That's what was so weird, since Lucky was in that car all the time. He has an allergy, too, you know," said Mickey.

Jane assured him she knew it was just a terrible accident. No one thought he should have known about the wrapper. She gave him a few encouraging Belinda-like words and said good-bye.

No, being a mean little shit didn't mean you were supposed to die. Sluggo just ran up against Lucky's sloppiness. Of course Lucky would leave his garbage in the car, especially a candy bar wrapper that he had to hide in the door pocket. He couldn't very well hold it in his hand and toss it in the garbage, could he? Even if the rumors buzzed that Lucky was faking that allergy, he would keep up his charade.

Jane's second stop before the tournament was the factory,

the nerve center of Lucky Productions. Lucky had assured Jane that he would get better security for the studio but Jane was pretty certain that the single key Lucky had given her would still work for the side door.

Four rental cars were in the parking lot along with two plain white vans that had green four-leaf clover decals applied to their side panels. Jane unlocked the side door and called out but got no answer. Perfect. Jane knew that her most valuable trait as a detective was her ability to see the objects around her, to notice the actual stuff of people's lives. Oh had told her that the first time they met, when Jane's neighbor had been murdered and Jane pointed out the missing Bakelite button on her vest. Jane also knew that for her, people got in the way of the stuff. When there were human distractions, Jane couldn't see or hear the stories the objects wanted to tell as clearly as when she was alone.

Jane's first stop was Lucky's office. The curtains were pulled back and two sides of it were exposed to the rest of the open space. Jane knelt down next to the trunk and used the key she had added to her necklace to open it. Like any treasure chest filled with beloved objects, odds and ends, tokens and totems, it was almost impossible to tell if anything was disturbed. At least there were no new notes containing nonspecific threats in sight. Jane closed the lid and relocked the box.

"I am disappointed in you, Jane Wheel."

Jane turned around at the voice behind her to see Sal standing in what would be the doorway if there were defined walls to the space.

"It's you?" said Jane, thinking how utterly cliché it was that the first man she had thought fleetingly about dating since her divorce would turn out to be the bad guy. So achingly predict-able! But why was he tormenting Lucky? At least the answer to that question might be interesting.

"What's me?" asked Sal, his smile remaining bright.

"You first," said Jane. "Why are you disappointed?"

"I find you here, all alone in the studio after Lucky told me somebody has been tampering with his stuff. And I just saw you messing with his trunk. I'm disappointed because when I first saw you I had kind of hoped you and I might get together. I've worked on enough shows to know that as soon as the boy finds a girl who he thinks is cute, she's going to either shoot him or get shot. I'm disappointed because I fell for that old plotline again. I should know better."

"I'm not going to shoot you," said Jane. "I'm not even the bad guy."

"Good. Me neither," said Sal.

Jane immediately believed him. She knew that made her both a bad detective and a sucker. Her trust was based solely on his curly dark hair, brown eyes, and the fact that he was actually wearing bowling shoes. Nonrentals. What kind of bad guy owns his own bowling shoes? And who risks wearing them out on the street unless he's planning on bowling?

"I was hired as Lucky's temporary assistant but I'm really here to find out who's playing all the tricks," said Jane.

Sal actually threw back his head when he laughed. "Why didn't you say so? I could have told you first thing, then you would have had time to go out on a date with me!"

Despite the fact that the office was merely curtained off, it was beginning to feel claustrophobic for this showdown or cute re-meet or whatever it turned out to be. Jane suggested they move into the open studio space and Sal followed her, picking up a folder from Lucky's desk. Jane could read upside down that it was clearly marked, BOWLING TOURNAMENT. Sal held it up. "What I was sent back for."

Jane sat down on the stool next to the now empty catering table. Three blackboard menus hung on the wall behind the table. They were marked "Daily," "Vegetarian," and "Special Diet." The first two had been erased and washed. Only the special diet board had writing on it. It was subdivided into peanut-free, gluten-free, and lactose-free. Jane pitied poor Sam needing to accommodate all of these special needs when he supplied the daily meals. His grandfather Mack wouldn't have known what to make of all the requests and demands.

"So tell me now. Who's playing all the tricks on Lucky?"

"Everybody. Anyone who comes in and finds the trunk unlocked. Or has one of the copies of the key we've made. We've been doing it for as long as I've worked for him. The thing is, he never noticed before. Not until we got to Kankakee. This is the first time he's been with it enough or sober enough or whatever."

"Those horseshoes? All hung upside down? He wouldn't have noticed that before?"

"Maybe. Not sure who did that one. It was more ambitious than most of the pranks we usually pull. We switch out those four-leaf clovers for three-leaf ones and once I actually took one of those mustard seed charms and hung it on the rearview mirror of the car and he never even noticed. Lucky's got his radar up on this trip."

"It's Kankakee," said Jane. "He's trying to get hold of his life and he thinks the key is here, so he's sharpened up." Jane stood up and went over to the menu boards, removing the "daily" board and studying the wall behind it. She ran her finger over the adhesive hook that held the menu. "Any locals in on the jokes?"

"Not that I know of. But you should ask Fran. She loves doing the stuff and might have recruited some of the Kankakee hires."

Jane rehung the blackboard and went over to Fran's desk. There was a wooden paper tray next to the landline phone. Jane lifted the ledgers off the tray, not sure what she was looking for. Strips of papers cut to look like the fortune-cookie fortunes?

Jane wandered back into the center of the main room. She turned to look at every view from where she stood. It was a magnificent space. She loved the brick walls and the skylights—all of the industrial trappings of the early factory, but with the potential to set off a few private rooms. What she could do with this place! Jane finished her 360 degree viewing by facing the set so recently decorated and tweaked by Tim and Maurice.

"The Last Supper," said Jane.

Sal walked over and stood next to her.

"Absolutely," agreed Sal. "Is that on purpose?"

"I hope not," said Jane. Maurice and Tim had assured her she'd get why it looked so familiar. They had said it was because of the curtains, which did add to the forced perspective. Stick twelve guys up there and the dais was going to become something other than the normal cable channel comedy special. Jane had heard that most comics had persecution complexes, but Lucky wasn't going to like the implications of this supper being his last, was he? And the world wasn't going to buy Lucky Miller as anyone's savior seated right in the middle of this tableau. Between the reviews he'd get—bad taste at best and anti-religion at worst and the bad karma he himself would perceive, Belinda St. Germaine might need to add a whole new chapter to her book for this one.

Sal got a phone call and checked the number. Although he sent the call directly to voice mail, he told Jane he had to get to the bowling alley. "My team needs me," he said, scrolling through texts. "I'm a hell of a bowler. Am I out from under your surveillance?"

"Not exactly, since you just admitted you were guilty," said Jane. "But I don't think you'll get far in those bowling shoes."

"I won't leave town, Jane Wheel," said Sal.

Jane assured him she would be right on his heels, but she wanted another few minutes in the building. She walked up to the front offices and checked out the storefront windows. Sitting down at one of the front reception desks, Jane called Mary Wainwright and got her voice mail.

"Mary, another real estate question," said Jane. "What did the old stone factory on Water Street make? No rush, just curious." Jane realized sitting at the desk that faced front, she could see the Kankakee River across the street. No one was playing basketball in the park, no one was playing in the sandbox. There was just a swath of green about to go gold and the river beyond. A nice-enough view. If it were possible to put a little roof garden on top of the building, the view would be even better.

Jane drove to the bowling alley with a mission-accomplished smile on her face. She had discovered who was behind the tampering with Lucky's lucky stuff and it wasn't anyone who intended real harm. If the note writer was part of Lucky's crew, it was someone who might have taken the whole merry prankster thing too far, but Lucky could relax and throw himself into his therapy without considering police action. If it was someone else who had left the notes? Jane would add up everyone who had access, question all of them about what they had done, and by process of elimination find out who was the not-so-clever shakedown artist.

The real mystery, the only mystery that was left for Jane to solve, was what had happened in Lucky's childhood that so traumatized him into forgetting his past. In chapter eight of her book, Belinda St. Germaine had listed several events traumatic enough to wipe the memory slate clean. The loss of a good friend, number six on the list, was enough to blind one to the time period. Even if Dickie Boynton hadn't been that close to him, it sounded like the two had been neighbors and perhaps Dickie had been the only friend Lucky had made as a boy. He still didn't seem like the friend-making type. Again, Jane wondered just who would be attending the roast and celebrating the spotty, mostly made-up career of Lucky Miller.

Jane thought about Nick's texts, the ones that so casually mentioned new friends at school. It was a gift that he liked sports as much as he liked science and math. It allowed him to live outside of his head, to relax in the company of peers, to enjoy a camaraderie that was based on something physical and immediate. His happiness didn't all depend on the solitary solving of an equation. Often it was triggered by a powerful kick or an effective block. When Nick's soccer coach switched him to defense a few years ago, Jane worried that he would feel bad, that her son would be disappointed not to be able to score as many goals.

"Keeping the ball out the net is as important as putting the ball in the net," explained Nick, one reasonable step ahead of his mother.

Like a pinball, her thought went from soccer to football, from Nick to Charley, and she remembered her husband explaining the anonymous linemen guarding the quarterback.

"They're his protection, his security, his insurance," said Charley.

Insurance. Security. Jane parked the car and Googled company names that had the word *security* in them. That was what Lucky's father's business was in Kankakee. Security Advisor. And Oh had told her that articles he found indicated he had most frequently listed his occupation as a salesman. *Maybe he sold stocks and bonds,* thought Jane, *but he also sold insurance. And insurance only pays out when something is lost or someone . . .*

Tim knocked on the car window and Jane, writing her thoughts and questions in her notebook, jumped.

"Come out and play," said Tim.

It had been a while since Jane had seen such a big smile on her friend's face. She opened the car door and Tim wrapped her up in a big hug. For a moment, Jane felt a twinge of envy. This was the kind of hug that preceded good news, someone else's good news. And although she wanted Tim to be happy, she was smart enough to know that another's happiness was what often took him away from her.

"Do you like Maurice?" asked Tim.

"I've just met him," began Jane.

"Lame answer," said Tim. "We both know that you are a firm believer in first impressions and like-at-first-sight."

"Yes, I like Maurice," said Jane.

"I knew it," said Tim. "What's not to like?"

"But I love you," said Jane. "And that behooves me to caution you about falling too fast for someone who lives thousands of miles away."

"Behooves?" asked Tim.

"It means that my feet would turn into round little hard-shelled hooves; in fact, I would be a total four-legged ass if I didn't act like your good and faithful friend and not just your yes-man bobblehead, agreeing with you all the time."

Tim nodded, forcing his smile into a more thoughtful expression.

"What if I were to tell you that Maurice and I have stayed up the last few nights talking about just those issues? Maurice lost his partner a few years ago, not that long after I lost Phillip. We're both old enough to know who we are, what we want," said Tim. "I knew with Phillip. I know with Maurice."

Jane wasn't sure she was ready to hear that Tim was moving to L.A. Not when she was this close to making a decision about where she was going to put down new roots.

"We're big boys," Tim said. "We can handle some time apart for now and our idea of spending some time here, some time there, allows us to see how we fit into each other's lives. And figure out how to merge our professions. And I was thinking, while I spent some time in L.A., you could run things here. Just for now, while you figure out what you want to do. Maurice thinks I ought to move to a bigger space here and expand—

offer rental pieces for production companies. He thinks there are enough movies shot in the Midwest that I could supplement sales with rental of props and furniture and . . ."

Jane half-listened. She heard Tim talk about living in Los Angeles for a few months in winter and Maurice living in Kankakee. Maurice was from Chicago and had close family ties there. He was also interested in going back to theater set design and Chicago would offer those opportunities. She heard Tim talk about new beginnings and how sometimes one had to shake things up.

"Breathe new air?" asked Jane.

"Yes, exactly. We have to breathe new air," said Tim. "Maybe you should try it, too," he suggested gently.

"So you and I are still partners in the business, in T & T Sales?" asked Jane.

Tim nodded.

"In that case, I've got the new location covered. Have you made the insurance claim on all of my lost stuff?"

Tim winced. "Yes. But I'll make sure it's more than a check. I'll make up the lost stuff, Jane, I swear."

"Let's go bowling," said Jane. "We'll talk about exactly what you're going to do for me later."

The automatic doors to the bowling alley opened with a whoosh and Jane felt a wave of nostalgia brought on by the sounds of the bowling balls hitting the wooden alley floors, the rolling, the crashing, the *thwaks* and *thuds* that couldn't be mistaken for any other sounds. Jane and Tim looked at each other. How old were they when they first got dropped off at the bowling alley with other kids for a summer afternoon of lugging a ball to the line and hoping it would roll straight down the center? A Kankakee childhood was not one programmed with summer camps and enrichment programs—at least not when Jane and Tim were growing up—and their parents, desperate to stave off the cries of boredom, looked for any activity that would keep their children contained, cool, and safe. Oddly enough, a bowling alley, so often the seedy location of many a noir novel or B-movie, was deemed acceptable as one of the safer spots in Kankakee for unchaperoned activity.

Jane didn't realize then, of course, that Don and Nellie had called ahead and told Lou, the bar manager, that the kids were coming and sounded the alert. Morrie, in charge of shoe rental, and Sylvie, the day waitress, as well as Angie, the bartender, were all charged with keeping an eye on Don and Nellie's girl and her friends. All of the *laissez-faire* parenting that Jane believed Don and Nellie participated in was a complete and total sham. When she was sixteen, Glenn at the gas station told her that Don had always called ahead when she was bringing her car in and that the night waitress at the bowling alley, Doris, had told him that Nellie always called when Jane was headed to the lanes with her high school friends. Apparently long before Hillary Clinton reminded the United States that *it takes a village*, Don and Nellie had been pioneering the philosophy in Kankakee.

Lucky Miller was circulating among the teams already in their second and third frames of competition. Nellie was not bowling herself, but managed to make it to the line for instructional purposes with several members of the EZ Way Inn team. Don was drinking a beer, standing back, and smiling at his wife, content to let her fulfill her role as "Team Manager," as it said on her shirt.

Wally's Tap had a team and the various crews from Lucky Productions were represented. Sal waved at Jane from lane fourteen, where an all-male crew wore black shirts with gold lettering, reading WE DRIVE AND BOWL LIKE CRAZY! The drivers were going head to head with an all-female team who Jane could only guess were the hair and makeup stylists since their tight-fitting green shirts said WE PUT LIPSTICK ON A BOWLING BALL AND CALL IT A.... Jane had no idea what the joke behind the fill-in-the-blank could be.

Jane looked for a team made up of writers, thinking they would have much cleverer bowling shirts. Malcolm was sitting with a group, but if they were indeed writers, they were not a credit to the profession since they all wore plain Lucky Production T-shirts.

A cheer went up from the drivers. Sal had just rolled a strike. He waved in Jane's direction and she waved back. Nellie saw her waving and motioned her over. Jane kissed Tim's cheek and pointed to Maurice, who was handing out shirts to two other teams who had yet to start their first match.

"Better get a team shirt before they're gone."

Tim shook his head. "We've already shared many things, but it's a little early to let him see me bowl."

After Jane saw Maurice greet Tim with as much enthusiasm and warmth as she knew he deserved, she turned her attention to Nellie, who was still waving at her, balancing on her tiptoes as if that added half inch would make her easier to spot.

"What the hell took you so long?" asked Nellie, then she momentarily turned back into the coach. "Jeez, Francis, roll the ball in a straight line, why don't you?"

"What did I miss?"

"Your boss Lucky's been blowing a lot of hot air. One of the office girls got a ball dropped on her toe and had to go to the emergency room. There was a lot of screaming and crying over that. Oh, and that guy over there, Mack's grandson or nephew or whatever the hell he is? He's been running around setting out the food and I think he's having a nervous breakdown. Other than that, it's your average bowling tournament," said Nellie. "Not again," she yelled at Francis when he failed to pick up an easy spare.

Sam was unpacking platters of food on two long folding tables, which had been set up to the south of the shoe rental counter. He had draped a colorful checked cloth over the surface and was shuffling and rearranging baskets and platters, looking at them from all angles. Although Jane wasn't sure that her mother's nervous breakdown diagnosis was accurate, he was definitely jumpy. When someone brushed by the table and tried to snatch a chip from one of the baskets, Jane could see, if not hear, him barking at the poor scavenger. He looked back and forth, from his table to the lanes where he studied the bowlers, looking from team to team, squinting at the score sheets that were illuminated over the lanes.

"Do you have money bet on this?" asked Jane, coming up behind Sam.

"What the hell is that supposed to mean?" Sam turned, then saw it was Jane and tried to recover himself. He was an average-looking guy who would have been cast as the best friend in a buddy movie, but never considered for the lead. Jane caught herself, realizing she often missed her old job as a creative director. She still studied people's faces as if she were casting for a beer commercial. In his grandfather's diner, Sam always looked cool and calm, but here, he was sweating profusely over his catering chores. When she first met him, Jane had guessed his age to be late twenties, maybe early thirties, but watching him squint and grimace and frown at the bags and boxes of food, she would have said his furrowed face was that of a man closer to middle-aged, whatever number that currently was.

"Do you need some help?"

Sam shook his head and offered her a sandwich. It was a peace offering and as far as Jane could tell, looking at the small sprouted wheat bun piled with fragrant chicken salad, it was an effective one.

"Delicious. You didn't learn this recipe from your grandfather; curry powder hadn't come to Kankakee in his day," Jane said, her mouth full of chicken and almonds and grapes and the delicate satisfying warmth of the curry. "Marco Polo had not yet arrived with spices. Is there cilantro in here?" she asked.

Sam nodded, distracted enough by the compliment to almost smile.

"I went to culinary school in New York. I came back here thinking it might be fun to open my own place, simple stuff, comfort food like my grandpa's, but a notch above, you know?" said Sam. "I got a lot of loans to pay."

Jane stopped savoring her sandwich for a moment and looked at the young chef. Sam wasn't just explaining his situation; it sounded more like he was offering an apology. Or a confession.

"Aunt Ruthie said I should try opening the diner, but the startup was going to cost a fortune, Then Lucky Miller came to town throwing money around and Aunt Ruthie said she knew how I could make even more. I thought she was crazy. She's pretty old and most of the time she doesn't know what she's talking about. She's always been loopy, you know, since she was a little girl. Her brother died when she was little and my mom said it made her battier than she already was. She was my mom's aunt so I guess she was my great-great . . ."

"Sam, was her last name Boynton?" said Jane, putting down her napkin.

"Where the hell is Sluggo? Why isn't he on the team with the drivers?" asked Sam. "He hasn't answered his cell phone, I can't get him at the hotel."

"Sam," said Jane. How could he not know that Sluggo died? Jane did a quick calendar check in her head. It had been two days, but it was possible that the Kankakee paper hadn't reported the death since they wouldn't have released the name until the family was notified. And maybe Lucky's people had tried to keep it out of the news. Anyone as superstitious as Lucky wouldn't want any bad karma to be associated with this project. But Lucky's people were in and out of the diner all the time. Wouldn't Sluggo's death be the main topic of conversation?

"What?" said Sam, "Why are you looking at me like that?"

Jane noticed that it had gone quiet in the bowling alley. Not silent, but as quiet as a still functioning bowling alley could get. Several of the teams had stopped their matches to gather in and watch what was unfolding on lane fourteen, where Sal and the team of drivers were matched up against the hair and makeup crew. Jane noticed Fran, the accountant, was also bowling on the makeup team.

Looking up at the scores projected overhead, Jane saw that the third member of the men's team had just completed his fifth frame. The score read *X, X, X, X, X*. Sal was halfway through a perfect game. No one spoke directly to him or about the phenomenon. Instead they high-fived each other and gave him serious nods. Jane knew that when someone was approaching "perfection," it was bad luck to say anything out loud. No one mentioned a perfect game to a baseball pitcher on his way to a no-hitter and no one was speaking to Sal.

By now, Sam had looked up and realized the focus of everyone's attention. He clearly was more interested in what Jane had to tell him about Sluggo. Because the place had quieted down so much, Jane could hear the whoosh of the automatic doors and saw a woman limp in, leaning heavily on a cane. Jane recognized her as one of the design assistants she had seen helping Maurice. On her right, looking uncomfortable carrying her purse and sweater over his arm, was one of the basketball players from the park.

"Lucky, you sonofabitch!"

Her voice sounded a little groggy, her words a bit slurred, but there was no mistaking her message. The crowds gathered around lane fourteen shushed her and she hobbled over to see what might be more interesting than what she had just experienced in the hospital emergency room.

"Jane, where's Sluggo?" asked Sam.

"He died, Sam. He left the hospital and had another allergic reaction in the car when another driver, Mickey picked him up and he didn't . . ."

Sam slumped into a chair next to the food table, dropping

the napkins and plastic forks he was holding in his right hand. The white papers fluttered to the floor and spread out around the table, and Jane, reflexively, bent to pick them up.

"I heard somebody say his EpiPen didn't work when he collapsed at the Steak and Brew, but I thought he was okay," said Sam, his voice almost a whisper. If Sal hadn't been rolling the ball and the alley hadn't gone dead quiet, Jane wouldn't have heard him.

"My partner was going to let me know if there was anything fishy in the medical report, but Sluggo *was* okay before he left the hospital. I saw him there. There was a candy wrapper in the car that caused a second reaction."

A roar went up as Sal's bowling ball smashed and scattered ten pins. Jane looked up and saw an *X* fill up the box on the score sheet.

"If you know something about Sluggo's death that would—" Jane said.

"Why should I know anything?" said Sam. "I don't know him, he just came in the diner and he seemed like a nice guy, that's all."

"I'm not sure why you're lying or what you're lying about, Sam, but you are lying. Not to speak ill of the dead, but no one I've met here ever said Sluggo was a nice guy. That is not why you're so upset," said Jane.

"You tell me what your partner says about Sluggo's EpiPen," said Sam, "and I'll tell you something back." Sam turned away from Jane and began to empty chips and vegetables into lined baskets. Digging deeper into one of his canvas bags, he hauled out all the fixings for guacamole including two large *mocaljetes* and pestles for smashing the avocados. Two young girls, one of them the actress who looked so much like young Ruthie hustled in and Sam gave them both the evil eye.

"Sorry, we're late. Suli called us from the hospital and asked us to look up some stuff and make some calls for her, so we got delayed," said the Ruthie look-alike.

"Don't care why, just get cracking on the guac. As soon as that guy misses a pin, everybody's going to remember there's free food and come over here. We better be ready," said Sam.

"Is that Suli?" asked Jane pointing to the woman with the cane.

"Yeah, and boy, did she have a time at the hospital. I mean they were real nice and everything, but the insurance cards Lucky gave us don't work and she had to use a friend's credit card to guarantee payment. She made me call the number on the card and it turns out there isn't any 'special coverage' like Lucky told us. I told my boyfriend who's got the lighting all rigged up and he's taking everything down in the studio right now. Said he can't risk his equipment or a lawsuit if anyone gets hurt."

"More guac, less talk," said Sam, from the other end of the table.

"I better get busy," said the actress-waitress. We're all going to need the free food. If Lucky was bullshitting on insurance, he's probably bullshitting on paychecks, too. Might as well let Sal get some glory before we spoil the party, huh?" she said, looking up at the overhead score, as another smash of bowling ball meeting pins inflamed the crowd.

X appeared overhead as cheers went up.

Jane looked up at the whoosh of the automatic doors opening to the lanes. Since the sixth frame, more and more spectators had arrived, all whispering about what was happening on lane fourteen, but no one spoke above a whisper around Sal. This new visitor was not, however, a regular fan of ten-pin bowling. Instead, Bruce Oh walked through the door, looking confused at the number of people surrounding one lane and, instead of heading over to the crowd as so many would do, he scanned the room. Jane waited for her partner to complete his survey and when their eyes met, she smiled and walked over to meet him. Perfect timing. She had figured things out but still needed the one missing piece she hoped he was there to provide.

"This is the team that is winning? That's why all are watching them?" asked Oh.

Jane pointed up to the score sheet. "Know anything about bowling?"

"Just enough to know that the player, Sal, might have reason to celebrate tonight," said Oh, reading the name and the score on the overhead projection.

"I'm afraid Lucky's not going to be celebrating. I think I figured out what he doesn't remember and maybe why he wouldn't want to remember, but since the crowd here will be ready to tar and feather him when they find out this whole roast thing is an empty promise, he'll probably prefer to forget everything that happens in Kankakee this time around, too."

"One bit of news that can't be called good, but at least isn't worse, is the medical report from Detective Ramey. He said that Mr. Mettleman's EpiPen could not have been emptied, at least not fully. They've gone over the tests that were administered when he was admitted to the hospital. He had the medicine in his system."

"That news might get me another chicken salad sandwich," said Jane, watching Sam pile the food on the plates. "But I'd like him to explain the details."

"As would I, Mrs. Wheel," said Oh, "since I have no idea what chicken salad has to do with anything. You might be interested in this advertisement I found. It ran in a business publication here in Kankakee. Oh handed her a photocopy from a newsprint page.

NOBODY LIVES FOREVER

ARE YOU ADEQUATELY PREPARED FOR THE WORST THING THAT COULD HAPPEN TO YOUR FAMILY? PERHAPS YOU AS THE BREADWINNER HAVE PROVIDED FOR YOUR WIFE AND FAMILY IF YOU ARE TAKEN BEFORE YOUR TIME, BUT HAVE YOU THOUGHT ABOUT WHAT MIGHT HAPPEN IF SOMETHING WORSE THAN DEATH HAPPENED TO YOU? IF YOU LOST YOUR WIFE? YOUR CHILD? NO ONE WANTS TO THINK ABOUT THE WORST, BUT WE CAN HELP YOU PLAN AHEAD FOR THE DARK TIMES.

CONTACT HERMAN MULLET, SECURITY ADVISER, ARCADE BUILDING, KANKAKEE, ILLINOIS.

"Yikes," said Jane, "talk about your fear-mongering advertising. It's effective though. No one would get away with a whole paragraph these days. They'd just use the tagline, *nobody lives forever*. That's the key—massage your worst nightmare and make the sale. What ghouls!"

"Hey, Bruce, what size shoes you wear?" called Nellie. "Boxcar's wheezing like a freight train. We're going to need a sub."

It had almost come around to Sal's turn again, so bowlers on other teams were wiping their hands and replacing their balls in the return to watch and wait. Lucky had been half watching, half listening, but Jane had seen that he had taken a few phone calls and was looking distracted and trancelike. Something must have triggered a memory. Or if one of those previous calls had been Suli calling him from the hospital to see why she couldn't get an answer about insurance coverage, perhaps Lucky was pretending to go into a trance. If Brenda were here, Jane was sure this would be exactly the time Lucky would choose to fake one of his allergic reactions.

An old woman had powered her wheelchair out of the dim barroom and wheeled up to Sam's table. She eyed the chicken salad sandwiches and Sam tuned on her as if she was a thieving crow. No one turned on a defenseless old woman like that unless she was a family member. Jane took Oh's arm and directed him over to the food table where she planned on introducing herself to the woman who she was certain must be Aunt Ruthie.

The old lady had a book of matches in her hand, which Jane thought odd, until she noticed the waiters and waitresses passing out matchbooks to everyone. A gum-chewing nineteen-year-old came over and handed matchbooks to Jane and Oh, who looked even more puzzled than usual when faced with what he assumed was a Kankakee custom.

"Thank you, but I don't smoke," he said politely, trying to return it.

"Who does?" said the waitress. Pointing to her mouth. "But this nicotine gum is delish. Does the trick."

"So why the matches?" asked Jane.

"Rudy keeps them around for when somebody's, you know," she said, pointing to the scorecard, but not risking the bad luck one encountered for mentioning the words, "Perfect game" or saying "300" aloud. "Everybody used to smoke, you know. So when somebody was bowling a . . . pretty good . . . around the eighth or ninth frame, everybody'd start holding up their lighters or lighting matches for luck when the ball rolled down the lane. It's a tradition. Rudy hasn't had to get these babies out in a while."

Jane saw that the matchbook cover had a thin layer of dust on it.

"Not sure any of the Lucky Miller people will know the tradition," said Jane.

"We're spreading the word. Besides, one person does it and everybody does it. Like kids. Everybody loves lighting matches."

Sal's tenth frame was getting closer. Jane looked over in time to see him dry his hands and shake out his shoulders. His face looked completely blank. She was reminded of hearing athletes talk about remarkable games, asserting that they hadn't thought about the record being broken, the strikeouts thrown, the three-pointers drained. Most of them talked about being completely detached from their bodies, unaware of anything outside or inside, operating on pure muscle memory.

Jane looked down at the matches in her hand, then looked at Lucky Miller who was turning his own matchbook over and over in his hand. *Everybody likes lighting matches.* Dickie Boynton ran away after he burned down his family's garage. Dickie, however, had not acted alone. Jane was sure that his pal, Herman Mullet, had been with him, either playing with matches or setting out to do some damage. And once damage had been done and Dickie had been blamed, Herman had told his father what happened and his father, ready to move on anyway, always one step ahead of the law on his securities and insurance schemes, protected his son by scramming out of town.

When Jane had found Lucky wandering the block of his old neighborhood, a fact confirmed by Mary Wainwright's check into the real estate history, he had seen a woman watching, a current resident, and told Jane a little girl had been watching years ago, when he was a boy. Jane saw that that little girl, all grown up and grown old, was still watching. Ruthie Boynton, holding her book of matches aloft in her left clawlike hand, hit the joystick on her electric chair with her right hand and motored toward Lucky.

The number of people at the bowling alley had easily doubled in the last half hour. It was a crowded Saturday afternoon anyway, with many locals thinking of the Lucky tournament as a spectator sport, hoping for a glimpse of the promised celebrities. When no celebrities except for Lucky who was fast becoming old hat around town showed up, some people left, only to return when cell phones started buzzing with the news of a perfect game being rolled. Spotting B-list celebrities was an okay way to pass a September weekend afternoon, but being present to watch someone roll a perfect game was history in the making. People were pouring through the automatic doors, video cameras in hand. Rudy and the other employees cordoned off an area around lane fourteen, so things didn't become too impossible for Sal, who simply repeated his motions on every turn. He applauded his teammates when they rolled well, and when it was his turn, he dried his hands, squared his shoulders, and allowed his body to do the work.

Tenth frame for Sal was approaching. He had started to stand, then looked down, paused and sat. The whispering filtered back to where Jane and Oh stood. A red-faced fifty-something man, wearing a Wally's Tap T-shirt, explained that Sal's shoe had come untied. Oh looked at Jane, puzzled.

"Why not tie his shoe?" asked Oh. "Delay of game?"

"Superstition," said Jane. "When you're on a streak, you don't change anything. You dry your hands the same way, you turn the ball in your hands the same, if you always sip your beer before you roll, you sip your beer. If he stops to tie his shoe, he might break the chain."

"And if he doesn't tie his shoe, he might fall and break something else?" asked Oh.

"Exactly the dilemma," said Jane. "But it gives me time to stop Ruthie."

Jane pushed through the crowd, confident she could overtake the wheelchair, but Ruthie did a little bob and weave maneuver through the crowd that the chair allowed and Jane couldn't imitate. People were pressing in now, as anxious to see what Sal decided about his shoelace as they were to see him bowl his tenth frame. Parents were pointing and aiming their children's heads to the projected score as if it were the aurora borealis. A once-in-a-lifetime spectacle. X. X. X. X. X. X. X. X. X.

Ruthie got to Lucky just ahead of Jane, who could now see that Lucky was completely in his trance, turning those matches over and over in his hand. The look on the old woman's face was positively victorious, as if she had planted Sal here, commanded the perfect game, and produced the matchbooks herself. Jane recognized the look. She had seen it on other people bent on setting records straight, exacting revenge.

"Herman Mullet," she croaked. "You burned down Daddy's garage and let Dickie take the blame. You thought you got away with it, didn't you? But I knew you'd come back. Criminals always come back to the scene of the crime." Her voice grew stronger and louder. Jane looked over to Sam, who was now also fighting his way through the crowd to his great-aunt. Jane knew he had his own reasons for wanting to shut the old woman up. He must have mentioned Sluggo, and the pranks played on Lucky and Ruthie told him they could play the tricks all right, but there was a way to get money out of Lucky. She could tell him how to blackmail Lucky.

Sam was the caterer and Lucky planned the food. He must have let him know he could eat peanuts. Or Sluggo told him since Sluggo was Lucky's source for what would happen to him during a reaction. Sam had messed with an EpiPen, on purpose or accidentally when slipping in the three-leaf clover, believing it was Lucky's kit. Maybe he played with the pen, thinking it wouldn't matter to Lucky. It would only prove he had faked his allergy. Just in case Ruthie's nonsense didn't work, Sam would shake him down for money, threatening to reveal that he was a phony. Poor Sam didn't know that Lucky wasn't afraid of being called a phony; his whole life was built around it.

Sal had stood up, but Jane couldn't tell whether he had decided to tie his shoe or not. The sound of matches being struck, lighters being flicked was loud and strange. A giant scraping, a sandpaper breeze. Jane, along with everyone else, turned to watch Sal. In that quiet moment, while everyone listened to the ball rolling toward the pins, Ruthie cried out, "You thought you committed the perfect crime!" At the word *perfect*, everyone groaned. Jane heard Ruthie screech above the fray, "You tried to burn up my brother, now it's my turn to burn you up!"

Jane saw Lucky shake his head. He yelled, "No, it was an accident. Dickie wasn't supposed to be in the garage. He ran in for his fishing . . ."

Lucky's voice changed into a scream and just as the ball crashed into the pins, Jane saw Ruthie hold her lit match to the bottom of Lucky's green plaid sport coat. Jane threw herself across two spectators who hadn't turned away from lane fourteen so were knocked to their knees as Jane threw her elbows forward. As the shouts began when the pins fell, Jane crashed into Lucky, knocking him onto the ground, and trying to roll him over and smother the flame. Nellie must have been watching Jane since she was right behind her with a pitcher of water, which she threw with uncanny accuracy, soaking both Jane and Lucky.

Jane had ended up lying across Lucky's body at a right angle and as she lifted herself up, she examined him for any sign of fire or smoke. The stench of burned wool was strong, but Lucky was no longer on fire, and he assured her, he had not been burned. He was, however, wide-awake and no longer in anything resembling a trancelike state.

"I didn't know Dickie was in the garage. I swear. We were playing around. My dad said Mr. Boynton would pay us if we burned down his garage. He had insurance on it. He was going to claim . . ." Lucky shook his head. The facts were still fuzzy. "I couldn't find Dickie when the fire started and he had said he was going in and I ran home and told my dad I killed Dickie. My dad said to shut up about it, I hadn't done anything wrong, and we were all going to disappear for a while. I remember, we were all packed and I hadn't even known we were moving. My mom just kept crying. I . . ."

The crowd around them was clearly torn. There were those who wanted to listen to Lucky's confession even though they had no idea what he was talking about, but there was, after all, a bowler on lane fourteen who had just rolled his tenth strike and was only two away from Kankakee bowling history.

Sam had restrained Ruthie, yanking the battery connector out on the chair, keeping his arm on her arm as he bent over listening to Lucky. Nellie and Oh had also gathered around Jane, helping her to her feet. Lucky pulled himself up to a sitting position. When he saw Nellie, he directed his words straight at her.

"I didn't mean to hurt Dickie. He was my friend. He liked to go down by the river, he taught me how to fish, he . . ."

Jane mustered up all of her inner Belinda St. Germaine and waited for Lucky to finish. Nellie, too, stayed silent, hawk-like, and watched Lucky.

"I remember. I thought I killed him. I had a . . . I guess I had a nervous breakdown. My mom took me to her sister in

Canada and they put me in a hospital and when I went back to my aunt's house, I told her I wanted to go back to my mom and dad and she told me I couldn't because there was a death in the family, so I just . . . I just thought my parents had . . . died. . . . But they didn't. A few years later, Mother came to see me, with a new husband. She told me my dad went to prison and I thought it was because of me and got all upset again and she said that it wasn't, it was because he was a crook. He sold people insurance policies that were no good, stocks that were no good, and he went to jail because of it. She said Dickie hadn't died in the fire. He died in the river. His dad wanted him to pretend that he died in the fire for the insurance money. He had taken an insurance policy out on him, but Dickie didn't want to be dead, he ran off to the river, but—" Lucky stopped talking and looked at Nellie. "What happened?"

"Dickie drowned. He camped under the bridge near his uncle's and it stormed and the river came up and got him," said Nellie. "It wasn't you." Jane was surprised to see Nellie pat his arm. Then she added, "So you didn't kill Dickie, but from what I hear, this crowd's going to tar and feather you for faking this whole damn roast. And that girl who broke her toe told everybody you faked up the health insurance and everything else you promised them. You better get the hell out of town," said Nellie. "I can already smell the tar heating up."

"Nope," said Lucky, shaking his head. "I ran away last time, but . . . wait a minute . . . Who died? Why didn't my aunt send me back to my folks? If I found out I didn't do it, what happened to my memory? Why couldn't I remember?"

"You died, Lucky," said Jane. "Your dad and mom had an insurance policy on your life and they filed a claim. When they moved to Louisville, they sent you to Canada and they filed a claim, said you drowned in the Ohio River."

Jane, Nellie, and Oh were sitting on the floor around Lucky, a small enclave protected by the molded plastic seats of lane three. Don must have been in the crowd around lane fourteen where shouts went up again. Now Sal was one strike away from a 300 score.

"Did they collect the money for me?" asked Lucky.

Jane nodded. "I believe they did. I think your dad might have decided to do it after the Boyntons' scheme with Dickie didn't work. See, your dad had taken the money for a lot of policies, especially on kids, and not really filed them with the company, playing the odds that there would never be an attempt to collect. He had taken a policy on you, though, because he got a discount and why not take advantage? Probably helped him sell policies if he said he had taken one out on you, too. And the one he took out on you was legit.

"But Dickie wasn't insured, and since he ran away after the fire, which Ruthie believed you set, they blamed you and your family for everything that went wrong in their own."

Ruthie was close enough to hear most of what Jane was saying. She bent over in her chair and leaned forward, making her raspy voice as loud as she could.

"I ruined your game, Herman Mullet. I ruined your perfect game!" she screamed.

Not exactly. Lucky didn't really have a game to ruin.

Instead, Ruthie Boynton ruined Sal's perfect game. In the silence as he went up to roll his twelfth ball, there was a collective intake of breath. And the scraping of matches being lit. Then Ruthie's words rang out in the tense quiet, her screech of *perfect game,* the ball was thrown and except for the crashing fall of nine pins, there was no sound at all.

21

Lucky Miller was not tarred and feathered. In fact, the citizens of Kankakee were fairly forgiving, considering they were not going to be treated to a bunch of insult comedians hurling jokes in bad taste at their own Lucky Miller. After all, the excitement and competition leading up to the event had been a lot of fun and most of the people in town who cared about any groundbreaking local events had witnessed an almost perfect game of bowling.

Sal showed an enormous amount of restraint after he bowled the twelfth and his score was recorded overhead as 299. He sat down and tied his shoe and accepted the backslapping and high-fiving, then went over to where Ruthie sat, finally subdued but not exactly repentant. Sal solemnly shook her hand and thanked her.

"I'd hate to think I peaked this early in my life," he said. "So if you jinxed me, it was meant to be."

If Jane hadn't been ready to say yes to a dinner date before that happened, she was ready now.

Before leaving the bowling alley, Lucky was able to grab

the microphone located behind the shoe rental. Over the PA system, he explained to those in attendance from Lucky Productions that the insurance glitch Suli had encountered was really a glitch. Although he admitted the show might not go on, everyone had been covered as promised and everyone would get paid as promised. Although there might be a slight delay.

"Including all the tabs you ran up all over town?" shouted Nellie.

There was talk about putting a plaque up at lane fourteen, but Sal asked Rudy not to. He seemed to be entirely serious about not wanting his life to be divided into before his almost perfect game and after his almost perfect game. It was, after all, as he reminded them, just bowling. Tim and Maurice came over, both a little breathless from the excitement. They had not been caught up in the excitement of the bowling, since neither had been paying attention to the X's going up overhead, but both had caught Jane's diving save of Lucky Miller and were duly impressed.

"Are you sure you're okay?" asked Tim, whispering to her, as Nellie was giving Maurice the third degree about what he was doing with all those tomatoes he bought at the farmer's market.

"Perfectly fine," said Jane. "Exhilarated."

She made her way over to the catering table and saw that Sam had been right. After Sal had finished his game, everyone had descended on the food, and the platters and baskets held only crumbs. Bruce Oh was having a quiet conversation with Sam. Although Oh looked serious, she could tell he was reassuring Sam he was not responsible for Sluggo Mettleman's death.

"The kit you took was Lucky's and the pen would have been emptied by Brenda before it was used on Lucky anyway. You do realize, though, if Lucky had needed it, you would be responsible for him," said Oh.

"It was stupid. But I wasn't trying to really hurt Lucky. He told me he didn't have an allergy, I guess because he knew I'd be making the food and he didn't want me to worry about stuff I saw him eating. I knew if I played with his pen I wouldn't be killing him. Sluggo said it was a way to humiliate him, though, if we showed that he didn't even use the stuff. It was just stupid. Like those horseshoes I had to hang in his office. It was just dumb stuff. Then Ruthie said I should blackmail him and then I could have the restaurant and pay my bills, but I couldn't even figure out how to do that right."

"That's a good thing, Sam," said Jane. "If you'd actually threatened him or asked for money or given him specific directions, the police would have been called in."

Lucky came up behind Jane. "No police. If I have any dough left after all the bills are paid, I'll back your diner, kid. Your grandfather was a good guy and you make a hell of a milk shake. In fact, next time I go into rehab, I'm thinking I might fly you out to cook for me. If I drink those milk shakes every day, I might not miss the Jackie D."

Lucky had declared an open bar for an hour and no one remembered that he had no way to pay the tab. The noise level built up again as a few teams decided to finish the games they had interrupted. Jane was pleased to hear the familiar crashing of pins resume. Sam had called Ruthie's home healthcare worker to pick her up and take her home after Lucky had tried to shake hands with her. She hadn't forgiven him. Old memories, especially the bad ones, the ones that have stood the test of time, don't erase or flex easily. Lucky was so pleased to have a grasp on his past, he didn't mind that Ruthie believed the worst of him. Jane was sure that Belinda St. Germaine would have her work cut out for her when Lucky came to grips with the fact that his parents actually gave him up, declared him dead, and collected on his life insurance policy. But right now, Lucky was content with a clear mind and a clean conscience.

Jane looked around the bowling alley and wondered if anyone had given much of a thought to their missing coworker, Sluggo Mettleman. No one had tried to kill him no matter what Jane had overheard him screaming into the phone. The three-leaf clover he had found? Any one of the pranksters on the crew could have dropped that into his bag, thinking it was Lucky's kit, but no one had tried to kill anyone. Instead of attempted murder, the Lucky Duck cocktail served up here had only contained the equally potent mix of revenge and greed.

In the midst of the noisy celebrating going on, Jane saw the automatic doors open and Mary Wainwright entered on the arm of her off-and-on-again escort, Chuck Havens, another familiar face from Bishop McNamara High School. Jane waved at them and Mary mouthed something to her across the room. Jane shook her head and lifted her palms.

Mary pointed to her throat, lifted the lapel of her jacket, and broadly gestured toward the placket that ran down the front. Jane laughed at the pantomime, but had no idea what Mary was trying to tell her.

Cupping her hands around her mouth and shouting over the noise as she threaded her way closer to Jane, Mary shouted one word. "Buttons!"

Jane smiled at what she thought she heard, then shook her head again. Couldn't be. Too perfect.

"Buttons! The stone factory made buttons."

"Buttons?" Jane called back.

"Mother of pearl. From the shells in the Kankakee River. Shell buttons!"

Jane looked over at Don and Nellie, who were now watching her exchange with Mary. Tim had also looked up when he saw Mary and Chuck enter and was shouting something in Maurice's ear.

"You're sure it was buttons?" asked Jane.

"Buttons," said Mary, holding up some pages stapled together and pointing at the copy of her research.

"Sold!" said Jane.

Later, at the Steak and Brew, over a table of drinks and food and in a much quieter venue, Mary and Chuck, Jane and Sal, and Maurice and Tim sat at a round table discussing the events of the day and the real estate deals to come.

Jane told them about her plan to buy the Button Factory, and make it into a live and work space. The modifications that had been done to turn it into Lucky's studio were perfect for Jane's new business plan. There was enough room to relocate and expand T & T sales and also to maintain the building as a small studio where, if the spirit moved her, she could rekindle some of her old contacts in advertising, produce a few commercial spots. Why not? In the new economy, Jane thought she just might be able to sell herself as a less expensive alternative to

some of the agencies in Chicago. And she was only ninety minutes out of the city. A roof garden with a river view, a loft space
to live in at the back, and a work space in the front all seemed
doable with her newfound real estate wealth and the insurance
check that would arrive soon to cover her lost collectibles.

"Hard to imagine you rattling around in a huge empty
space," said Tim.

"It won't be empty. Not for long anyway. I'm going to use
some of Carl's furniture and try out a midcentury modern life
for a while," said Jane.

"I knew you couldn't resist coming back to the Kankakee
theater world," said Mary.

Jane laughed. She really wasn't planning on trying out for
The Music Man, but if Mary thought she had a little competition for the lead, it would only make her better prepare for her
own audition. What Jane didn't tell anyone at the table was
that she had been taking a long hard look at Don and Nellie
and the EZ Way Inn since Carl died. Her parents needed
some help. This was going to be a transition time for them and
since Jane had Nick happily settled in school, her house sold,
and no belongings to weigh her down, why not stop in Kankakee for a while.

And that beautiful building had been a button factory.

"Meant to be," said Jane aloud.

Sal reacted to Jane's remark as one directed toward him
and he placed his hand over hers. She smiled, and patted his
hand with her other one before slipping both away to wave at
Detective Oh. She rose to meet her partner, who had just
come into the dining room.

"Detective Ramey sends his best wishes," said Oh, "and

he says to also thank you for not bringing any murdered bodies to his doorstep."

"I'm not sure I can take responsibility for that, but I'll accept the thanks for now," said Jane. She had told Oh earlier that she wanted to relocate to Kankakee, to make sure her parents were okay, and she had asked if they could still work together—when he felt her expertise was needed.

"Mrs. Wheel, you are the only partner I wish to have. Our business now has a branch office, which you will head," he had said. That was just before Nellie talked him into subbing on the EZ Way Inn team and Jane had watched Detective Oh bowl for the first time. Jane was not surprised that he was a natural.

When Jane got back to her parents' house later that night, she expected Don and Nellie to be in bed. She used her key at the front door and slipped out of her shoes, tiptoeing into the kitchen to make herself a cup of tea. She took out her notebook and drew a large square. She began doodling in walls and bookcases, office space and living space. She drew another elevation for her roof garden. Mary Wainwright was going to put Jane's offer in on Monday morning, but had already assured her that it would be accepted.

"Place has been on the market for over four years. Owner'll think he died and went to heaven when he gets this," said Mary.

Jane sent an e-mail to Nick, telling him she had a big wonderful surprise for him and that they would talk tomorrow.

"It's tomorrow already," said Jane to Rita, playing shaggy rug at her feet.

"Sure as hell is," said Nellie, padding in from her bedroom.

"That tea got caffeine in it? You'll be up all night." She fixed herself a cup and sat down.

"What about you?" asked Jane.

"I'm immune," said Nellie. "After drinking EZ Way Inn coffee all those years, whatever I had in me that reacted to strong stuff got killed a long time ago. I could chew grounds and still sleep. If I wanted to sleep that is, and I usually don't."

"Mom, how would you feel if I did move back to Kankakee? I'd still work with Tim and Detective Oh, but I have some other ideas for a business," Jane said. "I'd be around to help you and Dad out, too. If you wanted me to."

"That'd be all right," said Nellie. "Your dad would like it."

"Right," said Jane. It was no use. Jane was never going to hear what she wanted from her mother. Nellie wasn't going to give her the satisfaction of knowing she was appreciated, knowing she was doing the right thing. Nellie might want her daughter to come home and help out, but Jane knew she was never going to hear Nellie say it out loud.

"You guys all set for Carl's memorial?"

"Yup. We're opening up on Monday, with shorter hours that your dad and I can handle, and then on Friday, we'll have everybody in and serve food and talk about Carl and I suppose your dad will cry. It'll be a good way to say good-bye," said Nellie. "Your brother's coming in."

Jane nodded and told her mother that she and Michael had spoken on the phone.

"Carl cared a lot for you kids, you know," said Nellie. She

got up and took both cups to the sink and washed them out. "I believe your dad and I and you kids were the only family Carl had."

Nellie dried her hands, then opened a drawer next to the sink and took out what looked to Jane like a slip of paper. "I found this today and I want you to have it," said Nellie. "It's a four-leaf clover I found in a patch of weeds out behind the EZ Way Inn and Carl always kept it in the cash register. Said it protected him, kept him winning on the punchboards and the lotto tickets. Kept him lucky. Now it'll keep you safe. And lucky."

Jane stood up to follow her mother to bed. Rita got up, too, wagging her tail, facing the delicious luxury of having two humans who wanted her to follow them into bed.

At the door to her room, Jane faced her mother. She stood a head taller than Nellie and looking down at her mother's weathered face made Jane inexplicably sad. She felt like she was about to say good-bye, not good night, and she realized she didn't trust herself to be able to speak at all.

"I know," said Nellie, "I know." Then Nellie did the unthinkable and hugged her daughter. "Now go to bed and get some sleep. You got yourself about four part-time jobs and I heard a rumor you're buying a damn factory to live in."

Jane watched her mother tiptoe into her bedroom and close the door. *What in the world is wrong with me?* thought Jane, feeling like she wanted to sob and laugh hysterically at the same time. Here she was, a grown-up woman, a mother and a daughter and a friend and a partner and every day she faced all of those things a grown-up human being had to deal with. But the truth was, in the middle of the night, in her hometown of Kankakee, Illinois, Jane Wheel realized she was just another child who had been waiting a long time for a four-leaf clover and a good-night hug from her mother.